The Venango Way

Copyright © 2024 Michael L. Phegley

Michael L. Phegley

THE VENANGO WAY

Joe-Pye Press

200 Hanover Drive Evansville IN

For:

My mother

who told me I could do anything I set my mind to.

and

My father

who taught me the meaning of perseverance.

Thanks:

To: Dave and Michael who made the book better.

To: Missy and Roberto for proofreading and formatting.

To: Michelle for her unwavering encouragement.

To: Brenda for her support, patience, and listening skill.

To: Claire, Jack, Emma, Alex, and Ellie for making my life wonderful.

Why I Write Historic Fiction?
Why you should want to read it.

I've listened as people say: "I have no interest in history. It's boring. Teachers drilled me mercilessly on names and dates about people and places long dead and forgotten. It's just not relevant."

Those experiences can't be dismissed. Too often history teachers are hired for their coaching skills and only ever fired for loosing ball games. Too many textbooks are disinteresting collections of names and dates with too little context or connective tissue to bring them alive.

Stories, on the other hand, if told well, are like gossip. Everyone likes gossip. People can't get enough—especially gossip about our most intimate thoughts, feelings, or personal interactions.

Historic fiction is a story. Done right it is a story spreading gossip which turns out to be the truth about what happened, or at least the truth as we have the ability to know it.

Historic fiction is about how real people live their lives. Not merely famous or infamous people. Not just the brave or brilliant. Not only explorers, warriors, and kings.

All of us originate from ancestors who lived, laughed, struggled, and died before us. Pick any *time* in history. Your ancestors were struggling then, somewhere in the world. Aren't you interested in what they might have experienced? Pick any *place* in the world that you find beautiful or interesting. Someone at some time was there ahead of you. Don't you wonder who they might have been, and how it looked to them?

Historic fiction attempts to bring a few of those people and times to life on the printed page. It helps you experience other thoughts and feelings while developing an appreciation for different challenges, fears, and joys. Good historic fiction takes you through the portal of the printed page, escaping from your time to theirs.

If you're still not interested, don't buy my books. Don't read them. They weren't written for you.

Words

Our past has not always been pretty. I think it important that we not sanitize history. We need to recognize the inhumanity people often show one another. One way is to expose the meanness in words or more precisely the way people *use* certain words.

When writing history or historic fiction, I believe we should not remove offensive language. Rather we should expose its various destructive *uses*. We must be true to the reality that existed—good or bad—as we have the ability to know it.

This is not to promote *that* reality. To the contrary, it is to demonstrate the ongoing struggle to become civilized. We need to show how difficult a fight it has been and still is. We must expose the meanness not only in the words but in the casual, unconscious way we use those words to demean others.

I share my opinions on this subject to explain my occasional use of certain words in this text. Some readers may be offended. That is not my purpose. I attempt to be respectful, while being true to the nature of my characters. If I fail in my effort to portray each culture in a respectful manner, please accept my apology.

As a writer and a human being, I am a work in progress. You may share your opinions with me at **stormsatkendiamong @gmail.com**. Please, be gentle.

Waters

To fully experience this story, you must imagine the landscape of eighteenth-century North America before highways, railroads, and air travel. People and commerce traveled upon or along rivers and streams. Overland pathways connected these waterways. Small communities formed in such places, and over time some thrived.

The Hudson, Delaware, Susquehanna, Wabash, Kaskaskia, and Mississippi Rivers are the major waterways flowing north to south dissecting the area where this story unfolds. Other rivers like the Ohio, Illinois, St. Lawrence, Allegheny, and Monongahela flowed more east to west. These rivers and their tributaries were the transportation routes of the time. Controlling and defending these byways was critically important for people living here.

Even the smallest waterways called runs were significant. They powered the mills and watered the livestock. Primitive homes required a water source. Springs were particularly valued. Pioneer homesteads were not considered complete until a springhouse was built to cool the milk, cheese, and other food.

It is hard to overstate the importance of such waters. In his famous poem <u>Snowbound</u> (when a farm family's children search for their brook following a snow storm) John Greenleaf Whittier described it this way:

"We minded that the sharpest ear
The buried brooklet could not hear,
The music of whose liquid lip
Had been to us companionship,
And, in our lonely life, had grown
To have an almost human tone."

Our ancestors fought and died to secure and protect critical waterways. Today, sadly, we hardly notice and often neglect these historic treasures.

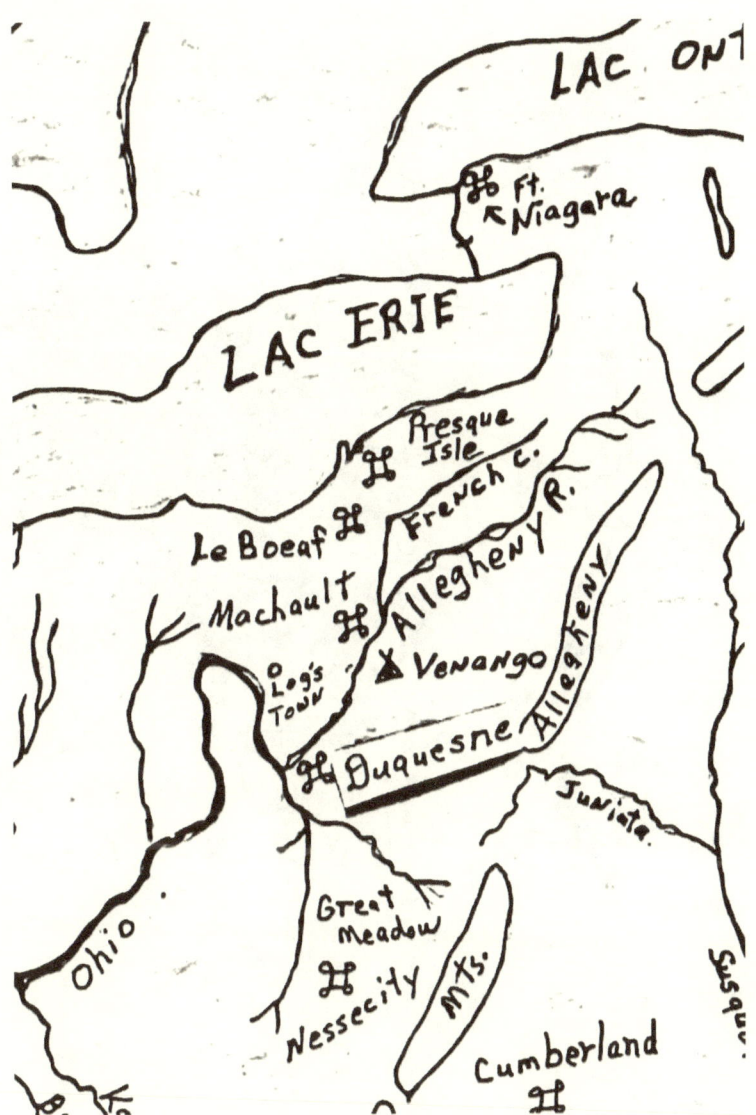

LAC ONT

Ft. Niagara

LAC ERIE

Presque Isle

Le Boeaf

French C.

Machault

Allegheny R.

Allegheny

O Log's Town

Venango

Duquesne Allegheny

Juniata.

Ohio

Great Meadow

Nessecity

Mts.

Cumberland

Susqu.

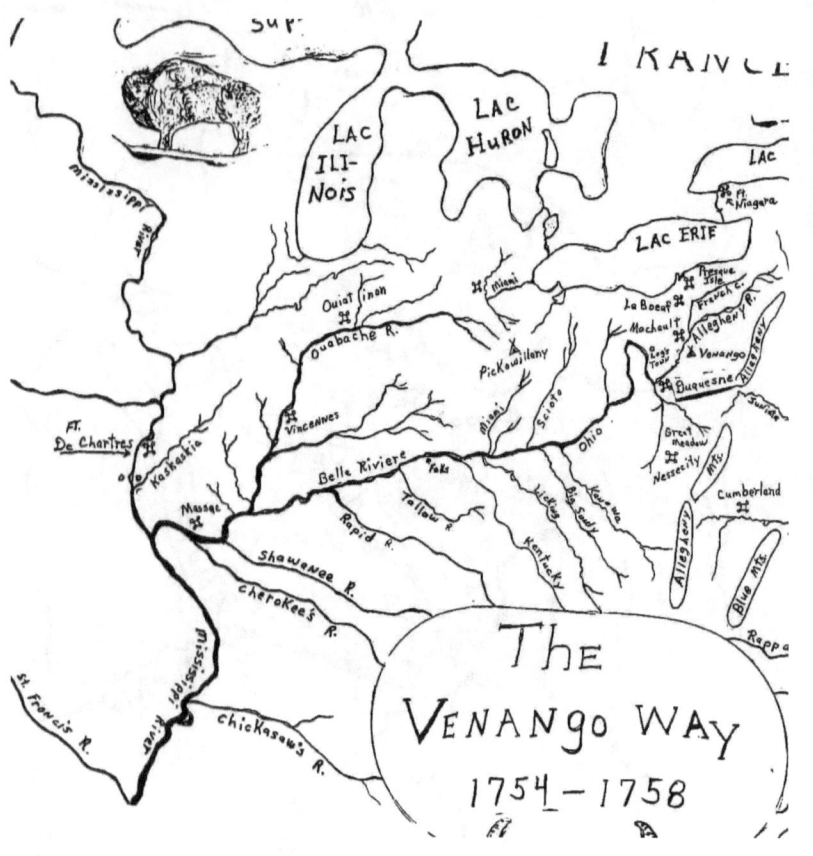

The VENANGO WAY 1754 - 1758

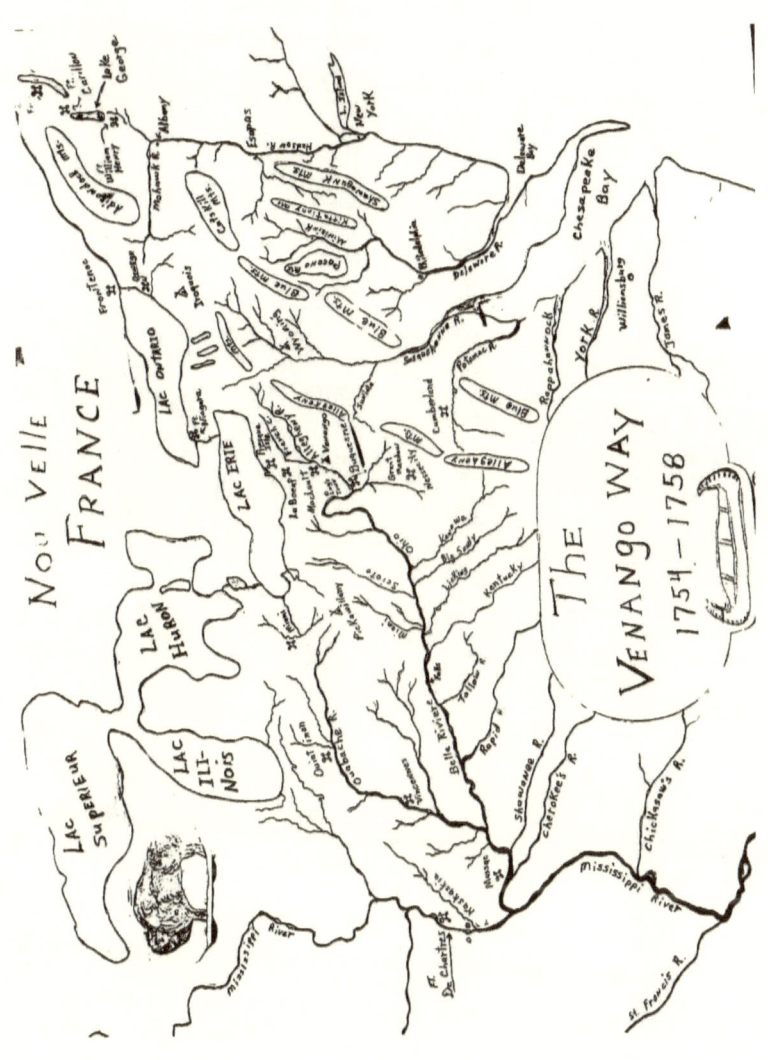

Chapter 1

November, 1679

Deep in the American Wilderness

$\mathcal{R}$ene Robert was confused. He must have gotten turned about. It was cold and damp. His moccasins were soaked through regardless of the bear grease he diligently applied each day. He'd been wading in the squishy muck of this too often marshy prairie. It was hard to find any dry ground here this time of year, though he guessed it might have been a different story a few months back in July and August. He had not found the portage he sought, though he supposed it must be nearby, as he had been told. Now all he wanted was to find his way back to camp. He had been gone most of a day. He did not relish the idea of a cold night alone. But daylight was beginning its fade, whether he liked it or not.

"If I keep walking, it will soon be night. If I fail to find the men, I'll be forced to get up a fire in the dark or maybe freeze to death if I can't. I better find a place to hunker down now."

Off to his right a clump of small trees towered above the brush and tall grasses. It was the first sign of anything above the tall grass he had seen for a while. The deer track he followed seemed to meander that direction. He decided to stop there. A short time later the earth beneath him solidified and he broke out of the tall grass onto dryer ground where willow trees grew. He noticed different bark on some of the tree trunks. He smiled when he noticed the reddish-brown bark of a tree he recognized.

"Wild cherry will burn hot if I can find any dry. Looks like a few limbs have fallen. This will work. Sassafras is somewhere close by. It will get a fire started. I can cut some of the tall grass

for bedding if I'm careful it doesn't catch fire. I won't get much sleep or rest but I won't freeze. Oui, this will work. I'm saved."

"Wait. What's that? Wood smoke? I smell wood smoke. Maybe I'm back to camp. Let's fire a shot; see if they answer."

He raised the musket he'd been carrying.

"I hate to waste lead."

He pulled the trigger. Flint hit steel. Nothing. The gun hadn't fired. He tried again. Same result.

"Powder's wet."

Quickly he emptied the flash pan. He pulled his powder horn around and unstopping its mouth, pouring a bit of fresh powder into the pan. This time the musket roared when the flint hit the striking plate. He listened. Seconds passed. Then a minute. The shot was not answered. None of his party had heard.

"Maybe that was a mistake. Reload and wait," he thought.

Quickly he reloaded. Then he crouched, waiting, listening. No one came or moved except for doves and pigeons on the wing. Geese and ducks honked and quacked overhead. They were all looking for a place to settle for the night, like him. The day continued its fade. Now he suddenly saw a dim light in the brush a short way ahead.

"Savages, he wondered? If there were many, they would already be upon me."

No sounds came except from the birds and there seemed to still be plenty of them. He moved forward a few steps. As he advanced slightly upgrade, he could see a campfire burning about 60 yards out in front.

"Whoever is there, they already know I'm here, no hiding that now. Might as well see what I'm dealing with before its pitch black."

Cautiously he moved forward a few steps at a time, not fast but no longer slow, pausing now and again to listen and watch. Nothing moved except birds overhead. Hundreds maybe thousands of them continued to fly through the twilight sky, some higher up noisily and brashly, others lower down with a quiet stealth, their only sound the swish of air displaced by their wing-beats.

He listened for anything moving at ground level. He heard the soft crackle of the fire burning a few paces in front of him. Nothing else moved or made a noise.

It was a small fire built long, but not long enough for a group. Just beyond the fire was a log and in front of it the leaves had been piled higher. A depression showed as where a deer had been lying in grass. Suddenly a log on the fire shifted, sending sparks straight up in the smoke rising toward a darkening sky. Owls called to one another. An elk bugled somewhere across the prairie. Still nothing moved close around.

"One man? Hoping to den up for the night. Probably ran off when I fired the musket. Maybe out there now watching me. Likely already a mile away looking to put distance between us before he sparks another fire. Can't blame him. Guess it depends on him whether he comes back or not. I think not. His fire's already started. Looks like he gathered enough wood to keep it through the night. I'm not going to get much sleep anyway; might as well use what God has provided."

Slowly Rene Robert strolled the last few steps into his new campsite. He looked first behind the log, with his musket at the level in case someone sprang up. No one did.

"I didn't think so."

He peered into the bare winter brush as far as he could see. He satisfied himself then sat the musket stock to the ground and leaned the barrel against a fork of a small limb extruding from the log, near but not too close to the fire. He paused, let out a breath, picked up a few of the stranger's sticks and placed them on the flames.

With that, Rene took possession. Now it felt like his fire. No one else seemed to care about it any more.

The log behind the fire was about two foot in diameter and the brushy top of the tree which it had supported before it fell was to the left of the camp. Directly behind the log, other brush grew thick, making that way a good escape route but a very noisy approach. The only real open quiet way to approach was how he had come in.

He took a small pack off his back, laying it beside his new bed in front of the log. He untied a short axe bound to the pack, removing the leather cover from its bit.

"Good I brought this. Beats the tomahawk for chopping."

He took his axe and musket a few paces back the way he had come in. Keeping the musket close, he selected some small brushy trees and fell them with a few stokes each, pausing between to listen. Quickly he dragged the brush into such a pile that it closed the open, quiet approach to his camp. Now he stood with his musket and axe inside a small open circle in the center of the pile.

"He may see me in the dark by the firelight, but he won't let fly an arrow through that brush. If he comes at me, I'll hear him, even if I'm dozing."

Rene Robert stepped back to his camp. Pulling a piece of oiled canvas from the pack, he spread it on the leaves and sat down upon it between the log and the fire. Soon he pulled a flask of brandy and some jerked deer meat and quietly began chewing and sipping. Night had arrived. The sky was overcast. No stars peaked out.

"Maybe it won't freeze tonight. But it would be better if it did. Frozen ground with even a little spitting snow is better than this cold and wet or god forbid this cold and rain," he thought. "Yes, lord, let the sky clear and cool the air tonight, but please, God, make it just a little."

The ducks settled. Geese honked, owls continued speaking one to another. Rene unbuttoned his capote enjoying the warmth of the flames from 'his' fire. The log behind him began to reflect heat. It also provided a break from the breeze, blowing from that direction, escorting the smoke from his fire slowly out toward the prairie.

"Could be worse. I'm glad I found this spot. My benefactor, whoever he was, is probably long gone."

Rene Robert placed his weapons close to hand. He retrieved a small log and placed it carefully on the fire. Then he lay back to snooze till the flames burned low. The cold or a sound would wake him. Either way he would know what to do.

"God protect me." He prayed, and closed his eyes.

As Rene Robert dozed beside the fire a flock of geese flew south in formation. Not long before they had passed over the south-east shore of Lac Michigan. Three evenings ago, they had overflown the tiny French trading post of St. Ignace established at Michilimackinac nine years since on the north shore. Near there, waters from Lac Michigan flowed into Lac Huron on their way to the St. Lawrence River and the Atlantic Ocean.

The lead goose could see in a glade below four specks of firelight beside a small north flowing river. He noted another tiny light emitting from a smaller campfire, as geese fly, only a short distance south. If he had had an eagle's vision, he might have also noticed sparks from flint against steel a distance to the east where a single man with chilled fingers tried desperately to spark a new fire.

The geese were tired. They had flown a long way. They were coming down for the night. At treetop level they watched for the right spot. There was the open water of a beaver pond on a gentle stream flowing south. Tomorrow they would follow that stream as it entered other streams flowing toward what America's first peoples called the Father of Rivers, draining almost one third of a continent into the Gulf of Mexico.

Down the geese glided for their individual water landings. Quiet night sounds returned: whip-poor-wills, owls, occasionally the nervous slap of a flat hard beaver tail on water—water which slowly, imperceptibly began its long journey to the warmth of the Caribbean.

A mile away, Rene Robert's flame flickered, slowly transforming its burning wood into glowing coals. He snoozed in its warmth. He dreamed of a portage he would find connecting the St. Joseph's River (flowing north) to a navigable stream flowing southwest. Such a portage would open new, exciting opportunities for the Frenchmen of Nouvelle France. His fire danced, shifting and changing as it burned.

Chapter 2

September, 1710

On the Ouabache (Wabash) River

Jean Verrou was tired. He had been paddling, poling, pushing and towing all day forcing loaded canoes upstream on the Ouabache (Wabash) River. They had beached their craft an hour ago. Jean had volunteered to hunt with Pierre. Pierre was the actual hunter. He led the way.

Jean carried a musket, a tomahawk, a couple sharp knives in sheaths on his belt and a small simple carry pack on his back. They hoped to kill a buffalo. They had seen such animals earlier in the day at a distance on a prairie beyond the west bank. They had traveled this river many times in the last ten years. They knew buffalo were sometimes plentiful in the fall.

It was September, maybe a little early for big herds. The crew had been eating mostly jerky venison for the past week. Everyone wanted fresh meat and most agreed they wanted buffalo more than they wanted elk though either would do.

Neither Pierre nor Jean wished to return to camp with anything less. Hunting, while others set camp, was an honor. Some voyageurs hired special men to hunt for them but this Canadian crew shared the task. Success, by vote of the men, brought additional opportunities. Failure would bring derision, taunting, and unpleasant duties for at least a week.

Pierre and Jean were on the east bank of the Ouabache at a small dry prairie of tall grasses. Jean knew that some priests and soldiers who traveled with the voyager crews found these prairies' abundant flora and fauna interesting and beautiful. But men like him generally took the beauty for granted and looked instead for opportunity.

Pierre glanced back at Jean.

"Looks good, does it not?" he said.

Jean nodded.

Pierre pointed ahead a few paces where they could see a manure pile, buffalo scat, dry, not from today, or yesterday.

"I saw elk droppings a way back, looked maybe a day old," said Jean.

"I saw it. Deer shit is everywhere," said Pierre. "But nobody wants venison tonight."

"Fresh venison's better than dry jerky."

"Not if you have your taste wetted for the tongue of a big shaggy. We have a little more daylight. You hang back. Just keep me in sight."

Jean nodded.

Pierre stalked ahead pausing every few paces to watch and listen. Jean followed at a slower pace, letting Pierre get ahead.

It was a pleasant afternoon neither warm nor cold. The grasses were midway in their transformation from green to straw color to rusty brown. The tall feathery seedpods bent low swaying in the undulating breeze. A wide variety of flowers bloomed within the tall grasses. Yellow compass plants and prairie dock, purple joe pye weed, white rattlesnake master to name a few of the dozens.

The sun, low on the western horizon, had lost its heat. The sky was clear. The prairie soon would cool.

"I should have brought my capote," thought Jean.

Today he liked the life he had chosen. He was twenty years old. He had taken his first voyage the spring of his 14th year. It was an exciting life for a young man and it might be getting better in the years to come. French trading posts were beginning to get built here and there along the hundreds of miles of trading route.

"New posts should make our trips easier and safer," thought Jean.

He had heard the priest in Kaskaskia discussing politics last week. This French outpost in the Illinois Country along the Mississippi River had been established a couple years before Jean's first voyage. He had watched its development for almost a decade. He remembered it from a few Indian wigwams, and a single priest, to now a village of half a dozen French style houses, common fields, common pasture, and the beginnings of a stone church.

The priests last week had been excited about recent news brought downriver. Antoine de la Mothe Cadillac had been reassigned by the crown officials in Quebec City to far off Louisiana at Mobile Bay.

"Maybe he will do us less harm there," said one of the priests smiling.

Jean could neither read nor write. He recognized Jesuits as educated men. He honored their position in the Holy Church. He respected their personal sacrifice, courage, and dogged determination. He feared their power and influence. But, he knew they were not infallible. He had witnessed too much.

"Priests and Commandants sometimes find themselves at odds when advising Royal Authorities," he thought. *"Their butter seems to be applied on different sides of the bread. Their fingers*

get sticky. Voyageurs like me, on the other hand, are happy to have any bread at all."

Jean watched Pierre stalk through the tall grass ahead. He and Pierre were unlike most voyageurs. They listened and watched when any authority spoke, and they listened most carefully when the words were spoken in whispers. Opportunity was often discovered at such moments. Awareness helped one make wise decisions. Jean knew that sometimes a good decision could do much to keep a simple voyageur alive.

For years, opinions along the trade routes had wavered back and forth about de la Mothe Cadillac and his relationships with the Jesuits and Royal Authorities.

The French officer had arrived in 1694 as a new Commandant at Fort de Buade at St Ignace on Mackinaw Straight, when the fort was yet new and when the Jesuit Mission had already been in existence at that place for two decades. The priests at St. Ignace were happy for additional protection but quickly became jealous of competing new authority.

Priests had ruled at St. Ignace since the time of Joliet and Marquette. La Salle visited the Jesuits there in 1679 before he discovered the portage between the St. Josephs' and Kankakee rivers, before he built Fort St. Joseph to protect the important portage, before he paddled down the Illinois and Mississippi, and before he died somewhere along the gulf coast of America.

Jean knew the legends. All his life he had listened to men tell tales of the great generation of explorers who had claimed this land for the French King Louis XIV. Those stories from the previous century were replete with rumors of lost gold or silver mines. Some coureur des bois (woods runners) still sought that gold and silver today. Truth be known, Jean himself had faded to sleep many nights dreaming of such discoveries. It was one of

10

the reasons he continued to work the rivers and listened intently to whispered conversations while others were drunk on brandy or wine.

Now King Louis was getting old. Power and influence were shifting. Most Frenchmen sought their fortune in the trading of furs. The commerce was brisk and profitable. The trading posts and missions were growing the business and many were enriching themselves or their benefactors. Anything, anyone, or any change, which might upset or threaten this accumulation of wealth immediately found detractors, who could quickly become enemies.

De la Mothe Cadillac was a man who noticed opportunity for improvement. He was a commandant who possessed a soldier's eye for good defensive positions. More importantly, for France he saw the 'big picture' strategically. He predicted and planned for future conflict, which he suspected would develop between great European powers now actively competing for influence in America. Short-term profits for a few, he believed, must give way for the greater glory of France and the King. If that sacrifice also benefited the career of Antoine de la Mothe Cadillac, so much the better.

Jean did not see or understand world events or business, as did the priests and commandants. He did, however, recognize tension, hear rumors and witness developments along the waterways he traveled. He was a stakeholder in these decisions like any Frenchman paddling these rivers. He kept a close council, usually with only Pierre, but he watched, listened, and formed opinions.

Pierre was crouching now in the grass. Beyond was a thicket of cottonwood and pecan trees. He motioned to let Jean know he planned to circle them to the left. Jean nodded and Pierre moved off quietly in that direction.

Jean noted some more dry manure. The sun was lower. A breeze blew from the west blending river and prairie fragrances: fish, mussels, dry grass.

Jean returned to his thoughts. He knew de la Mothe Cadillac was responsible for building Fort Pontchartrain at Detroit. Jean had watched Detroit develop as he had watched Kaskaskia because of its location between Lac Erie and Lac Huron.

Detroit rapidly grew in importance. Many Indian villages moved closer to Detroit. The Jesuit Mission at St. Ignace withered. The priests blamed de la Mothe Cadillac.

The sun, a ball of bright orange, sank now into the western horizon. Jean was beginning to lose confidence in Pierre's hunt. The rustling grasses swayed and meadowlarks sang. Jean began to fear failure and taste dry jerked deer meat. He did not like either.

After de la Mothe Cadillac left New France to become the Governor of Louisiana, his ideas continued to influence decisions in Canada for a time. In 1712 Fort de Buade was abandoned in favor of a new Fort Michilimackinac built across the strait of Mackinaw to the south shore. St. Ignace suffered again.

Fort Miami was built on the Maumee River to protect a portage to the important Ouabache (Wabash) River. In 1713, Fort St. Louis at Starved Rock on the Illinois River (built a generation before by La Salle and soon abandoned) was rebuilt and resupplied.

Jean and Pierre saw all this as progress. But, certain Jesuit priests burned with jealousy.

Chapter 3

April 15, 1734

At Kaskaskia in the French Illinois Country

*F*orty-four-year-old Jean Verrou woke to the glorious smell of frying bacon. Outside in the darkness a mocking bird called loudly from the pear tree. Ruth puttered in the kitchen of the two-room French built house.

Jean stretched his arms above his head slipping quickly from the bed into his clothes. It would be a long day and work would begin at first light. Jean wanted time to enjoy his breakfast. Passing through the kitchen, he nodded to his wife, opened the door and walked outside. He paused on the porch to take a deep breath and another stretch.

"Smells like rain," he thought, stepping off across the yard.

A few moments later Jean returned glancing to the east. Stars, continued to show clearly. Whip-poor-wills called from the rivers to accompany the mocking-bird. A cock crowed somewhere in the Village.

The ground was moist but without a frost. No doubt there would be fog from the rivers, but the sky seemed clear above.

"Maybe, no rain today after all," thought Jean.

He lifted the door latch stepping inside. The glorious aroma greeted him again. His mouth began to water. He was hungry.

"Morning stars are beautiful today inside and out," he said, smiling at his wife. She stood between the stone fireplace and a small wooden table. She smiled back, accepting his compliment.

Morning-Star was her Indian name. Jean used it at home or sometimes shortened it to Star. At church and around the priests, he called her by her Christian name, Ruth.

Morning-Star had been the 30-year-old Widow DeLisle when Jean had married her six years ago. Chickasaw Indians had killed her previous husband, sixty-year-old Boucher DeLisle, during a spring convoy transporting Illinois flour and pork to the Isle of New Orleans. That previous marriage had lasted fourteen years. Star had birthed two children with DeLisle: a daughter Gabriel who had died early of a fever, and a son Baptiste who died age eight, two years after Jean married the widow, adopting the boy.

Two children, three-year-old Alex Verrou and Mary Verrou, age one, slept now in opposite corners of the bedroom. Jean was a very fortunate man and he knew it. Boucher DeLisle had been a good 'habitant' (tiller of the soil). The Widow DeLisle was a pretty woman and she had brought respectability, a house, two oxen, farming tools, and property rights to the marriage. Yes, Jean Verrou was a fortunate man.

Jean sat down and began eating his breakfast: eggs, bacon, bread, hot sassafras tea, cool red wine. It would be a long time till the noon-day meal. The work would be hard but not as hard as forcing loaded canoes upriver. Today was the appointed time to repair community fence around the plowland long-lots. Every habitant was expected to help, and it was required by law.

Kaskaskia had come a long way since its beginning over three decades before. Jean had watched it grow first as a visiting voyager paddling through on long trips and recently as a local habitant tilling the soil and raising a family. Much had changed.

After Antoine de la Mothe Cadillac become governor of Louisiana alterations in management were quick to follow in that part of the French-American colonies. The Illinois country previously governed by New France from Quebec was annexed to become the Upper District of Louisiana with its north boundary above the Illinois River. Jesuits, at Kaskaskia were not rid of their old nemesis yet. The priests were quiet for a while after that.

Control of all commerce in Louisiana was given over by the King to a Scot businessman named John Law and his Mississippi Company (or Company of the West as it was sometimes called). New Orleans was founded on the Mississippi River in 1717 with high hopes and little planning. It grew slowly with fits and starts and always seemed to need outside support. The Illinois Country saved the new town (and hoped for shipping center) from repeated threats of starvation. Convoys of flour and pork came over a thousand miles downriver through hostile country arriving often just in the nick of time. Soon the Illinois country had a reputation in France as the breadbasket for Louisiana.

About the same time Governor Boucher, in Quebec, dispatched Jean Baptist Bissot, Sieur de Vincennes from New France to establish Fort Ouiatenon on the Ouabache (Wabash) River near its Eel River Tributary. This location was just north of the boundary separating New France and the Upper District of Louisiana (Illinois country). The Ouabache (Wabash) River was growing in its importance to the lucrative fur trade industry. Profits from this trade financed almost everything in New France and continued to draw investment from rich men back in Paris and Versailles.

Jean Verrou was still paddling the rivers two years later in 1719 when Commandant Boisbriant was dispatched up the Mississippi to build a new fort to protect the one village in all Louisiana, able to grow enough good wheat to feed more than its' self. At Kaskaskia he soon built a (temporary) fort directly across the Kaskaskia River on its east bank. He named it Fort De Chartres. Two years later he moved the fort four leagues (12 miles) north on the larger Mississippi River, approximately one mile inland from its east bank, where it still sat today.

Soon three new villages were begun. Chartres at the fort, Prairie Du Rocher two miles east at the Bluff (a limestone landscape feature carved eons before edging the Mississippi river bottom for fifty miles) and St. Philippe two leagues (six miles) north. These three plus the fort, Kaskaskia and Cahokia, (a French Seminarian Mission 14 leagues (42 miles) north) constituted the Illinois country during the formative decade of the 1720s.

The new Commandant could formalize property rights. Fields were laid-off by survey in the French style: ribbon shaped long-lots. One of the first habitants to get his land rights legally registered was Boucher DeLisle at Kaskaskia.

Jean Verrou knew these things and felt the future looked bright for his family. He had positioned himself well for an illiterate voyageur, who had started life with nothing.

He thought about this now as he ate his breakfast. Even his friend Pierre worked the river less as he aged. It was a hard life working the river. Pierre presently was occupied building the pirogues needed for the Mississippi River trade. Demand was high. He lived in the Indian village at Kaskaskia, was still healthy, and sometimes helped Jean if an extra hand was needed and terms could be reached. The two old friends, however, drew a little further apart each year.

"I need to invite Pierre to a meal sometime," thought Jean as he drank his wine.

"That new Fort at Vincennes will help security on the Wabash. People say it's built halfway between here and Detroit. That's a hundred miles closer than Ouiatenon. Those fence posts will

not cut and set themselves today. I think I hear people moving on the road."

"They're going. I better go too," he said to his wife.

He rose, taking his hat from its peg, and walked out the door of his house. There was light in the east. Whip-poor-wills had stopped singing but several more cocks were announcing the sunrise, which had not yet arrived. Men were moving along the road toward the common plowlands.

Regardless of how these small villages, their white-washed houses, long-lot plowlands, farm tools, and picket fences might look like others in France, there was one very big difference. These tiny few villages were surrounded by thousands of square miles of American wilderness. Beyond the coastal areas and a few river routes that wild land was still unknown to white men and most of the other people living in it were not their friends.

Chapter 4

$\mathcal{J}$ean walked to the barn, threw the wooden latch back, and entered. Moments later he led forth two small, yearling bullocks he'd been training as a team. They were yoked together in the French fashion with a heavy hickory poll lashed across both sets of horns. In the center of the yoke-stick an iron clevis was affixed where a rope or draw bar could be attached between the animals.

Shim and Shave had been yoked together with a series of smaller yoke-sticks for part of every day since they had been young calves. At first the training was for short periods to graze on hay, eat grain in the barn, or be led to the stream for water. Gradually Jean had lengthened the periods of time Shim and Shave were 'in yoke' until not long ago they reached the half-day mark in the pasture grazing together.

Thereafter, Jean began working the young oxen on light pulling tasks about the house and barn. He used them yesterday hitched to the cart when he went to the river to pick up posts to be set today. Now he hitched them again to the cartload of red-cedar posts.

"Up," he said, flicking Shim lightly with a long stick. The team plodded forward.

Jean was proud of Shim and Shave. Selecting and training the bullocks had required time and patience. The oxen were not full grown but they had the makings for a well-matched team.

It was the first time Jean had raised and trained his own oxen. The team would not be ready for the charrue (French wheel plow) this spring. They would earn their keep working in other ways this season. But next year, full grown, they would replace the aged team, which

Boucher DeLisle had purchased long ago to work his fields.

"When I plow with my own team the fields will feel, for the first time, like they are really mine," thought Jean.

Boucher DeLisle, from the grave, haunted Jean just a little. DeLisle had been a respected member of the community. He was a good habitant always willing to help his neighbors. The priests had liked him. Even the Commandant had sometimes sought his advice on local matters. And then he had suddenly been killed by the Chickasaw on that Spring convoy floating Illinois flour and pork to rescue New Orleans, the capital city which always seemed to need saving.

For years since marrying Morning-Star, Jean felt he had been living in the shadow of Boucher Delisle. Occasionally a neighbor would comment on how Boucher had worked his fields or performed a task. Jean always felt the sting of comparison. He knew they were judging him. He was not Boucher. He was not their old friend and neighbor. Jean had not even been a long-time habitant or a permanent resident of Kaskaskia. He had been a voyageur.

His 'kind' usually stayed near the friendly Indian villages or the fort on the Mississippi. They were normally here today and gone tomorrow. They were useful when needed on convoys downriver or when fighting savages: Iroquois, Cherokee, Chickasaw, Fox and other unnamed tribes west of the Mississippi. But, voyageurs didn't usually marry local widows, with land rights, houses, and barns.

Jean was correct. His neighbors were watching and judging. So far, he had surprised them. He was still here. He stayed sober. He worked his fields.

Kaskaskia was a small village. It had been over six years since Jean had married the widow. Boucher Delisle was still well remembered and as far as some of them were concerned Jean Verrou lived in his house.

As Jean and his team of yearling oxen approached Star stepped out onto the side porch with a musket, powder horn and possible bag. She smiled at her husband and eyed his new team. She could see his pride, and she was proud of him for it.

Jean stepped closer, took the items and placed them carefully in the cart. As he finished, she touched his arm and skipped ahead to open the front gates.

A high picket fence enclosed their lot in the village including within: house, barn, poultry coop, garden, small corral, stone well, orchard trees, and out-house. It was its own small fortress and it was not unique.

Fenced lots were the custom for good reason. The village streets were within the fenced commons (public land), which everyone was free to use for pasturage, forage, or wood gathering. Peoples' livestock (hogs, cattle, horses) roamed free within the commons.

Today, more than usual, animals were about, the village streets having just been moved out of the fenced common plowlands. Custom provided that the stubble fields from last year's crop must be made available for public grazing mid-December to mid-April each year. This practice increased forage for animals during winter and also fertilized the plowlands with manure.

After a few days repairing fence, weather permitting, the plowlands would be available to begin this season's fieldwork.

The ancient French system for land use worked to everyone's' benefit. Doing your share of the work built your reputation. A good reputation was essential to a family's credit and respect within the community. Jean Verrou intended to do his part.

"Bonjour Monsieur Verrou," said a man in the road ahead.

"Bonjour Louis," answered Jean.

Jean and his team were traveling from his house along the road from Kaskaskia to Fort De Chartres and beyond to Cahokia fifty miles north. The two-wheel dirt track was the only roadway existing in North America west of the Susquehanna River fifteen hundred miles east.

Jean had followed the road a few times to Prairie-Du-Rocher thence to the fort and on to the Indian village two miles north. Beyond that point Jean had never had reason to travel though he knew the remaining part by reputation.

Four miles above the Indian village was the small community of St. Phillipe established by Phillipe Renaut. Renaut was one of the most powerful men in the Illinois Country. He had been granted a huge rectangular tract of land measuring one league (three mile) along the Mississippi and two League (six miles) inland. This grant by the Company of the West was intended to benefit and support his mining operations. Renaut had imported fifty black slaves to work in his mines and fields so work here progressed quickly. From St. Phillipe the road swung east above the tall limestone bluff and continued on high ground most of the way to Cahokia the Seminarian Mission and the most northerly village in the Illinois country.

The roadway ended at Cahokia. However, not far away the Buffalo Trace headed off to the east following the general direction which millions of buffalo had trod for centuries across tall grass prairies toward salt licks and winter grazing in Kain-tuck-kee. About halfway to Kain-tuck, this track crossed the Ouabache (Wabash) River fifty leagues (one hundred and fifty mile) east. Here was the new isolated French village of Vincennes or at least the cleared lots where the houses were being built.

Jean knew Frenchmen who had already traveled overland to Vincennes, but not many. It was a dangerous trek. Travel by river was safer and maybe faster.

Jean seldom had reason himself to travel the road more than he had this morning, half a mile from his house, to where his long-lot fields were located within the common plowlands. His fields stretched between the two rivers Mississippi and Kaskaskia. The road cut across the fields closer to the smaller river.

Thanks to the location of his long-lots between the rivers, Jean had no fence to be maintained by himself on either end. He owed that also to Boucher Delisle's sound wisdom, so today he would go beyond his fields to the common fence on the north side of the plowlands and help his neighbors work there.

Crossing his long-lot now, Jean inspected his stubble fields. Hoofmarks had cut and compacted the soil repeatedly over the winter as the animals nibbled down the forage. Fresh hoofmarks were evident where recently the livestock had been driven through on the way to the commons for summer pasture. The new tracks, Jean noted, were cut an inch or two deep, clean on the edges, with no water collected in them.

"This ground is ready for the plow soon as we finish with the fence," he thought.

Jean was anxious. He wanted to get going on this year's work.

"Maybe after the heavy plowing is finished, I can sell Boucher's old team."

The red-cedar post hit the bottom of the trench with a thud. Five-to-six-inch diameter, eight-foot-long posts made a heavy load to lift and drop into a two-foot-deep hole. Jean had hefted and dropped that one by himself. Louis had not offered to help as he had been doing before.

Louis Bourdon was over sixty-years-old this year. He was tiring out as this day waned. Louis would do his share in other ways, Jean had worked with him enough to know. No one would ever call Louis Bourdon a shirker. But, as days like this wore on, he slowed down on heavy lifting.

Louis and Jean worked together often. They were neighbors in the long-lot plowlands with Louis holding the location to the south of Jean's. They enjoyed working together.

Louis didn't talk a lot but when he did talk Jean listened. He had learned a great deal about working ground from listening to Louis, who had been doing it many years.

Louis likewise enjoyed listening to Jean's stories about the life of a voyageur. Louis had traveled only slightly, almost none, since he had come with a young wife, three children, and a younger brother to settle at Kaskaskia 30 years ago. Before coming here, he had lived in his father's home near Quebec City almost three hundred leagues (nine hundred miles) and three portages north. In Canada, Louis learned to till the soil on his father's long-lot fields.

Coming to settle in the middle of the wilderness had been the adventure of Louis Bourdon's life. In the beginning, he had expected to die or be killed many times. But in recent years since the fort was built and the soldiers came, he felt better. Besides he had beat the odds. He was already an old man with eight children, still living so far as he knew. Only three lived at home. A daughter had moved to Fort Detroit. Another had moved to the Arkansas Post; a son Joseph had left for the new Post Vincennes a month ago. Two other daughters lived in Chartres near the fort with families of their own.

"Here comes Parlier," said Jean, looking across the field.

A rider on horseback approached at a trot. It was Jacques Parlier, the habitant whose location was to the north of Jean's in the plowlands. Jean also shared work on occasion with Jacques Parlier but he enjoyed it less.

"Bonjour messieurs."

"Bonjour Parlier, what brings you?" said Jean.

"Bad news. Three bateau touched for a short time at the landing. Voyageurs said they'd come down from Vincennes. Yesterday morning just before they reached the junction with La Belle Riviere (Ohio River) they found two bodies snagged in a pile of drift. Recognized one as part of six men who left Vincennes nine days ago in two bark canoes headed for De Chartres. Must be a war party to take on six men. Likely Cherokee, like last fall."

"Any other news from Vincennes?" asked Louis.

"They said the fort is built. But, it is not much beyond a blockhouse and a few pickets. Four proper French houses are being built, but none have a roof yet. They do have a priest but no church is built or even begun. I asked but they didn't know Joseph by name. One had been to the blacksmith and he said there was a lad working there which might be him."

"They did say the Piankashaw have a new village just below the place and they are very friendly people. The voyageurs didn't stay long. They shoved off hoping to make the fort before dark. The Royal Marines will probably be here in the morning asking for militiamen to go with 'em for a scout. That's all I know. Got to spread the word."

Jacques Parlier trotted his horse west along the fence line heading off toward the Mississippi. As he passed by, he studied Shim and Shave who were tied to the cart.

"Think that little team will be as good as Boucher's old pair?" he called back.

Jean didn't answer. Instead, he kicked some dirt in the hole around the post and Louis started tamping it, compacting it, into the bottom of the hole with his well-worn tamping stick. Jean picked up Louis' old shovel and added more dirt as Louis tamped with the stick. Four-inch layers of soil backfill were added for a while like this, Louis pausing occasionally to eye and adjusted the post.

"I'm sure that's probably Joseph working with the Blacksmith," said Jean.

"I hope so," said Louis, "that was his plan. But, do you think Vincennes can hold that little fort of his till he gets it better built?"

"He has his orders. I guess he can. His father held on to Ouiatenon. It's been there for thirty years."

Louis paused to look toward the east and take a deep breath.

"Maybe Vincennes 'the younger' has upset the normal order of things again," said Louis. "Who knows how some of these tribes think. Maybe he has offended the Iroquois again. God knows the Fox, Cherokee, and Chickasaw think they own the world. They don't care

25

much about the King's proclamations. And then we have the English trying to turn our own Indians against us, stealing our trade every chance they get, offering cheaper English goods. I hope the commandants and the priests know what they are doing. They sure have pissed off some tribes before. Hell, years ago the Fox were our trade partners at St. Ignace. I knew an old coureur des bois (Canadian who lived among the Indians) who was there when they moved their village to Detroit. He went along. He said after they got the village built and a crop of corn harvested, the Fox tribe got into a scrap with the Miami. The temporary commandant at that time was a new hand. I forget his name. He sided with one, then the other, and pissed-off both tribes. The Miami finally came back around to trade with us again, but the Fox never did. They still hate us. They may not be powerful enough to destroy us all, but they sure as hell kill us when they get the chance."

Jean knew Louis had lost his younger brother battling the Fox. He said nothing and waited.

"It's been six years since Francois went off with Lieutenant Melique and his seven soldiers to scout trouble up the Missouri a few leagues. Never saw them alive after that. Wish I had not been along when they were found."

"I know," said Jean.

"We used to lose seven or eight or even ten men at a time in ambushes like that. Regularly".

"I know," said Jean, "but the expedition three years ago took a little starch out of them."

"I was there you recall," said Louis, "we didn't kill near enough and we still lose at least one or two people every year; I'm thinking mostly to the Fox. Not to speak of the people we lose downriver to the damn Chickasaws".

Louis paused to look at Jean.

"That last expedition was likely my final. I don't move so quick anymore over distances. But I'd be willing to go one more time, if we were going against the Fox. I'm tired of 'em picking us off one or two at a time. Do you figure it really was Cherokee like he said?"

"I don't know, Louis, could be it was the Fox who did it and laid down a false trail hoping we would blame it on the Cherokee. But from where the bodies were found, likely it really was them devils down south. The soldiers will have to sort out who we blame. Sure as hell someone did it. Someone will have to be punished for it. I just pray we get the right ones."

Louis stomped a clod into pieces and tamped it into a small finished mound of dirt around the post.

"After a couple rains that should settle well enough," he said.

Louis Bourdon did not like criticizing Royal Authorities or thinking much about murdering savages.

Chapter 5

July 2, 1743

Kaskaskia, French Louisiana

*A*lex Verrou was settling into a trot. The bell at the Church of the Immaculate Conception reverberated across the bottomlands, calling its parishioners to mass as it had in Kaskaskia for two years, since King Louis XV sent it up the Mississippi by bateau, a gift to the church in the Illinois country.

Thirteen-year-old Alex Verrou was very proud of the bell the King of France had sent. However, Alex was not headed toward church. He was trotting the opposite direction toward the Kaskaskia River.

Two boys, Etienne and Maurice, were waiting beside the pirogue.

"Bonjour," said Alex, running down the riverbank, tossing his possible bag into the craft, climbing aboard, skittering aft, applying his weight out into the water, and raising the bow of the pirogue a little off the sand beneath it.

Neither of the other boys answered. Etienne smiled, nodding to Maurice. Together they pushed the skiff out into the Kaskaskia River, clambering aboard, first Maurice and last Etienne, just as the bow slid from sand into the clear water.

As the craft drifted, Etienne and Maurice picked up their paddles, dipping them into the water and pulling hard. Alex let his paddle slide back with the current, turning it as a rudder guiding the pirogue away from the bank, upstream, toward Mill Run, half a mile ahead on the opposite shore. All three boys now shifted to their normal paddling stroke, with Alex guiding the craft and Etienne squinting ahead ready to fend off any snag waiting submerged below the river's surface.

Handling the pirogue was serious business. The boys planned to become voyageurs. They thought of themselves as already accomplished river-men, but today they were fishing, which was business of a different kind.

The river's current was slight today and the boys closed the distance toward Mill Run in a few minutes. Before arriving at the creek, Alex steered the pirogue under an overhanging monarch of a tree, its white bark gleaming in morning sunlight.

The big sycamore had been a landmark, guiding the boys back to their limb-line. Upstream from the tree an alder bush overgrew the bank. Here, last evening, tied to one of its limbs the boys had attached a short drop line terminated by a fishhook, baited with chicken gut. Twenty similar drops were set now, scattered on both sides of the river for a league (three miles) upstream. This morning, the boys were running their limb-line sets for fish, as they had run trap-line sets last winter for fur bearing animals: fox, mink, muskrat. (Beaver had been trapped out near Kaskaskia twenty years before the boys were born.)

Fishing was valued in the village as an important food source, especially large channel-cat and sturgeon. Fish of one-hundred-fifty-pound weight were not uncommon.

If not eaten locally, large fish could be sold at the fort. Most people worked the big river, which is why the boys fished the Kaskaskia.

The smaller river flowed into the Mississippi two-thirds of a league downstream at La Pointe de Bois, where The Kaskaskia Commons changed gradually from pasture to wetland to sandbar, then disappeared into the mixed water from both rivers. On the smaller water farther from Fort de Chartres, the boys had less competition and therefore fewer conflicts over locations for their sets.

Etienne brushed a few overhead alder branches to the side and grasped the heavy line, pulling it up carefully, hand over hand. In a moment, he could tell there was no weight to the line and no struggle at the far end, so, he quickened his retrieve till the bare hook came to him.

He frowned, shrugging his shoulders as he reached back toward Maurice who was leaning forward with more chicken innards in his left hand. Maurice took the hook and line, stringing new bait on the hook and tossing it over the side, as Etienne and Alex directed the pirogue from under the bush back into the river.

Maurice watched the re-baited hook sink, disappearing into the depths. He picked up his paddle. The boys headed upstream toward the next limb-line, hoping for a better result.

Two hours passed while the boys checked sets. As they paddled away from the ninth drop-line on the east side of the river, they had only five catfish in the bottom of the pirogue. The largest fish was short of fifteen pounds, but well over ten. The smallest would not make two. The other fish were closer in size to the little than the big.

"Running small today," said Etienne.

"Oui," said Alex.

"Let's stop at the turn and hunt up the creek for a while," said Maurice.

"Why?" asked Alex.

"Just to see what we can find and be out of the pirogue for a while," said Maurice.

"We haven't paddled a league and you want to get out and walk?" said Etienne. "Some voyageur you will make."

Alex and Etienne chuckled as they all paddled steadily toward a big hickory. On the left bank they could now see Obishan's creek emptying into the river. Maurice mumbled a response under his breath but he was careful not to miss or short a paddle stroke, which might invite more comments.

"Maybe I don't want to be a voyageur," he thought, *"if I have to put up with assholes like you two."*

All three boys were smiling to themselves as they neared the big hickory, quietly paddling in unison looking indeed like the young voyageurs they wished to be.

The limb-line this time was tied to an overhanging willow tree. As the boys approached, the limb began shaking and bobbing above the water. The fish below had not been on line all night. It had fight left. From the size of the limb and the bending and bobbing it did as the fish fought this might be their biggest catch today, if they caught it. It wasn't in the boat yet.

"Back off," said Etienne.

All three boys back paddled, and Alex maneuvered the pirogue back into the current, away from the willow. The limb shook above the water.

"That may be a big fish. Let's let him wear down for a spell," said Etienne.

"Let's go across to the creek and get out of this pirogue, maybe hunt a while," said Alex.

"Excellent idea," said Etienne.

All three boys pealed with laughter as they paddled across the river, never missing a stroke or bumping the gunnels.

"Let's spark a fire and have an early shore lunch. Give that old boy some time before we bring him in. In an hour or so he will tire and we don't want to lose him," said Alex.

The other two nodded. All three began scouting the bank area for dry wood. In two minutes, they were on shore, a small pile of driftwood beginning to grow on a flat sandbar a few steps upstream from Obishon's Creek.

Etienne reached into the pirogue and brought out the two smallest catfish. In seconds he knocked each one in the head with a heavy rock from the river and went to work gutting and skinning the fish. Suddenly he was hungry.

Maurice bent over and quickly laid twigs and duff together into a fire set. His flint and steel were soon striking and sparks flying.

Alex procured a skillet, a pouch of wheat flower, and a small gourd of bacon fat from the pirogue. He had come prepared.

"I love this shit," said Etienne.

"The life of a voyageur," said Alex.

"Coureur de bois," said Maurice.

The fire was started and Maurice piled on bigger sticks.

Alex and Etienne dragged in a couple, small driftwood logs, big enough for each boy to sit dry while waiting for the hickory to burn down to a bed of hot coals. Some things take time.

"We won't always have a skillet, you know," said Maurice.

"We do today," said Alex.

"Old Pierre made this pirogue, did he not?" asked Etienne.

"Oui, he did, before the first war with the Chickasaws," answered Alex.

"Pierre still does good work," said Etienne. "He burns and chips out the interior better than anyone else. He takes the time. The skin here looks to be no more than an inch thick."

Etienne ran his hands over the pirogue, as it lay pulled up on shore.

"He smooths it down real nice inside and out. Leaves it lighter-weight than most."

Etienne appreciated craftsmanship.

"Pierre always leaves that burnt brown on the inside. His pirogues look like someone has aged whiskey in 'em but they are smooth not rough. You know?"

"Oui, he does good work," said Alex, "maybe even better now. He was never fast even before."

Pierre had taken a hard blow to his left knee from a war-club in the first Chickasaw War. It had never healed straight. He walked now always with the aid of a good walking stick, and often wincing in pain.

"Well, that was a bad war. Pierre is lucky he had your father to drag him out of there and help him home," said Maurice, looking at Alex. "Lots of the wounded were left behind that time. Many ended up burnt at the stake like Commandant Artaguette, the Jesuit Father Senat, and Sieur de Vincennes (François Bissot Sieur de Vincennes)."

33

"Oui, it was a bad war," said Etienne, "my mother still cries and lights candles for Uncle Antoine. Louis Bourdon's son Boucher died on the way home."

"No, that was the second campaign against the Chickasaw in '39 when I was ten years old," said Alex. "I remember that time when father came home and told Louis: Boucher had took the fever on the way home. His wound was not too bad but the fever caught hold of many on the way back because there was so little to eat. They ran out of supplies. They fought for months that time. Even the New Orleans solders ran out of food before they got home, and the fever killed many of them, too."

"Well at least during the second war Governor Bienville got his soldiers upriver on time and Commandant La Buissoniere waited for the link up before anyone attacked the Chickasaw," said Etienne. "That turned out some better. But the first war was a mess. I heard a couple old men talking not long ago after mass. We didn't have enough men the first war, only fifty Frenchmen including those Vincennes brought with him. Even with a thousand of our Indian allies it was not enough. Artaguette should have waited or come back home."

"Well," said Alex, "Father said something had to be done. Back then, the Chickasaw were attacking our convoys every time they went down or came upriver. Especially when our Bateau were coming upstream. Lots of men were killed on the river every summer then. We were having trouble getting goods shipped to us. At least after the second war the Chickasaw respect us. We didn't destroy them but we hurt them bad. Now, we have an understanding with 'em about our right to use the river. The last few years there is less trouble, at least for big convoys."

"Grease is hot," said Etienne.

He slid the filets into the skillet, listening to the sizzle.

"We going along on the drive?" asked Etienne.

"I think so," said Alex. "I asked Father. He said he would think on it."

"Never been to Vincennes," said Maurice.

"None of us have been anywhere except de Chartres," said Etienne.

"I've been to St. Phillipe," said Maurice.

"In a pirogue with your mother to visit your aunt when you were two. That don't count," said Etienne. "Besides St. Philippe is only two leagues (six miles) north of the fort."

Alex turned the frying fish filets in the skillet with the aid of some tongs he had cut and bent from a flexible willow limb.

"It's time for us to do something more than work fields, mind stock, trap, and fish," said Alex. "If Father doesn't take us on the drive we can just go to the fort and sign on to a voyageur crew heading to Detroit, Fort Niagara, Montreal, or Quebec."

"They'll sign us up. Last time I went to the fort, I had three offers and Father knows it. He will let us help him. He knows we are ready. If we do well, I know he is talking about a cattle drive to Arkansas Post so we can bring back horses. It's dangerous but we can make some real money on a drive like that one."

"Has anyone ever done it? Is there a trail?" asked Maurice.

"Sure, where do you think the horses we have came from," said Etienne. "Years ago, Michigamea scouts guided soldiers from de Chartres overland. They found a tribe in Arkansas Country who had many horses for trade, got 'em from the Spanish."

"Will someone guide us to Vincennes? It's a ways out across the prairie that direction and it's pretty dangerous out that way too, last time I asked," said Maurice.

"Piankashaw guide from the Fort. He knows the way. We will go in a couple weeks when the prairie has dried up a bit more," said Alex.

"Will he know how to keep ticks off?" asked Maurice. "Lots of ticks in those tall grasses."

Alex didn't answer but he took the skillet from the fire and passed it to the other two. Carefully each boy took his share onto some elm bark pieces Etienne had peeled from a nearby tree. Quietly they began to blow and nibble on hot fried fish. It smelled good and tasted better.

Across the river the limb-line attached to the willow had stopped bobbing but a taught line still swirled in slow circles from the deep water.

Chapter 6

"*I* will take Alex with me on the cattle drive to Vincennes," said Jean.

Morning-Star looked up from the iron pot on the hearth where she stirred stew with a wooden spoon. Without comment she tuned back to take the pot and set it to the side. The fire had burned low and the coals had cooled from red to grey. She picked up a stick and stirred the coals.

"He is ready," she said.

"I know," answered Jean. "I was his age when I signed on for my first trip upriver. Last time we were at the fort a couple voyageurs approached him when they thought I was too busy to notice. I didn't let on, but I listened and watched. I may have missed some words in my business conversation but I heard Alex say plain, *"not this year"*."

Morning-Star glanced up from the fire. She smiled at Jean who smiled back. Star turned again to the fire, picked up two small pieces of wood, adding them atop the coals. Reaching for a fireside bellows, and without looking at Jean, she said, "if we were living with the tribe, he might already be a warrior."

She went to work slowly with the bellows blowing the coals to life under the fresh wood.

"I know," said Jean. "The soldiers at the fort will try to recruit him, if they haven't tried already. I want to keep him here, working the fields with me, but he will want adventure. All young men do."

"Challenge grows the man," she said.

"Well, there's plenty of challenge right here at home," said Jean. "And money to be made here too. Lower Louisiana can't seem to get enough of our flour, pork, and indigo. Everyone in St. Philippe is growing cotton now. Put that together with salt from the works across the river, and you have a convoy ready to head south. Add in some tallow and bear meat from Greasy Bend downriver, and the merchants in New Orleans will fight each other to buy your whole cargo before you ever tie at a dock. Hell, last time a convoy went south, merchants were waiting out at the Red Church on the German Coast to come aboard and inspect the commodities. That's ten league (30miles) upriver. Those Germans at the Red Church are getting some good cropland cleared but they still can't compete with us for wheat and corn."

Jean paused to take a breath. Morning-Star began rearranging rocks at the fireplace, without looking up. Star liked rocks, of a certain size, loose, around her cookfire. Such rocks, arranged just so, reminded her of her mother's fire where Morning-Star had learned to cook before marrying the Frenchman, Boucher DeLisle.

"Alex could get work building pirogues and bateau for the river trade like Pierre," said Jean. "The gristmills can't keep up grinding flour and corn meal. We can take on another field allotment, get us a few slaves like the Jesuits have done, and maybe raise cotton too. Or we could raise more cattle, horses, or hogs. Or he could help me train more oxen as a business. Hell, there are lots of ways to make money right now. He doesn't have to go upriver trapping or trading fur or transporting goods back and forth. Adventure is fine but there is a time to use your head."

Jean paused to take another breath. He walked to the door, taking his hat from the peg. He glanced back toward Morning-Star. She was busy arranging rocks.

Jean lifted the door latch and stepped outside. He called back, "I have work to do," closing the door behind him.

A week passed. The sun was hot and the scythes had been whispering all afternoon. Alex made a pass with his blade, scaring a small green snake, which quickly slithered away in the stubble. Alex smiled.

"Close one," he thought, *"you should find better cover."*

Alex grounded his scythe to wipe his brow on his sleeve.

"Let's rest," said Jean.

Jean walked to the cart nearby, leaning his scythe against it. He sat down beside the cart appreciating the meager shade it could offer out in the open plowland fields. Alex followed, placing his scythe carefully against the cart and flopping down beside his father. He was tired, his arms and back were sore.

Shim and Shave, heads down, looking almost asleep, were hobbled nearby.

"Get the water barrel," said Jean.

Alex rolled over, reaching under the cart to roll out a two-gallon wooden keg. The small oak barrel was sweating through in the heat. It was lightly moss-covered having been seldom ever kept in direct sunlight and often stored half submerged in the well. But it did its job and kept water cool when it was handled correctly.

Alex pulled the wooden bung and slung the keg up on his arm to drink. The water tasted good. He passed the keg to his father and Jean drank too. When he finished, he handed it back to Alex who drank again replaced the bung and rolled it carefully back into the shade, taking critical note of how the shade line might move under the cart as the sun sank toward the west.

"If I hire your friends, I won't be sorry, will I?" asked Jean.

"No," Alex answered.

"You know what is said? Two boys hired is like half a boy and three boys is no boy at all," said Jean.

"I've heard you say it, no one else."

Well, I say it because it's true and it's what my father always said."

"I know, and it might have fit a couple years back but not now—not with us."

"No, I think you are right, not ever again for you three. I'll be proud to have 'em with us. You can tell 'em."

Alex was lying on his back watching a cloud sail across the sky. He smiled but Jean didn't notice because Jean was looking across the field watching Jacques Parlier's two black slaves swinging their scythes in rhythm, cutting Parlier's wheat.

"We will need to lead each cow by road from the commons through the plowlands to the north corral. Sixty head will take time. You may start that job Monday. We head north on Thursday coming.

This was a hot dry day. But, in the shade under the cart, with a breeze blowing across open bottomland fields, it was a good deal cooler.

"Too bad we cannot take a nap. We have work," said Jean, pulling himself up by holding onto the cart.

Alex quickly scrambled up, standing beside his father, almost as tall. Away, in all directions they could see dozens of men in other long-lot fields steadily swinging scythes. Today wheat was important to them, to Kaskaskia, and to all French Louisiana.

Chapter 7

The Drive Begins

$\mathcal{A}$ small black steer bawled and shook his head as Maurice led him out of the cornfield. A bouncing lead-rope had proved difficult to catch slithering along the ground in rows of tall cornstalks. The steer had led him a merry chase for a few minutes and then balked and wouldn't move. Luckily for Maurice, Etienne followed with a stick.

As they trotted the steer to the cart Alex awaited, a worried look upon his face.

"I thought I was going to have to leave these others and come help. I knew this was a bad idea," said Alex.

"Well, it would have worked if Maurice had tied him better," said Etienne.

"I didn't tie that one. You did," responded Maurice.

"I did not."

"I think you did," said Alex, smiling.

"Well maybe I did. The important thing is I got him back."

"With my help."

"The important thing is he wasn't in the cornfield long," said Alex. "Old Jacques likely won't be out here for a while. He is getting lazy these days, letting his nigras tend his fields. They have already hoed that corn the last time for this season. The soil is dry; the cattle are leaving a shallow hoofmark. With a couple rains no one will notice. He didn't knock down too many stalks, did he?"

"No," said Etienne. "No damage done."

Etienne winked at Maurice, who smiled back.

"Bon," said Alex. From now on, we bring one at a time like Father told us. A steer could get lost in that tall corn and do a lot of damage before we could find him next time. Have you got him tied now?"

"Yes," said Maurice. "I tied him myself this time."

Alex stepped to the back of the cart and inspected the knot. He nodded, glancing at his friends.

"Those corn leaves cut you up a bit Maurice. You're bleeding like a stuck hog," said Alex.

Maurice had two deep scratches across his face but he smiled.

"Up," said Alex.

Shim and Shave plodded forward, pulling the cart down the road with three securely tied steers following.

The boys walked along spread out to the left, right, and behind the cart. They wanted no more mistakes today.

Thursday arrived with a clear bright sunrise. Roosters crowed from the village.

"Keep Old Skinny to the front," said Jean, speaking to Alex. "She will keep to the road while we have a road. The others mostly will follow her. Etienne, you and Maurice swing wide on the drag and sweep up stragglers. I'll work the west side of the herd and go after strays. The bluff will keep them corralled on the east side for today."

The boys, mounted horseback, listened but they pretty much knew the plan already. Etienne's horse turned in a slow circle and shook its head. Maurice and Alex kept a tight rein. Their mounts stood quiet, shifting weight and using their tails to swat flies from time to time.

"This evening we will turn them east along the common fence at Prairie Du Rocher," said Jean. "We'll bed them down in the outside corner where it meets the bluff. I scouted it. There is a little stream and we can keep them bunched up. The fence is tight. The bluff is solid limestone at its base and it rises straight up. Hopefully we won't lose any before we get them trail broke. This morning let them graze as we ease along. By noon when it's hot, they will get the idea and we will push them from time to time, but not too much. Let some of them keep their heads down today. Let them string out in a long line but not too wide or long. Today needs to feel natural like a buffalo heard moving slowly toward water. You'll get the hang of it."

The boys remained silent but they looked anxious to get started. The gate on the north corral had been opened by Jean. Old Skinny had already led most of the cattle out. With heads down the cows were grazing nearby. Jean, looking north, drew a long breath stretching his back as he sat in the saddle.

"Okay, Alex, ease up to Old Skinny, get her head up and start her walking north," said Jean.

He clucked to his horse and turned him west. Suddenly he pulled back on the reins skidding his mount to a stop.

"One last thing boys, for today go easy on the yipping and fast moves. These cows are not wild but they are cattle."

The day passed. The herd was bedded down. Darkness had settled.

"Do you hear that?" said Alex, standing near a dying campfire.

"Sure," said Maurice, "they've been playing for a while."

"Fiddle music travels a long way at night here on the bottoms," said Alex.

"Especially echoing off that limestone bluff," said Maurice.

"Well, those are dancing tunes. Someone is having a party and it is not even Saturday night," said Alex.

"You want to saunter over and have a look at the ladies?" asked Maurice.

"Yes, I do, but I don't want Father marching after us when he finds us gone, and dragging me back by the ear. Trust me, you don't want that either. Besides our night watch might get a little sleepy if we don't get some rest before we go out in the dark to watch those cows," said Alex.

"Wish we had a fiddle," said Maurice.

"Why, none of us play?"

"Well, maybe we could learn," said Maurice.

The fiddle music was clear, though faint, across the distance. An owl called from closer somewhere on top of the bluff. The herd was nestled against the rock face. The fire had no flames. Alex looked up into a clear star-bright sky and wondered for a moment what they might find in the prairies ahead.

Chapter 8

$\mathcal{H}$ebert The Younger had joined the herd with fifteen of his own cows at Prairie Du Rocher, the tiny village, now disappearing into the horizon behind them. The road had turned west toward the Mississippi and Fort de Chartres. Old Skinny was leading the way. Jean and Hebert were riding wide on the left and right flanks. The three boys followed sweeping up stragglers.

Hebert's new cows were already blended into the other cattle. They had stopped glancing behind.

"Beginning to look like a cattle drive, isn't it?" said Alex, as his horse trotted up beside Etienne's mount.

"I don't know. I never seen a drive before this one," said Etienne.

"That's because there has never been one here before," said Alex. "Father said he saw cattle driven near Quebec when he was a boy."

"Were the herds this big?" asked Etienne.

"I do not know."

"Hey, look over there," said Etienne, pointing. "That's something, is it not?"

"Oui, it is."

The boys were looking at the only Dutch style windmill this side of the Delaware River, two hundred leagues (nine hundred miles) east near Philadelphia, in the English colony of Pennsylvania. A breeze turned tall, white sailcloth blades powering the mill and gleaming in the morning sunlight. Beyond the Mississippi, green hills rose and cumulus clouds floated in a blue sky. It was a painting waiting for an artist who never came.

"The mill is grinding flour," said Etienne, "or cornmeal."

"Likely not," said Alex. "More likely sawing logs."

"Whatever it's doing it has a lot more power than the horse-powered mills."

"Oui, but there are many horse-powered mills, and only one windmill," said Alex. "and horse-powered mills work even when the wind does not blow."

"Oui, but you don't have to feed hay and grain to a windmill."

"No, that's true," said Alex, "but horses don't usually get broken in a windstorm."

"Well, they sometimes run off in a big storm."

"Well, windmills can get struck by lightning."

"So can horses, especially when standing under a tall tree."

"Well, what I know is we have the only water-powered gristmill at Kaskaskia," said Etienne.

"For now," said Alex. "I've heard talk of a water-powered mill being built near Prairie du Rocher and maybe even one in the hills across the big river. The more crops we raise the more mills we need. New Orleans wants our wheat flour. Their women bake bread daily."

"Well, we Frenchmen love our bread, everyone knows that. How could we live without it?" said Etienne.

"The Indians do," said Alex. "They use corn to make bread."

"French wives in South Louisiana don't serve cornbread to their families."

"The West Indies wants cornmeal to feed their slaves," said Alex. "Convoys go downriver spring and fall now-a-days. Father says he may take on additional long-lots as soon he can train more oxen."

"I heard the church Fathers are shipping some of their wine now," said Etienne.

"Why not, the Jesuits make plenty every year from those wild grapes they've trained to grow on arbors. It's good wine," said Alex.

"I like it," said Etienne. "Of course it's the only wine available outside the commandant's quarters and one or two other homes where I am seldom invited to dine."

"Well there is plenty of wine in New Orleans," said Alex. "But, despite that fact, Father says they are developing a taste for the wine of Kaskaskia. He said the habitants at Vincennes grew a good crop of tobacco last year too. The flavor from those leaves excited buyers in New Orleans. Father wants to look at tobacco growing when we get to the Ouabache (Wabash)."

"Whoa," said Etienne, as he reined his horse left, leaned forward and went riding off to redirect a straggling heifer going astray.

Chartres was the name people called the village, which had grown up at the front gates of Fort de Chartres. The town had expanded toward the river, which was at first a mile west. In recent floods the river had cut new banks toward the east. Today there was less than half a mile between the village and river landing, where dozens of bark canoes, bateau, and pirogues were hauled up on bank.

The road Old Skinny trod passed by the fort twenty yards east of its back gates. People from the village, soldiers from the fort, voyageurs, Indian scouts, individual coureur de bois, even a few black slaves released momentarily from their toils were all up on the back wall of the fort to watch the strange procession.

A sleeping drunk was almost trampled before he could get himself dislodged from his wallowed nest in the grass. He stumbled toward the walls of the fort cursing and crying. Guards opened the gate they had just closed and dragged him inside, closing it with a thump. Onlookers roared with laughter

'Hey, get your musket Pierre," yelled one man. "Yonder comes a half dead antelope leading a heard of buffalo."

"Bring your milking stool Pierre," called another.

It went on like that as the herd passed. There was a great deal of laughter. Many of the ladies and children were present. Comments were mostly controlled. It was all in fun, guards and soldiers were with the commandant to be certain it stayed that way.

There was fiddle music but the commandant had issued strict orders: no weapons or cannon were to be fired in salute.

It was a hot day. The herd took minutes to pass. Dust was kicked up, most of the fun had soon been had, and much of the crowd began drifting away. The fort's commandant remained standing on the wall near the gate as the three boys approached bringing up the rear. As they came even with the roadway leading into the back gate he snapped to attention and gave a hand salute as they passed.

A few minutes and a quarter mile up the road Maurice glanced back. The fort looked smaller. Above its walls was the flag with the blue fleur-de-lis and white background suddenly unfurled and snapping smartly in a breeze. A man stood where the commandant had. Then he disappeared behind the wall.

Chapter 9

The Parisian

𝒰nnoticed by the boys, another rider had joined the herd as Old Skinny marched them past the fort. Now the stranger came galloping his horse back to where Alex rode drag out on the right.

"You are Alex?" he asked.

"Oui."

The stranger was young but older than Alex by a few years. He was scrawny but fit and weathered.

"Jean sent me back to ride with you for a while. I am Bossbriant the Younger."

"I thought you were The Parisian."

The stranger gazed at Alex for a moment.

"I have seen you before at the fort," said Alex.

"Oui, some habitants do call me The Parisian." The young man stared at Alex a moment more. "Maybe most, maybe all," he said. "Yes, I am The Parisian if you like." He smiled to himself and shrugged his shoulders. "Your father said to tell you he wants you riding flank on the left when we go past the Indian village."

"Why didn't you say so when you rode up?" said Alex, kicking his horse into a gallop.

"I wanted to introduce myself," called The Parisian.

A quarter mile ahead Old Skinny was walking past the village at that moment.

A few minutes later, as the last of the herd passed the Michigamea Village, the stranger had ridden his horse over near where Maurice rode. From yards away he called: "I am Bossbriant the Younger. I have signed on to go with the herd to Vincennes."

Two hours passed. They left the Indian village behind. Alex was back on drag with The Parisian who wanted to be called Bossbriant the Younger. Maurice and Etienne were riding as flankers. Hebert the Younger was on point, and Jean had ridden ahead to St. Philippe where the herd would be kept tonight in holding pens.

The Michigamia were Morning-Star's people. Alex had many cousins, aunts and uncles among them. He had been to the village twice as a boy with his mother. He wondered about that now. Why did they not visit his mother's people more often? Why did he not know them better?

The Michigamia were Christian Indians. Many French coureur de bois did live at the village. Those Frenchmen married into the tribe and raised families of metis (mixed blood) children just like Alex but yet different. They were raised more in the Indian way. Those Frenchmen and those children were more Indian than French.

Alex, though he shared the native blood, had been raised as a French habitant. The two cultures traded and learned from one another, even intermarried, but in many ways, they kept themselves separate.

"I feel like I am living in two different worlds at the same time," thought Alex.

"You are thinking about the ladies at the fort. Oui?" asked the smiling Parisian, who was suddenly again riding his horse close beside Alex.

"No," said Alex.

51

"Why not? They were beautiful, oui?"

"Oui, they were," said Alex. "but they were French ladies and married. They are not for me to think about."

"So, the Jesuit Fathers have taught you," said The Parisian. "But they do not know some of those ladies as well as I. Or maybe the Jesuits know them even better than myself."

"Why does everyone at the fort call you The Parisian?" asked Alex.

The Parisian did not answer.

It was hot and dusty. The sun was low, a red sky was beginning to develop out west. The land they traveled was flat, scoured and re-scoured from time to time by the big river. Red-winged black birds trilled from a nearby marsh. The big bluff they now moved back toward dominated the eastern horizon.

"I was a boy when they brought me to Louisiana. I was swept up from the streets of Paris by the gendarmes (French policemen), along with whores and thieves. The Company of the West had promised King Louis they would populate Louisiana with Frenchmen. Any French person delivered to the docks in New Orleans counted. The Company intended to keep control of all Louisiana Commerce for themselves. I was of no consequence."

"I've heard the stories," said Alex.

"Well, this is my story," said The Parisian. "Let me tell it."

Some of the French ladies at the fort and the French villages came off that ship with me. We were loaded straight onto a bateau and sent upriver to Fort de Chartres. Slaves rowed the bateau but I was sometimes told to row as well. I wasn't sure which I was to be, slave or Frenchman.

In Paris I was called a name I did not like. I met Hebert the Younger on the trip upriver. He had been to New Orleans. I heard him tell his name and explain of Hebert the Older. I also heard of Bossbriant the first Commandant at Fort De Chartres. When I arrived, I told people my name was Bossbriant the Younger. It seemed a good name to me and I wanted a good name.

"It didn't work?" asked Alex.

"No. The people would not have it. They laughed and soon I was known as The Parisian."

"It might have worked if you had picked a name of less importance."

"Oui, that was my mistake. I keep hoping as time passes, he will be forgotten and I might yet use the name."

"That might work in Canada but not in Louisiana," said Alex. "Why not stick with The Parisian?"

"Oui, I may be forced to."

"Sounds about right to me," said Alex.

"It is better than what they called me in France," said The Parisian.

Chapter 10

St. Philippe

𝒜 setting sun behind them, the herd meandered northeast closer to the limestone bluff.

"Look at the size of that place," said Maurice, riding beside Alex.

A large stone house stood ahead. A huge barn and several other frame and log buildings were spread out behind. They were all enclosed with picketed fence.

"Is that a house?"

"I guess so," said Alex. "Old Renaut's I suppose."

"Oui. Could be no other."

"No."

"It must pay to be a friend to King Louis," said Etienne who had reined his horse over near his friends. "Look at the size of that lot they have enclosed. It must be five arpents (4.25 acres). And that doesn't include the corral." He paused. "There's Jean."

Ahead, Alex could see his father driving Old Skinny into the corral. The other cattle up front in the herd were funneling in behind her through a narrow gate.

"Hold up," he said to the others.

But it was too late for him to tell the Parisian who was then riding the right flank of the herd. He had already pushed the cattle on that side a bit too fast. The cattle bunched at the gate, were too close together and spooked.

Alex watched as a dozen or so steers bolted and ran off up the right side of the corral fence out into the prairie beyond. The Parisian, realizing his mistake, backed his horse away from the bunched cattle. He started to rein his mount right, then turned him back toward the herd, watching the near cattle, now with a careful eye. But he kept glancing over his shoulder moment-to-moment observing the runaways trotting off to the southeast.

"You boys stay with the herd," said Alex. He reined his horse right and went galloping off to swing wide around the herd and go after the strays. It would be dark soon and black cattle would be hard to find at night.

He had lost sight of the strays as they turned behind the corner of the corral. When he got to the corner himself, he could see them again, far off. They had dropped down along a marshy lake, which ran south in front of the bluff for a distance. He reined his horse west to pass around them wide on that side, avoid pushing them away, and bring them back toward the pens.

Twilight was arriving. Hundreds of swallows soared low above the lake, gracefully swooping down now and again to skim the surface, leaving a tiny wake trailing behind marking for a second their flight path. Bitterns and frogs 'croncked' along the banks of the old riverbed turned shallow lake.

Alex got round them to the south and approached the strays at a trot. As he closed the distance, he slowed to a walk. Suddenly he pulled up his mount and glanced all about. There were only six steers.

"Where did the others go? Are they in that brush? Did they get further down?"

He peered off into the darkness behind him toward the south. Then he studied the brush again close around, near the water.

"Could they be mired in the mud?" he wondered, *"they can be that stupid."*

It was dark and he could barely see the six in front of him.

"Easy," he said.

"Let's take it easy and meander back to the herd."

But, he did not move his horse. Instead, he sat quiet on the animal for a full minute. He heard a splash.

"Fish," he thought, *"or big bull frog."*

He listened to the cattle ahead. They were calmer now, swishing their tails and moving about in the grass. Crickets began to fiddle in the nighttime coolness.

Finally, he clucked to his horse, loosened the reins and began guiding the strays serenely back along the brush-line toward St. Philippe and the cattle pens. As he moved the cattle, he saw something stir in the darkness to his left.

It was Etienne and Maurice emerging from the shadows, slow and inconspicuous, horses at a walk. They fell in behind and move up alongside Alex.

"Is this all of them?" asked Etienne in a hushed voice.

"I don't think so," said Alex. "I thought I saw more leave the herd."

"Me too."

"Want me to get ahead and turn them when they get close to the pens?" asked Maurice.

"Oui."

Maurice rode off quietly to circle out around the strays once again. Luckily the moon was up and it was becoming easier to see in the darkness. Soon, The Parisian was swinging the gate, closing in the six strays he had caused to bolt and run off.

'Merci, messieurs. These strays in the pen may get old Jean off my ass."

"Where is Jean?" asked Alex.

"He and Hebert went up to the house. Have you ever seen a house so big?"

"No."

Wood smoke was in the breeze and someone was cooking meat. From off a little way beyond the barn they could hear the squeak of a fiddle being tuned.

"What are we supposed to do now?" asked Etienne.

"Jean did not say. He just said for me to wait here for you messieurs to bring in the cattle."

"Well, here we are and those six are all the runaways we could find in the dark. Now what?" asked Etienne.

"We wait," said Alex. "At least for a while."

"Don't you want to get a look in that big house?" asked Maurice.

"Sure I do, but we have not been invited."

"People living in homes like this expect polite behavior," said The Parisian.

"Who lives here now?" asked Etienne. "Bienvenue or Buchet?"

Everyone in the Illinois country knew that the original owner Philippe Renaut (for over two decades Director of Mining for the Company of the West, a personal friend to King Louis XV, seeker of gold and silver, founder of this village) had sold out two years ago and left on last spring's convoy to board a ship in New Orleans and set sail back to France.

"Buchet," answered Alex. "Bienvenue lives elsewhere in the village. They split the long-lots but Buchet bought the house, buildings, and horse mill."

"Who bought all the slaves?" asked Etienne.

"I don't know," said Alex.

"You think old Renaut misses his house?" asked Maurice.

"I doubt it," said Etienne. "He is probably living with King Louis in the palace."

"You think the palace is bigger than this?" asked Maurice.

"It is bigger," answered The Parisian.

"Bonsoir, messieurs," said a young voice from the darkness.

It was only then they noticed a slight figure standing nearby in the obscure light.

"Monsieur Jean has sent me to fetch you to the house, suis moi (follow me)," said the boy.

"Now we're going to see how the rich live," said The Parisian.

They followed the boy up along the fenced lot to a narrow gate and entered the compound, which enclosed the residential property. This lot was indeed five times the normal one arpent residential lot of most French residences. But, everything in the Illinois Country associated with Monsieur Renaut had been done on a grand scale.

As they approached the house, a smaller whitewashed picket fence surrounded home and garden separating the two from the remaining barn lot, agricultural buildings, and slave quarters.

The boy led them through another gate, along a stone path through the garden leading toward a back entrance. Alex recognized the dark shape of a long grape arbor and noted the faint smell of roses, growing corn, onions, and herbs. He could hear the fiddler begin to play from behind the barn.

The imposing stone structure rising before them was truly larger than any other home northeast to Quebec, south to New Orleans, or east to the English colony of Pennsylvania.

Their escort preceded them up the steps and walked into the dim light of a large kitchen attached to the main house by a breezeway (covered roof with open-air sides during summer).

As they entered the kitchen Alex recognized their guide was a boy of very dark skin.

"*A slave,*" he thought.

"Bonsoir," said an attractive black woman standing by a table set with more food than any of them were accustomed to. "Bon appetite."

They learned during supper that the black boy was known as 'Little Pierre'. Now he led them once more, this time through the breezeway and into the rear of the main house. Little Pierre held a candle lantern high to light their way through a dark narrow hallway. Ahead Alex could see a much larger room opening before him. This room appeared to be more brightly lit, no doubt by many candles and reflections.

Laughter could be heard from somewhere deeper within the house. Suddenly Little Pierre stopped. He opened a door in the wall to his right. It obscured the light from the well-lit room ahead.

Pierre handed his lantern to Alex and motioned him up a cramped dark stairway. Alex took the lantern ascending the steps into a large room above. The room had white walls and a large window. The furnishings were simple: three beds, a table, three chairs, a small writing desk equipped with pen, inkwell, and a fourth chair.

"I'm not sharing a bed," thought Alex.

When everyone including Little Pierre were in the upstairs room, the boy took the candle lantern from Alex and used it to light two others atop the table and desk.

"Bonne nuit," he said, descending the stairway with his lantern.

During the night Alex was awakened by a sudden flash of light through the window, then another. He opened his eyes to darkness within the room and heard the rumble of far-off thunder followed in a few seconds by the second rumble.

Alex turned over in bed away from the widow, but lightning flashes continued reflecting off the whitewashed walls almost as brightly as before. He pulled his blanket over his head and snoozed, listening to the grumble of the approaching storm and the snoring of The Parisian.

After a while he awakened again, this time to the sounds of heavy raindrops rattling the wooden shingles of the roof. The Parisian still snored. Alex drifted back to sleep.

When Etienne shook Alex awake next, dawn had arrived without the cocks crowing to announce it. Rain still poured outside. Raindrops, in occasional wind-gusts, pelted the widow.

"Look at this view," said Maurice.

Alex pulled his shirt over his head and let it settle across his shoulders and stepped over to look out.

Through the downpour they could see the wood shingled rooftops of almost all the small villages of St. Philippe. Beyond, summer crops in the fields were soaking up the welcome moisture. Directly below grew a continuation of the kitchen garden and an orchard of several trees spread away to the fence on the village side.

"I could get used to all this," said Maurice.

"Let's see what that gal in the kitchen has for breakfast," said Alex, heading for the narrow stairway.

The wind blowing through the breezeway this morning was wet and cold, making the warmth of the kitchen welcome for a July day.

"Bacon, always smells good," thought Alex.

The large fireplace was engaged with a number of pots and pans at various heights and positions above the hot coals. Three black women bustling about the room tending tasks made the kitchen already crowded.

Pierre jumped up from a bench where he'd waited.

"Suis moi," he said, motioning them to follow him through another doorway onto a covered porch at the southeast side of the cookhouse. It was cool and damp but out of the wind and wet. There were rough wooden tables and chairs set against the stone wall. Little Pierre

61

revealed a covered basket of warm bread sitting atop one of the tables and soon he was serving hot food and drink from the kitchen.

"I could get used to this too," said Maurice.

Chapter 11

Finding Strays

"You take Etienne and Maurice. Go down the west bank," said Jean to Hebert. "I'll take The Parisian and Alex to the east bank. Buchet said it's one league (three mile) to the lower end but it will be marshy at the south after all this rain. May take a bit longer this morning. If it gets too wet to meet up, sweep wide to the west and meet back here by dark."

They were all mounted horseback at the corner of the corral where they had last seen the strays all together. The count this morning had determined five remained missing from the herd. The rain had stopped but they had lost time and cattle can wander into trouble, especially at night in a storm. The search parties trotted off separate directions.

"Father isn't saying much," thought Alex.

He wanted to ask Jean about the house and what it was like but he sensed this might not be the right time. His father was riding on his left and The Parisian rode to Alex's right, neither had much to say this morning.

The low clouds were moving off above the bluff but still no sign of a sun in the east. Overhead blue sky portended a bright day when the clouds moved out.

"It's gonna get hot," thought Alex.

The Oxbow Lake was fed at its north end by a stream coming off high ground through an ancient cut worn in the bluff eons ago. Water, which once might have reached the Gulf of Mexico, now would evaporate away in the lake and lowlands before it could reach the present Mississippi riverbed.

The stream however had a good flow at the north end of the lake. As they approached, Alex was surprised to see someone had built a new mill on the stream a little distance north from where they were crossing.

"Who built that?" he asked his father.

"Renaut," answered Jean. "The summer he sold out."

Alex didn't ask more. They traveled in silence, looking for strays. Time passed slowly.

During the day they jumped a dozen or more whitetail, a fox, a pair of skunks, and several coveys of quail, but no sign of stray cattle in the brush or on the horizon. They were heading back now with the bluff on their right and the sun low to the west. It had been a hot humid day. The wind was still. Mosquitoes were beginning their evening rise from the marshlands. Suddenly Alex heard some rocks falling from the bluff. He glanced up to catch for a second the sight of what he thought was a man darting behind a tree. But it was a long way off.

"Sun and shadows can do strange things this time of day," he thought.

He said nothing, but he continued watching. Hawks soared directly above, silently circling, hunting their prey.

It was dusk when they returned to the big house.

"Take care of the horses," said Jean to The Parisian, handing over the reins.

"Alex, you come with me."

Jean had said fewer than a dozen words to The Parisian all day and most of those had been late in the afternoon.

The tension however seemed suddenly to be gone from his voice.

"Where we going?" asked Alex.

"I thought you might like to see the parlor."

They followed the perimeter fence around to the road at the front of the home entering through a wide gate. The house was magnificent from this exposure. They strolled through a fragrant flower garden on a stone pathway to the front door. Ascending limestone steps, they knocked. Soon the door opened and they faced an old black man leaning on a cane.

"Entre," he said, recognizing Jean.

They entered into a foyer with a grand stairway ahead and two doors to either side. Two other doorways were visible down narrow hallways flanking the stairs. The foyer itself was bigger than some homes Alex had known.

His father led him into the room on the left. Candelabra hung from the ceiling, some candles already lit. Framed paintings and silvered mirrors hung on the walls. It was more beautiful than anything Alex had ever imagined. But somehow it made him uncomfortable. He didn't belong in this world. It was too far removed from where he existed and yet here it was not six leagues from his home in Kaskaskia. Why was it here? What kind of man would presume to build such a home in this place? What kind of people would feel the need or the right to live in it?

Alex heard laughter come again from the deep interior of the house but this time was different. It was feminine, young and beautiful. Alex was developing an ear for such sounds and his imagination was stirred. But, he felt an increasing need to leave. He wished to spend no more time in this disorienting dream world. He wanted a return to his reality.

"Thank you, Father, it is beautiful. May I go back now?" he said.

In a blur, he was out the door, strolling quickly along the path through the flowers. He turned at the gate to look back up at the house. As he did, he noticed a pretty, young girl watching him from a second-story window. Embarrassed, he turned back and walked quickly away.

He found The Parisian and Maurice outside on the kitchen porch at a table, Little Pierre carrying food to them. He sat down at a table nearby and was soon brought his own plate of stew. He buttered some brown bread from the cloth-covered basket, which never seemed to be empty. A glass appeared, seemingly from nowhere, and Pierre was already filling it with wine before Alex had eaten the first spoonful of stew.

"Some people here do live well," he thought.

"We found two," said Maurice, looking up from his plate.

"When, where?" asked Alex.

"At the far end when we started to make the wide sweep. They just showed up ahead of us," said Maurice. "Etienne went on further south to see if he could find sign of the others. He's not back yet."

"I'm back," said Etienne, walking out through the kitchen doorway, a plate of food in his hands. "I never saw sign of any others. They'll be wild in a week if they don't run home or get eaten."

Etienne set his plate next to Alex's, pulled a chair over and sat down next to his friend.

"I guess The Parisian will still be in the doghouse a while longer," he said under his breath.

Alex smiled.

"It was a quiet day."

"I'll bet."

"Kaskaskia no longer has the only water powered mill," said Alex.

"What are you talking about?" responded Etienne.

"I saw one today. Monsieur Renaut had it built before he left."

"Condamner (damn)," said Etienne. "I might have known a man who had a lead mine and the slaves to work it would not be satisfied with a horse powered grist mill like everyone else."

"I guess not," said Alex.

Chapter 12

Preparations

*F*irst light found the boys on the kitchen porch finishing breakfast.

"Is it my imagination or is this morning's fare expanded?" asked Maurice.

"Ham and bacon—three different jams— and honey. I think you are right," said Alex.

"I'll wager King Louis doesn't eat this well," said Etienne.

"I will take that wager," said The Parisian. "How much do you wager?"

"You're in trouble enough," said Alex, "don't be trying to get Etienne's money."

"Etienne has money?" asked Maurice.

"It was not my fault those cows escaped," said The Parisian. They're wild. And why are they all black and hard to find at night?"

"They are not all black; a few are brindle colored," said Maurice.

"Very few."

"Some."

The Jesuits brought the cattle of the Illinois country to Kaskaskia from Canada, some said originally from Scotland. They were hardy animals well adapted to cold winters. In truth, they were mostly black, with black horns, and smaller than English cattle, though these boys had no way to know. Only The Parisian had ever seen another breed.

"We've only lost three," said The Parisian.

"Three in three days with a road to follow," said Etienne. "Wait till we get lost in the tall grasses and the wolves start trailing us. At this rate we could lose half the herd before we get to Vincennes."

"Or our hair," said Maurice, "if the Fox or Cherokee catch our scent."

The conversation waned for a moment as the boys let that thought settle.

"Hebert said we were to meet him in the tack room," said Etienne.

Except for Maurice they rose, stepping off the porch and strolling the path through the garden heading for the barn. Maurice cut another slice of bread, slathering on butter and jam. Then he followed along after the others nibbling most of the way.

The tack room was large, like everything else on this plantation. On a rough table were spread a variety of weapons: knives, tomahawks, pistols, Michigamia war clubs, muskets. The tack room doubled as an armory today.

These young men were familiar with the tools. Violence was not a daily occurrence in their lives but neither was it a rarity. Each had personally known men killed. Etienne had an older sister who vanished one day, years before, while picking berries. This was part of life in the bottomlands along the rivers. Wild animals and savages were a constant people accustomed themselves too, like fevers in late summer or blizzards in winter.

Except for The Parisian, the boys had received training most of their lives. From a young age they had been encouraged to stalk through fields and forests hunting game for the table. They knew the difference between the hunter and the prey. The boys were hunters. They choose not to think of themselves as prey.

Everyone already had carried a knife and tomahawk on their belt as they entered the barn. Only Etienne had packed a pistol as well—a small one he had been wearing since leaving Kaskaskia—a lady's pistol given to him by his mother.

Leaving the barn, they were all better armed than before, including Etienne. Between them they toted out much of what had been on the table though they were still confused concerning how they would carry the weapons horseback while herding cattle.

Their mounts had been readied for them. The horses were tied to a hitching rail. Three new horses were loaded as pack animals, and Little Pierre now led that string from the barn mounted himself on a big bay.

Twenty-five additional cattle had been blended into the herd yesterday by a couple of Joseph Buchet's slaves. Antione Bienvenue and a black man had brought over twenty-five new cattle this morning to be added.

"$60+15+25+25=125-3=122$," calculated Alex.

"Why's Little Pierre mounted?" asked Maurice.

"Must be going along," said Etienne.

"I'd rather we take that nigra cook," said The Parisian.

Alex could see Jean up near the house talking to Messieurs Buchet and Bienvenue.

"What is so important?" he asked.

"Jean's a little upset about the boy," said Hebert. "We were promised two additional men with the cattle. Buchet claims Pierre is twelve years old but he looks no more than ten to us."

Hebert checked the cinch on his saddle.

"The second man, Tobias, is a slave, but he looks to be a good hand. He brought over the cattle this morning by himself. Bienvenue arrived after."

Jean finally came toward the corral and the messieurs retired to the house. Alex and Hebert met him halfway.

"We taking him?" asked Hebert.

"Oui," said Jean. "Buchet said if the boy doesn't earn his keep, I can sell him in Vincennes and keep the money. He is writing authorization now."

They walked down to the others standing near the corral.

"Parisian, you take Old Skinny out and lead her down the road," said Jean. "Etienne and Maurice will ride drag, the rest of us will ride the flanks and string them out before we get to the cut in the bluff."

"Allons-y (let's go)," he said.

The Parisian led them out. Jean rode to the house where the old black fellow handed him a scrap of paper. He read it and placed it in his possible bag. One by one they took a position as the herd funneled out of the corral and headed northeast toward the bluff.

"The herd needs to be on the high road by noon," said Jean to Alex and Hebert. "I'll lead us up the cut."

Not long after, the herd was strung out along the road moving at a steady pace. The day was hot and humid. The ground was mushy and wet instead of dusty. The limestone bluff towered in front casting a shadow, which Old Skinny and The Parisian were already shaded by.

Jean was forward of the herd at the base of the bluff where the stream, which powered Buchet's mill, flowed out into the flat bottom ground. A narrow valley known as 'The Cut' rose ahead of them. The road followed the stream into The Cut winding its way up through tall oak, hickory, and beech trees.

Jean suddenly halted his mount, pulled his pistol and fired a shot into the air. Alex pulled up to listen. As the echo faded a second faint pistol shot answered from somewhere in the trees atop the bluff.

Jean rode ahead, the cattle herd followed, funneling themselves up into the gap and disappearing into the trees.

Alex moved from direct sunlight into the shade of the bluff. The cattle were bunching just ahead as the herd narrowed themselves to fit through the terrain.

"It's ten degrees cooler," he thought.

As he entered the trees there was room for only two or three cattle wide in some places following the road beside the stream. With each step they were climbing upward. It was dark within the forest, out of the sun.

"It's dropped another ten degrees."

As his eyes adjusted, he gazed upon a different world. It was a place of ferns, wild ginger, and moss. The creek rushed bank full from the recent rain. Its gentle roar, today, drown out the normal sounds of this valley. What little light dappled the carpeted forest floor came filtered through multiple layers of tree canopy and vine. The very humid air itself seemed green and hushed.

It took an hour to work the herd up through The Cut. Finally, the ground plateaued widening out all around. The road turned north following the bluff-line, on this higher ground toward Cahokia.

Traveling under the huge trees made it a continual twilight and Alex noted a different problem. In this forest you could never see the whole herd at one time. A part of the herd was continually out of sight down a slope or obscured by understory brush.

Fortunately, cattle are natural herd animals. By instinct they prefer keeping to a path. The road was nothing more than a wide dirt track kept trodden by foot, hoof, and a very occasional set of wooden wheels.

Hours passed. Increased daylight appeared ahead. The cattle were breaking out of the trees into an open prairie. Soon Jean had circled the herd at a tiny stream, with riders forming an outside perimeter to hold them in place. Alex held his position, while the animals milled about.

He noticed Little Pierre and his string of horses moving off upstream. Jean was trotting his mount around the herd. As he passed every other man was pealing back away and following Little Pierre.

Jean was approaching Alex now.

"Stay on watch till you are relieved," said Jean, "We need to keep them here tonight."

He kept riding, passed, circling.

"Who answered your shot at the bluff?"

"Scouts," answered Jean. "Some of your cousins."

Jean moved on toward Etienne. Soon the cattle were settled, some lying down, some grazing, others slurping water. Upstream Alex could see smoke rising and floating off to the east. Occasionally he thought he caught the scent of woodsmoke and roasting meat.

"It might be my imagination."

There was a purple sky. Doves flew to water.

Chapter 13

On to Cahokia

Two days passed on the high road to Cahokia. Tomorrow they would add more cattle to the drive. The Seminarian Brothers at the Church of the Holy Family had gathered thirty head they wished to cull from their herd before winter came again.

Etienne was riding drag with Alex. The cattle moved through another big woods. The terrain of this upland region had varied. Forest gave way to prairie and then back again, with marshlands here and there to make things interesting. About the time the drovers got acclimated to one type of topography it changed to another.

"No dust today," said Etienne.

"It'll be back," said Alex.

"Well, I may welcome it. It's better than the damn mosquitoes."

"What do you think of the scouts," asked Alex.

"Haven't seen much of them. They come at dusk, palaver with Jean, leave to sleep in the woods, and we don't see them again till the next evening."

"Mother sent them," said Alex. "They are Michigamia, my cousins."

"Even the black one?" asked Etienne.

"Metis (mixed blood), Indian mother," said Alex "born in the village, claimed by the tribe, raised by the entire tribe. I don't know much about Michigamia ways but I know a little. That boy is Indian and not even the priests will challenge that."

"I guess," said Etienne with a sigh. "I wish I were going with you tomorrow. I'd like to see Cahokia."

"Somebody has to stay with the herd. Should be an easy day; sit with cattle while they graze a meadow around a water hole. They'll be tired, hungry and thirsty. The hard part will be driving them away the day after."

"I'd still like to see the village."

"It's a village like any other. You just want a peak at the gals."

"You don't?"

"Doubt we'll see any; we're not going to a dance."

An hour after sunrise Etienne, Tobias, and Maurice circled the perimeter of the herd. It was a tranquil scene, cattle grazing, birds singing. Etienne glanced toward the camp.

Hebert snoozed in his bedroll. Pierre tended a smoky fire. Alex, The Parisian, and Jean mounted their horses and rode out.

"I wish I were going with them."

They followed the road half a league (mile and half) where they caught a view from the top of the bluff. As they trotted along, they gazed out across bottomlands toward the Mississippi river. In the distance they could see the long-lot common fields. Smoke rose from the chimneys of summer kitchens and outside ovens.

It was a pretty village from above with Cahokia creek and another smaller run flowing through the scene.

"They have a bridge across that little creek," Alex noticed.

Cahokia was older than Kaskaskia by a year or maybe three depending on whether you asked a Jesuit or a Seminarian. It had prospered less and was separated from the French communities nearer the seat of power at Fort de Chartres.

Cahokia was situated on the Mississippi. There was an island separating the village from the main channel of the big river. The bluff rose to its east about two-thirds of a league (two miles).

The drovers came off the bluff riding down through another cut similar to the one they climbed up near St. Philippe. Here, today, the stream was not rushing with recent rainwater. As they began their descent the water gurgled its way quietly along from rock to moss covered rock, through quiet green pools. Grey squirrel barked and skipped limb to limb in the hickories overhead.

Suddenly the surrounding trees burst alive with screaming, brightly colored parakeets.[1] It was a noisy, active flock of three or four hundred green, yellow-headed birds, which descended through the trees in an instant and then flitted here, there, and seemingly everywhere.

Alex had seen these annoying birds before. They could strip a peach orchard of young fruit in fifteen minutes. In a woods like this their calls obscured all other sound leaving animals and hunters alike disoriented for a time.

As suddenly as the birds came, the tumultuous flock flew away, final stragglers only seconds behind the leader.

---

[1] Carolina Parakeets later hunted to extinction.

Quiet returned to the valley as the riders rode out onto the flat bottom-ground, their ears adjusting to the sudden change. Alex heard crows cawing in the distance.

In a few minutes they were crossing the Riviere du Pont (the name of the smaller stream) on a wooden bridge, horses at a walk, hooves clomping on heavy plank floorboards. Upstream two young women waded barefoot in the water, skirts tied up between their legs to keep them dry. A wooden cart beside the creek held several baskets filled with clothes.

"Guess it's wash day," thought Alex. But he wasn't looking at the laundry. Neither were the girls. The two brunette teenagers seemed captivated by the sight of strangers, and they stared boldly and mostly at Alex.

"Bonjour mesdames," said Jean.

"Bonjour messieurs," they responded in unison.

The clomping hooves muted as one by one the horses crossed over the bridge, walking the dirt road once again. The riders rode on toward the village. Alex glanced back only once. The jeunes dames (young ladies) were still gazing.

Soon the drovers approached a horse-powered gristmill at the edge of the village. A priest and two black men mounted horses and came out to meet them.

"Bonjour messieurs"

"Bonjour Father" answered Jean. "I am Jean Verrou."

"Then you are here for cattle," said the priest. "They are in the Prairie des Buttes Common."

He spurred his horse and loped off back toward the bridge, his robe flapping in the breeze. The two black horsemen and the drovers followed.

78

At the crossing they slowed their horses to a trot clattering over the bridge one after another on the wooden planks, making a considerable racket. They passed by more quickly than Alex wished.

He did however manage a smile at the ladies this time, and to his surprise both jeunes dames (young ladies) smiled back.

The Prairie des Buttes Common was over two thousand acres of pasture, woodland and wetland. The cattle were in a holding pen at the back near the bluff. The gate to the pen was opened and Father Mercier rode his horse inside and Jean followed.

Quietly they perused the animals moving out among them slowly.

"Name is Jerome," said one of the black men, "I'll be coming along with these cows. Father says we're heading to Vincennes."

"I'm Boisbriant the Younger," said The Parisian."

"I'm Alex."

The other man did not speak.

"Slaves," thought Alex.

Jerome looked to be a hearty man in his thirties, maybe older. Alex had trouble guessing age among the black race. Like Indians it seemed to him blacks aged slower than white people until all of a sudden at an advanced age they wrinkled up seemingly overnight. Frenchmen he thought aged gradually but from Alex's observations the white men wore weathered faces much earlier in life.

Jerome sat his horse confidently. He wore a knife and a pistol on his belt. He carried a bedroll behind his saddle.

"These cattle are a little skittish but they are sound," said Jerome "They will make the trip. I chose them myself."

Jean and Father Mercier meandered their mounts back and were passed through the gate.

"Alex, you and The Parisian get these cattle back to the herd. They seem a little edgy to me but these fellows from the mission will help you. I'll be along later."

With that Jean and the priest rode off at a canter back toward the village.

An hour later the new cattle were trotting past the bridge on their way east with drovers flanking and behind. A few steers bolted to go over the bridge but Jerome headed them off, having anticipated their move.

Alex searched the Riviere des Pont carefully upstream and down. No laundry, no girls. He glanced up toward the village. He saw picketed enclosures, rooflines and a church spire from the mission.

The Church of the Holy Family had also received a bell as a gift From King Louis XV, and before that, candlesticks from Louis the XIV. But, it seemed Alex would not see the bell or anything else this visit. He was leaving Cahokia behind, heading east toward the bluff, the herd, and far off Vincennes.

Chapter 14

Leaving Cahokia

*J*ean rejoined the drovers as they managed the cattle up the vallee (valley) to the uplands. At the top the quiet black man left, without word or a wave, heading back down to the mission. Jerome continued on with the drovers and cows. In a short while they could see more cattle ahead.

"125 -3=122 +30=152," Alex did the calculations in his head. *"I wonder how many we will lose?"*

There would be no more additions. They would find no further cattle herds to draw from. There were no other French villages between here and Vincennes 150 miles away.

The fresh cattle were trotting ahead into the meadow where the herd had been kept and now were scattered about heads down. The new stock arrived in a tight knot but soon dispersed themselves as the drovers quit pushing them forward. Quickly they too had their heads down tearing at grass or drinking water.

"Jerome, you keep an eye on your cattle. Make sure they don't wonder."

"They are not my cattle, monsieur. I think they belong to you now."

"Well, you keep an eye on my cattle then."

"Oui, monsieur."

The sun had passed its zenith a couple hours before. It was a warm day. A fresh breeze blew here above the bluff. Red-tail hawks shared the sky with white-headed eagles.

Jean trotted his horse toward a new camp, in the shade of a lone red cedar, where Little Pierre had resettled during the day. Fresh venison roasted on a spit above the fire. Bread had been baked. It was still warm.

"Nice spot," said Jean to Pierre, "who got the deer?"

"Tobias," said Pierre, "he is a good hunter."

Jean produced a bottle of wine from his saddlebag as he dismounted.

"From the good Fathers at the mission," he said.

"That won't go far," said The Parisian.

"Well, we won't be telling the others," said Jean. "And I'll be drinking the largest share."

The meal was soon over and Alex lay down in the shade. A full stomach, the smell of cedar, and a cool breeze soon lulled him into a nap.

Alex awoke to a gentle shake of his shoulder.

"Go relieve Maurice."

Alex rubbed his eyes and sat up. It was not yet dark. Frogs croaked from the spring fed pond nearby. He rose and took the reins of his horse from Little Pierre who had saddled the animal for him.

"Merci," said Alex.

He mounted and rode out into the surrounding meadow. Mosquitoes greeted him as he left the smoky fire behind. Swallows swooped about overhead, with nighthawks soaring higher up. Alex circled the herd counterclockwise and found Maurice riding next to Etienne on the far side.

"Maurice, I'm here to relieve you."

"What about me?" said Etienne.

"Guess you stay with me for a while longer," said Alex.

Maurice trotted his horse toward camp. As he faded away into the shadows, they saw him waving his arms suddenly above his head.

"What's he doing?" asked Etienne.

"I don't know," said Alex, and then they saw them.

"Bats," they said, echoing one another.

Suddenly hundreds of bats had arrived in the meadow. The tiny nocturnal creatures darted about on wings aflutter. Flying close to the grass, they zipped in and out between cattle and riders, avoiding collisions by inches and buzzing past up into the night sky.

Unlike the parakeets earlier today the bats were silent in their work. They went about their business in the darkness. Most, not all, creatures quickly acclimated to their customary nightly presence.

"How was the village?"

"Like any other."

"Any jeunes dames?"

"Deux" (two)."

"Jolie (pretty)?"

"Oui"

"Well?"

"Had no time. They were washing clothes. I was herding cattle. I never got a word in."

"Worth going back for?"

"Maybe, someday," said Alex.

An hour later Maurice smoked his pipe, watching a card game The Parisian was attempting to teach Jerome.

"Hold up that game and gather round boys," said Jean. "I need your attention."

Hebert and Little Pierre sauntered over closer to the fire. The Parisian put away his cards. Jerome sat up to listen. Maurice continued to smoke the pipe but he was all ears.

"Tomorrow, we start across the prairie. You already know it's a long way to Vincennes. There are four river crossings and a few smaller streams, which can get big in a rain. There are also a number of wet prairies, which can get real swampy in bad weather. That's why we are going this time of year. It should be dry. But we've had some rain of late and we may get more."

"We'll be crossing some big tall grass prairies. Cattle can get lost in that grass this time of year, just like people. Riders can usually see above it but we may not always be able see what is fifty feet away down in it."

"The buffalo have their trail. Indians keep it trod. We'll need to keep the cattle strung out on it and not let them slide off and follow any forks which end up at some swamp, spring ,or salt lick three leagues off our way."

He paused to look at Jerome.

"Now I'm going to give you some local news," said Jean. "Two of the mission slaves went missing last week. One was across the Mississippi fishing. The other was hunting to the north of the Indian village, half a league above French Cahokia.

"Maybe the one drown and the other ran off or maybe they ran together." said The Parisian.

"To where?" asked Jean.

They all thought about that for a moment.

"No," said Jerome. "I knew them. They feared the Fox who eat Christians. The Chickasaw and the Cherokee are allied to the English. Better to be a slave here."

"A man who works the mines maybe would take such a chance," Jerome continued. "These were field-hands; they worked above ground. They worshiped at the church. They had families. Better for them to stay in Cahokia."

Jerome examined each man in the shadows of the firelight.

"They are dead or carried off."

Chapter 15

The Prairie, Day 1

On the upland prairie it was hot almost as soon as the sun rose. It would get hotter as the day advanced. The sky was blue. Wispy clouds appeared, sailed along overhead for a time and after a while evaporated.

The little bluestem grass of this particular prairie brushed the cattle under-bellies as they walked along.

"We shouldn't lose any cows here," said Maurice.

He rode beside Jerome on the right flank of the herd.

"No, not here," Jerome answered.

The herd moved presently northeast. Old Skinny walked a game trail but not yet the ancient Buffalo Trace, which would lead the herd east if the drovers could keep them on it.

"Have you ever seen the companies' lead mines?" asked Maurice.

"Oui."

"Have you been down underground?"

"No. I was sent to bring men back to work our fields at harvest."

"Do those slaves get to work above ground often?"

"No. Usually, we get a few at harvest and plowing time. Sometimes they are taken to the salt works to help boil the brine or cut and haul firewood. Last year the company rented some out to the traders down river at Greasy Bend."

(Greasy Bend was a bear slaughter business for hides, salted hams, lard and rendered cooking oil. Casks of bear oil were prized in New Orleans after repeated skimmings at Greasy Bend removed the unusually strong wild stench.)

"Do they like the work at the bend?"

"They like our fields best. They work hard hoping to impress the priests. Occasionally the Fathers will purchase one."

"What's that?"

Maurice was pointing to a strange looking plant growing along a wet slew they were moving past.

"Cattails."

"No, the closer one like those ahead."

He pointed to a plant with a bare six-foot stem rising from broad cabbage type leaves at its base. It displayed large bright yellow flowers at the end of leafless branches.

"The priests call that one prairie dock. There is some growing near the Riviere des Pont in Cahokia. Father Mercier made a painting. It hangs in the mission."

"It's different," said Maurice. "I've never seen it before. Do Indians use it for anything?

"Not that I know."

In front of them was a considerable bed of prairie dock. Beyond, the cattails indicated wetter conditions but that gave way soon again to grass. All around them grew more little bluestem. It waved in the wind, bending toward the east. The prairie appeared the same in every direction to the horizons. The herd was strung out along the trail keeping to higher ground.

"Six," said Maurice.

"What?"

"Hawks," he said, pointing all around.

They were big hawks, bobbing along, coasting very slowly, and riding into the wind just a foot or two above the grass. A narrow band of white flashed above their broad shifting tail feathers.

"The predator seeks his prey," thought Maurice.

Suddenly one of the hawks dropped feet first through the grass. Sharp talons silently opened and closed. Up and away flew the bird on flapping wings, a wriggling black snake firmly in its grip.

"Got him," whispered Maurice.

Chapter 16

Out on the Prairie, Still Day 1

*B*uzzards circled in the distance. Jean had noticed them over the near horizon an hour before. Their appearance had grown larger as the herd moved toward them. He had quickly lost count. There had to be fifty circling like a funnel cloud above a single point on the prairie ahead.

"Must be a big kill," thought Alex.

All the drovers had seen the birds. It was the most activity on the big prairie rolling out in front of them. The sun was well up and the humidity seemed to rise with it.

"Wonder what the wolves have left. Deer most likely. Got to be big. More deer than anything else." thought Tobias. He was a good hunter as little Pierre had said. He enjoyed being away from the village. He was also curious about Vincennes. He was glad the Father had sent him.

"What do you think it is Maurice?" asked Etienne, trotting his horse alongside.

"Don't know. Elk maybe buffalo."

"Could be. We'll find out if the track keeps heading that way."

Well Old Skinny seems to be pointing the herd straight as an arrow right now."

"If she changes course somebody's got to go see."

The prairie was quiet. The wind blew out of the west. Crows cawed.

"I saw a badger down in the grass back a-piece," said Maurice.

"What was the mean little devil doing?"

"He'd been digging like they always do. I saw the hole and fresh dirt first. Thought it was a ground hog's hole. Then I saw the squat little shit hunched down in the grass like a snake coiled to strike. Three feet from my horse's hooves. Thought it was a skunk at first. But there was more white and grey than black. Then I saw those beady little eyes looking back at me. There wasn't any fear in 'em. I knew then it weren't no skunk."

"Might be it was a ground hog's hole. Badgers can dig 'em out and eat 'em," said Etienne.

"See that tall grass over there?" asked Maurice.

"Oui, I've been noticing that there's getting to be more of it."

"We're making the transition," said Maurice. "That's big bluestem, it's twice as tall. Have you noticed the other tall grass with the seed heads that are puffed out?"

"No."

"Well watch for it. I don't see any right now. It's switch grass."

"Why do you care?"

"Just interested. I like to study things," said Maurice. "The difference can sometimes be important; attract different animals and birds and such. Some grasses make better weaved baskets. Sometimes you can learn something from the savages that may help you. Besides I think I might like to be a healer or a medicine man. They use all kinds of plants."

"Oui, they do, but if you mix the wrong things in your tea or poultice you might be sorry."

"Well, I didn't say I was a healer. I said I might want to become one. I won't be mixing you up no tea tonight."

"I won't be drinking any," said Etienne.

They were close now. Jean could see clearly a cloud of big black birds circling above. Others on the ground hopped about, flapped their wings, and screamed at one another for their share of the kill. Together, from a distance they had resembled the tail of a whirlwind dancing in the plowed lands. Up close it was ugly.

Old Skinny had left the trail to give the birds a wide berth. The herd had followed. Jean instead rode closer to scatter the birds and confirm the kill. Begrudgingly they finally moved off far enough.

"Buffalo. Saw no sign before. Where are the others? There must be more."

Jean sat up in his saddle to scan the horizon. He saw no sign of other 'big shaggy'.

"Maybe an old bull off by himself. Wolves probably got him." Jean rode back toward the herd. Hebert met him with a question on his face.

"Buffalo," said Jean. "By tomorrow night they'll have him cleaned to a pile of bones for the mice to gnaw."

Not all the riders bothered to come see, but Etienne did. He came back to tell Maurice.

"Buffalo, a big one. Must have been wolves that got him. Not much else could or would take down a big bull this time of year."

"Indians would."

"Oui, could be. Not likely. Too much waste."

"Voyageurs would."

"Oui, but where is the river they travel?"

"Wolves?"

"Oui," said Etienne.

Chapter 17

Day 2 on the Prairie, Already Turned East

*E*tienne rode drag with Alex this morning. Like the day before it was hot. The herd had turned east. His eyes watered. He couldn't see much looking into the sun.

"I'll be glad when 'Old Sol' gets a slight bit higher."

"Me too," said Alex.

"Tobias is a pretty good provider," said Etienne.

"He seems to be a good all-around hand," replied Alex.

"Oui. But he's particularly good at hunting up a meal," said Etienne. "Last night's supper was delicious."

"Well, that's Little Pierre's work. That boy can cook. His momma taught him well."

"You think his momma was the jolie (pretty) black cook?"

"Oui, do you agree?"

"I do. She looked the right age and she directed his work more than the other women."

"Who do you think his daddy was?"

"Don't know. Haven't heard him speak of a family."

"You think he's happy being a slave?"

"I don't know. But he is one."

"He is, and a mighty good cook."

A covey of quail flushed suddenly in front of Etienne's mount. The horse shied away and crow hopped a few times. Etienne kept his seat but just barely. He was becoming more comfortable in a saddle.

Alex chuckled.

"Thought you were gone that time."

"This beast is spooked by everything," said Etienne.

His mount pranced and shook its head. Etienne kept a tight rein. The bit did its job. The horse settled.

"I like canoes better," said Etienne.

"Be hard to use one here," said Alex.

By noon the grassland had changed. It was Tall Grass Prairie now. The growing season was advanced. The cattle moving through were obscured and visible mostly by the movement of the grass. The heads of the horses and the riders were above the surface of this sea of green, but in another month the horses would sink from view as well.

"In a few more weeks it will be unbearable out here," said Alex.

"Oui, you get no breeze down in the grass. The daytime sun bakes you."

"I hope we set camp early today."

Ahead they could see more vultures circling, but not as many as the day before. The herd soon closed the distance. Alex watched Jean investigate and return to his place on point. As the rear of the herd came up, Etienne rode over and came back.

"Deer," he said. "Last night maybe this morning."

"Wolves?"

"Most likely."

Hours later Alex saw a line of trees ahead.

"More shade will be welcome."

There had been trees scattered along the path they followed, solitary oaks and osage, but only a few. Alex and Etienne paused now in the shade of one, a giant oak situated on a hill. In the warm breeze they surveyed the horizons.

"The river?"

"Oui."

"Our river?"

"The Kaskaskia."

"We could follow it home."

"It is rough country for cattle and men on horseback. Better to go back the way we came."

"How do you know? You've never followed the river this far up."

"I heard Father and Hebert discussing it before we left home. Hebert knew a trapper who worked the river."

"Well, if I had a canoe, it would easy."

"You could build one."

"I could."

"You wouldn't get to see Vincennes."

"No, but maybe that will prove not such a loss."

"You would never know. You would just have to take my word for it."

"I could ask Maurice. Or I could just wait till next year when I sign on as voyageur and paddle north on my way to Detroit."

"Well, this is your last chance this trip to paddle home. The other rivers we cross will flow to the Ouabache (Wabash)."

"I could go that way."

"It'd be longer. By the time you can get a canoe built we'll be back home anyway."

"Well, I could do it and get home, but I want to see Vincennes."

A half hour later Jean turned the herd upstream a little way, to where the river made a tight horseshoe bend. The water was deep and wide. He intended to hold the cattle here tonight.

"We'll make camp behind the herd," he explained to Hebert. "Keep them between us and the water. They won't swim unless we force them. It will take only two men for night watch and both will be always close to camp."

"You getting spooked?" asked Hebert.

"I'm getting a feeling," said Jean. "Just a feeling. Scouts haven't been in yet. They acted a little nervous last night when I talked to them."

"Do you trust them, Jean?"

"I do. They said they hadn't seen any sign of trouble. But, Jean Pierre—he's the full blood—says there is less game than usual for this time of year."

"Well Tobias don't seem to have trouble finding plenty."

"No, he doesn't," said Jean. "Probably nothing to worry about. Just a feeling. We'll see what the report is tonight."

"Where do they go every evening after they leave us?"

"They do a few wide sweeps around us during the night. They keep a dark camp, catch sleep when they can, stay wide on our flanks in the daytime. Somebody watching us might not even know we had scouts."

"I forget they're out there. I seldom see them come or go."

The commandant suggested it. Less they are seen the better it is for everyone, including them.

Next morning the drovers brought the herd to cross the river back where the buffalo had splashed across for centuries. It was a good place to cross. Jean and Hebert positioned themselves on the far side to get a headcount as the cattle negotiated the stream.

The drovers yipped and whistled them across a few at a time, letting them drink on the way. When it was done Jean looked at Hebert.

"One hundred fifty," he said.

"Me too. Did we miscount?"

"No, not both of us."

"How in hell did we lose two?"

"In the tall grass unless they swam over the river last night."

"Nothing to be done if they're back in that grass. We'll take a look upstream this side for a little way. That's all we can hope for."

Jean and Hebert mounted and trotted off to the north. Jean shouted back to Maurice.

"Keep 'em moving, we'll be back in an hour."

By mid-morning Jean and Hebert were not back. Tobias was on point. Alex and The Parisian were on the left flank of the herd. Jerome and Little Pierre with his packhorses were riding the right. Etienne and Maurice brought up the stragglers, pushing them to keep up with the others.

"Think they'll find them strays?" asked Maurice.

"I'd bet them cows are back in that tall grass, and we're likely to lose half a dozen more today if we're not careful. The Parisian is asleep half the time he is in the saddle. He's good at it but I saw him yesterday with his eyes closed for fifteen minutes. The horse is doing his work."

"Well, I wish Jean and Hebert would get back. Where they at, do you suppose?"

"How would I know? Maybe they got lost. It would be easy enough when you get off the trail in this mess."

"It is pretty when you look out over it though. Don't you think?"

"No, I don't. Maybe, you do. But, my friend, you may have been touched by too much sun."

"More vultures," said Maurice.

"Oui, they seem to always be ahead of us."

"Or far away. I saw two flocks this morning way off."

"Well, what do you think it is this time? Want to make a wager?"

"You sound like The Parisian. He's always trying to get a wager," said Maurice.

"Look there." Etienne pointed.

Tobias was yelling something and circling his arm in the air.

"He wants us to circle the herd."

"Why?"

"I don't know but he just rode back from checking what the vultures were feeding on."

"I don't like this, "said Maurice.

"No," said Etienne. "We can lose another five or six in this maneuver without Jean and Hebert. Keep your eyes open."

In a few minutes the herd had been circled, head catching tail. Drovers positioned themselves on the outside perimeter to hold the cattle in place. The animals milled slowly around in the center with no place to go.

Tobias spoke a minute with Jerome who then rode over to the vultures, while Tobias rode toward Alex.

"What's happening?" asked Alex.

"I think we found our strays."

"Where?"

"Under that pile of birds."

"Wolves get 'em?"

"It weren't wolves. Their throats were cut not ripped."

"Why?"

"Message for us I would say."

Jerome was galloping his horse through the tall grass toward them.

"Somebody doesn't want us here," said Jerome.

"Who?" asked Alex.

"I don't know," said Jerome.

The two slaves looked at one another and then at Alex.

"What do we do now?" Asked Alex.

"Monsieur Jean told me to watch his cattle so I guess we get back on the trail till he catches up," said Jerome.

"Should we wait for him?"

"Not here. We will search for a better place and make an early camp. The messieurs should catch up by then. Tobias, you lead the cattle out."

Tobias trotted his horse into the herd and cut out Old Skinny.

Jerome began a circuit to tell the others.

Alex looked back the way they had come.

"Where are they?"

Chapter 18

Day 3, Burnt Prairie

*E*tienne looked back around noon to see Jean and Hebert riding up from behind. They were still a ways off, trotting their horses, in no particular hurry. In a few minutes they caught up to the herd.

"Did you see the strays?" asked Etienne.

"No, did you?" asked Jean.

"Jerome and Tobias did."

Jean and Hebert rode off toward Jerome.

"Where have you been? What took you so long?" Etienne wanted to shout after them. But he didn't.

"Where they been all morning?" asked Maurice, riding up alongside.

"They didn't say," said Etienne.

"What took them so long?" asked Maurice.

Etienne leaned forward and galloped his horse off toward Alex.

"Hey, don't leave me back here too long," shouted Maurice.

It was late afternoon. Jean had been searching for the right spot. He needed a place to bed down the herd. He didn't want to lose any more cattle in the dark, but he hadn't found any good options. The grass was tall, the next river far. He rode over to Jerome on the right.

"Keep the herd in sight but swing wide. We have to find a place for tonight. We can't be choosy," said Jean. "I'll go left."

Jerome rode southeast and Jean headed his horse north.

An hour passed. Jean found only more of the tall grass tangle with a mud hole here and there. Glancing toward the herd, he caught sight of Jerome riding toward him at a cantor. Jean rode to meet him.

"Did you find a good place?" asked Jean.

"I found a place? It's a burnt prairie with a little slough on one side."

"How big a burn?"

"Big enough. I think. Just over that ridge."

"Let's turn the herd," said Jean. "Take us to it."

The charred prairie was big enough, a hundred arpents maybe more. Jean could see it now and imagine it then — a big tree on a sand hill, dry grass, lightning, a fire burning all around, extinguishing itself at the slough and the green grass when the rain came.

"Pierre can set camp under the tree. The swamp isn't a horseshoe but it bends some around the hill. See there. We'll just have to watch the two ends so the cattle don't get around us."

He smiled and nodded to Jerome.

"Bien (good)."

Cattle sniffed the ground walking through the burnt prairie toward the water. Birds sang. The tree on the hill cast a long shadow.

The herd soon settled. The cattle were spread out downhill toward the water. Jerome and Etienne were on watch at either end.

Pierre gathered wood for his fire. The horses were hobbled. The Parisian snored nearby. Alex and Maurice sat with their backs against the tree, enjoying the breeze.

"Be dark soon," said Maurice.

"Oui, I hope he brings in more venison."

"I'm hungry. I'll eat anything Tobias kills and Pierre cooks."

"Who's out there besides us?"

"I don't know."

"Why kill those steers and leave them for us to find?"

"To eat some I suppose, and to let us know they did."

"Why?"

"To show us they can. Who knows. Indians do all kinds of things for their own reasons."

"Your father and Hebert don't seem too concerned about it. But it worries me."

"I think it worries them too. That's why they went out afoot. Jerome will bring in the meat."

"Where are our scouts?"

"I don't know. I never see them. They may have already talked to father today. They usually come to him while the herd is in motion."

"Well, what's our plan?"

"Same as always I suppose."

"How far is it to Vincennes?"

"Three or four days, I think. Hebert said it was seven or eight days from Cahokia if things went well. We've been moving steady."

"So, we're about half way across these grasslands?"

"I think so."

"Smart place for an ambush."

"I suppose. You wishing you hadn't come along?"

"Oui. I think maybe I am wishing that."

It was roasted rabbit they ate with bread made from cornmeal instead of flour. A typical meal for slaves or Michigamia but not for Frenchmen.

"Better than jerky I guess," said Alex.

"I thought it was alright," said Maurice. "But not up to his usual standard."

"Well it could be he has spoiled us," said Alex, "better get used to it. Voyageurs always eat Indian foods."

"Well, we're drovers not voyageurs."

"What do you think drovers eat?"

"Never known any drovers; guess it depends on where they are. Till now we've been eating pretty good."

"Well look at where we are right now," said Alex. "Better get used to it."

Alex was awakened by Maurice before midnight. The quarter moon was high and the stars bright.

"We're to relieve Jerome and Etienne," said Maurice.

Alex stretched his arms and rubbed his eyes. Someone was smoking a pipe standing near the tree.

"*Hebert*." he thought.

As he rode out to Etienne, he was surprised at how well he could see in the burnt prairie. He recognized Etienne on his mount. He could see the outline of the herd and a few individual cattle standing alone.

"Time to get some sleep," said Alex. "Have you seen anything?"

"No. The cattle have been quiet. Nothing but frogs croaking and bats fluttering about."

"Bats? Out here? Thought they lived in caves."

"I don't know where they live," said Etienne. "But they're out here. You'll see them. Maybe they fly in from far off, maybe there is a cave or a hollow tree, but they are here," said Etienne. "Jean say anything about the strays?"

"Just that Indians do strange things, like I said before. He and Hebert seem to be keeping a night watch of their own at camp," said Alex. "This makes a good place to bed down, doesn't it?"

"It does. I didn't like the idea of night watch in that tall grass."

"No."

A scream came suddenly from out of the darkness.

"Rabbit?" asked Alex.

"Oui, I heard a couple earlier."

"There are lots of rabbits."

"Oui, and lots of bobcat, wolves, foxes, owls, not to mention a few panthers."

"Go get some sleep."

After Etienne rode back toward camp, Alex could hear the bats flutter as they flew around him and out over the swamp. He could smell the burnt prairie and the muck from the stagnant slough. He also caught the unmistakable whiff of skunk from somewhere.

It was a warm night. The heat of the summer was building on itself. Even the recent rain had not changed that. There was no river breeze. Night sounds were different here, hushed and mysterious.

The watch seemed long. The minutes passed slow. He walked his horse between the swamp and up near camp, then back again, over and over, sometimes talking to the cattle, sometimes listening.

Finally, a mockingbird sang from somewhere in the darkness. Soon thereafter a shade of light showed on the eastern horizon. In the shadows away from the cattle Alex caught the sign of movement. Three, no, four creatures moving cautiously; Deer come to drink.

The slough awakened with small birds singing and flitting about. Cattle moved down to water. Dawn had arrived with no cocks crowing out here, even in the distance.

Chapter 19

Day Four—The Big Spring

Mid-morning the herd was moving easily along.

Sweeps of tall yellow wildflowers rose above and within the big blue stem and switch grass. Etienne had to admit to himself that Maurice was not totally full of shit.

The prairie panorama did have attractiveness, especially this time of morning with a wide blue sky above. But Etienne knew also two other facts. One: he was never going to admit as much to Maurice. Two: the beauty was a mirage that would soon disappear into hot, humid air which would be dripping from his brow.

Jean had discussed the situation this morning in camp. His feeling was no longer just a feeling. Someone was out there somewhere nearby. Their intentions were unclear but not particularly friendly. Options for the drovers were limited: move on, do your job, stay alert, don't wonder off from the herd. It had not exactly been the grand plan Etienne had hoped for when Jean had begun his talk.

The herd was topping a rise in the terrain that had been gradually and gently upward all morning. Now topping the ridge, Etienne could see a grand view opening to the east for miles. Ever more tall grass with solitary trees here and there and a single copse of trees off to the south maybe half a league. Old Skinny ahead seemed to be bending the herd in that direction. Jean had been riding behind Etienne on the right flank. He rode up now from behind.

"I'm going to check out those trees before the herd gets there," he said, as he rode past. "Go tell Little Pierre to come up. Tell him to come on if I motion."

Jean rode on at a gallop.

"What's that all about?" wondered Etienne. *"We going to set camp early? It isn't even noon yet."*

He dropped back, whistled, and waved for Pierre to cross the herd with his horses and come to him. Pierre soon was riding beside Etienne.

"Jean's checking out the trees ahead. Says you're to come on if he waves you in."

Little Pierre looked ahead to the trees. Jean suddenly appeared and waved him on. Pierre trotted his string of packhorses forward. Jean rode on out to speak to Hebert who was riding point.

Hebert gave the motion and started circling the herd where it was. Jean led Pierre and the packhorses back to the trees.

"What is so important?" said Etienne when he got close to Hebert.

"He's found a spring. Jean wants time to fill the casks before the horses and cattle muck it all up."

Etienne went back to his position with the cattle.

In a few minutes, Little Pierre came back riding his big bay and spoke with Hebert and Jerome. Both men went riding off to the trees, leaving Little Pierre to cover their positions with the herd. Alex edged over when he could.

"What is so important, Pierre?"

"A spring, we are filling the casks."

"What else?"

"Campfires, Monsieur Jean found fresh ones."

"How many?"

"Two."

"How old?"

"Dunno."

The spring was a big one, feeding a small pond. It was already mucked up and muddy from the cattle when Alex and Etienne watered their horses. They had to ride down onto a muddy shelf below the surface of the prairie behind them. It felt like they were down in a giant ground hog's hole. All around the soil was compacted and kicked up to the outside, where for thousands of years before them buffalo, deer, elk, and other creatures had watered. A thin band of trees surrounded it all with a stream flowing out on the downhill side heading southeast.

The campfires had been built within the trees but below the surface of the prairie. It was a good site, fresh water, firewood, flames hidden from view.

"Think these are our stalkers?" asked Alex.

"Likely so," said Etienne. "Look."

Etienne pointed to the edge of the trees where the scouts were speaking to Jean. He didn't look happy. The Michigamia turned and trotted away soon, disappearing into the tall grass.

"That's only the second time I've seen your cousins," said Etienne.

Jean saw the boys watching and rode over.

"We took a wrong fork back near the burnt prairie. We're damn near two leagues off our route. We should have never been here. We'll have to go back. This way turns into a huge swamp."

"What about the fires?"

"I don't know, boys. Probably our cattle thieves, but why they didn't drive them steers back here and jerk the meat is beyond my understanding."

"We've got to turn the herd and get a move on. We've lost the whole morning." He rode off to tell the others who were already moving the herd further in the wrong direction.

Rather than confuse the cattle, they made a wide swing before retracing their old path. A couple hours later they were back at the burnt prairie.

They found the correct fork in the Buffalo Trace or at least the one that seemed most traveled. It was hard to tell. They had encountered dozens of such forks and often times it was a guess. They had made other mistakes but this was the first which had cost them half a day.

The sun was high. The mirage had vanished. Etienne was not anticipating a pleasant afternoon. He was correct, and he didn't know the half of it.

Chapter 20

Night in the Tall Grass

*I*t had been a long hot afternoon. The herd was crossing another wet slough. The cattle were knee deep in muck. The sun was setting.

Alex and Etienne rode drag trying to keep the cattle close together in the tall grass.

"This is the third swamp we've crossed today," said Etienne.

"The land is flat, no place for the rain to go, streams are muddy and sluggish," said Alex. "The country doesn't drain itself like hilly country does."

"It's getting late. We better find us a place to bed them soon," said Etienne. "How many you think we lost today?"

"I don't know. I'm guessing at least a few."

'Perhaps more," said Etienne.

Jean was out in front of the herd. He had given up on another burnt prairie. He had even given up on getting out of the tall grass. He was just hoping for some dry ground under them before the sun went down. He should have stopped an hour before when that last dry ground had come. He was cursing himself now for pushing on. Ahead he saw two broad oaks rising out of the grass.

"Please lord let it be dry beneath them."

Before Jean got to the trees, his horse's hooves stopped splashing and began clomping, once more on solid ground. The trees were fifty yards apart with no others in sight. They grew on a slight knoll in this wide wet prairie. The grass on the dry ground was little different than the wet except directly under each tree where it was thinned.

"Best we can do tonight. We'll set camp under one and circle the herd close around the other."

It was night when they got it accomplished. Little Pierre was striking a fire in the dark, for the light mostly, it would be dry jerky for supper.

Jean called a four-man watch for tonight. Drovers soon were circling the herd slowly in opposite directions passing each other in the darkness every few minutes.

Listening was a big part of the job. In the grass after dark, movement was easier heard than seen, especially in the muck of the slough. Surprisingly, Etienne felt more confident they could hold the herd here.

"Jean may be right. If something gets past us, I think we'll hear it as soon as it starts sloshing around out there. We can go get any strays before they get lost. This could work."

Hours later they were relieved in the dark and trotted their tired horses over to the tree camp in the shadows. The fire was a bed of coals. Alex rekindled it for some light. They found their bedrolls and settled down.

"How many you think we lost?" asked Etienne.

"None," answered Alex.

"None tonight I think," said The Parisian, "but how many today?"

"Get some sleep," said Hebert. "We'll be back on watch before long."

Near dawn they were back circling the herd. First light brought the tree camp alive. Soon the other drovers joined them to move the herd on its way east. Alex was half asleep in the saddle.

He woke with a start. He noticed a great blue heron flying gracefully overhead on giant, angular, slow-motion wing beats.

"Must be some open water somewhere," he thought. But he did not see any.

During the next hour the prairie rose out of the wet ground to become dry again. A scattering of trees once more began to appear. This savanna in the Illinois country was unique. Farther west, the climate was too dry, north it was too cold, south too hot, east of the Oubache (Wabash) was a land of trees and beyond that mountains. Only here grew the Tall Grass Prairie. Certain plants growing were found nowhere else in the world.

Only Father Mercier back at the Church of the Holy Family seemed to suspect such things. No botanists had ever visited this place. In fact, these drovers were some of a very few white men who had ever crossed this plain. For that matter only The Parisian and Hebert were full blooded Frenchmen

What Alex noted was heat, ticks, mosquitoes, snakes, too wet, too dry, and grass so thick the cattle got lost in it. He was tired. He was weary of living the life of a drover.

Working the fields as a habitant back home sounded good to him right now. It would be nice to fish the Kaskaskia from a pirogue again. He longed for the shade of a cottonwood and a cooling river breeze. He would be glad to get back to it.

Afternoon brought a continuation of prairie except the tall grasses mingled more often with patches of little blue stem and large sweeps of splendid wild flowers. The slight difference, however, opened the space, allowing a breeze to flow within rather than over the grass. Cattle and horses seemed to be intermingled with the plants rather than swallowed up by them. Animals and riders alike were suddenly less stifled.

"Not so damn thick," said Etienne, riding beside Maurice. "I can breathe again."

"Oui, this is much better than we've had all day." They were riding right flank and Jean was cutting across the herd toward them. Vultures circled overhead.

"Boys, there is nothing you need to see ahead. A dead man was under that flock. Not much left of him now. Jerome and Tobias are burying what there is left. You keep the cattle tight behind Hebert and Old Skinny. Are your pistols charged and handy?"

"Oui, monsieur," said Etienne.

"In my possible bag," said Maurice.

"Get it out Maurice. Check your charge and keep it close. Seems our stalkers may be more dangerous than we thought. We'll talk later."

Jean leaned forward and galloped his mount toward the boys riding drag.

"Who do you think it was got killed?" asked Maurice.

"How in hell should I know? I can see most of our crew."

"One of the scouts?"

"I doubt that. Jean said there wasn't much left. We just saw both scouts this morning. Even a big flock don't work that fast."

Maurice had dug out his pistol and powder horn. He emptied the flash pan and recharged it. He moved his knife sheath back on his belt and replaced it with the pistol on his left side opposite his tomahawk on the right. Pistol first tomahawk second and knife last. He was ready. But he was scared.

"You ready?" asked Etienne.

"Oui," said Maurice.

Maurice glanced about and kept a tight rein on his horse.

Etienne had traveled since the beginning of the drive with his weapons always at the ready. He appeared calm. But his horse was suddenly fidgety, tossing its head and prancing. Etienne was nervous and the animal knew it.

Chapter 21

The dead man was black. Who was he? Where had he come from? Who killed him? Why? No one seemed to know for certain. Jerome thought it could be one of the men missing from Cahokia but there was nothing from the tattered clothing to say for sure.

Jean suspected the Fox were back to bedevil the area. Hebert thought more likely it was the Cherokee since they had killed the voyagers last fall on the Ouabache (Wabash).

There were black men living in Vincennes. The dead man could have come from there.

"If it were a large war-party they would have been on us long ago," said Jean. "There were two fires at the spring but little other sign to give us information. The scouts have found nothing for us to go on."

"It's likely a small party of two or three young braves out to build a name for themselves. If they were mounted, we would see the tracks. So, they're on foot. I'm guessing they don't much want to confront a bigger group of mounted men."

"They may have been out all summer living off the land. They have at least one scalp now, maybe a few. They have sent a message. They have stories to tell if they get back to their village to tell them. If I were them, I'd be getting cautious and thinking about home."

"Well you're not them," thought Etienne with his head down. *"They might want to be great warriors and come home with a hundred French scalps. And maybe they don't want to walk home."*

"We will have to watch the horses closer," said Jean.

116

Etienne glanced up. Jean looked back squarely at him.

They were camped on what was called the Little Ouabache (Wabash). They had found themselves another big bend in a river. It was a good camp with sycamore and ash trees shading it. They were downstream a little way from where the buffalo trace crossed the river. Just beyond them was a big swamp where great blue heron had built a rookery. Forty or fifty huge nests, bigger than an eagle's nest, were visible from here, built high in the tall trees.

It was dusk. Maurice watched the big birds fly in as the sky gradually faded from lavender. The Parisian snored a few feet away.

Tomorrow Jean and Hebert were planning another head count as the herd crossed the river. Maurice was more interested in a head count for drovers.

"What they going to do if we've lost a few cows," he wondered, *"go look for them?"*

"Last time they did that they were gone half a day. Why do they need to know how many we've got? I say drive the ones we have and let's get on to Vincennes. The only count that matters is the one when we cross the Ouabache (Wabash)."

The cattle were lowing down near the river.

"They seem nervous tonight," thought Maurice.

Owls and whip-poor-wills were back in the nightly chorus along the river. At least those were familiar sounds. Maurice thought of home as he listened, dropping his head, falling asleep, his back resting against a tree.

First light brought a large woodpecker to a nearby tree limb already riddled with holes. His hammering soon woke the drovers Jean had hoped to let sleep a while longer.

"Just as well."

"Let's go boys. We're awake now."

An hour later, back at the ford the headcount was completed. One hundred forty-seven. They had lost three.

"I feared worse," said Jean.

"I expected five or six," said Hebert.

Neither suggested a search. The Parisian was on point, Alex and Etienne on drag. Jean rode out to the left flank and Hebert rode to scout directly in front of the herd.

They all knew they needed to get across another muddy stream this afternoon before dark. It would likely be wet and swampy in the lands between. Everyone was hoping for high ground again tonight.

"This land would be impassable in the wet season," said Alex.

"No one will ever try that," said Etienne. "You would need a canoe to cross the rivers and even some of those sloughs would be chest deep."

"There would never be a need," said Alex. "In the wet season you could cross maybe when it gets iced over enough but then you got the fear of a big snow that might catch you and the cold. I don't see any need to ever cross these prairies except this time of year when the mosquitoes and ticks can get at you."

Unexpectedly a shadow spread across them and then they heard a muffled sound of a million wing-beats rapidly getting louder. They glanced up. Thousands—rather hundreds of thousands of birds were flying over in a huge flock like a dark cloud. Soon the flock obscured the entire sky blocking the sunlight and creating a wavy shadow on the land.

The cattle were nervous and kept glancing their large eyes upward. Bird droppings fell like rain on everything below. It seemed to last forever but probably was over in ten minutes or less.

The sky cleared except for loose feathers, which floated down like downy flakes for ten minutes longer. The shadow was gone. The storm had passed but the air did not have a fresh rain smell.

Alex looked at Etienne and laughed. They were both busy cleaning themselves of bird droppings.

"I heard someone shooting," said Alex. "I bet we have a good supper tonight."

"I hope it was pigeons getting shot."

The boys looked out across the herd trying to count heads. "I think everyone is still with us."

"Not the biggest flock."

"Big enough."

"They can be a real plague if they land on the crops."

"Oui but they taste great. We should have shot a few ourselves."

"I'm sure Tobias got off a few blasts of buck-shot. Even one of those should bring down enough birds for everyone to eat. And I heard him shoot at least five or six times."

"I'm hungry. I'm tired of dry jerky. I'm betting Little Pierre knows what to do with those pigeons."

Chapter 22

Beyond Big Muddy

$\mathcal{T}$he herd crossed the big muddy creek late afternoon and soon found a narrow vale of little blue stem. A tiny stream flowed through with enough force to keep itself clear. There was a single oak on high ground. Much to the delight of his drovers Jean decided to make an early camp. Little Pierre would have time to work his magic on the birds.

Etienne helped prepare the spits. There would be two on a long fire. Alex kindled a blaze and piled on the wood. In an hour ten pigeons roasted above hot coals and Little Pierre puttered over them with a hog bristle brush and a pail of his most excellent sauce.

A savory aroma drifted through camp out into the prairie. Nine hungry drovers anxiously waited. For the moment all thoughts were on supper.

The meal did not disappoint. More birds were added to the spit. Everyone would have his fill this evening.

Twilight brought a barking fox in the grassland. Marsh hawks floated low over the prairie. Meadowlarks called. A warm breeze carried the scent of wildflowers and summer grass.

Morning found the herd moving through a mixed prairie: tall yellow compass flower, drooping prairie coreopsis, indian blanket, orange butterfly weed, big blue stem, switch grass, little blue stem, buffalo grass, rattlesnake master, an ecosystem bursting this time of year with living creatures, a native land of prey and predator, wild country evolved over centuries.

"Only the cattle and drovers are out of place," thought Maurice. *"Then again maybe not. Aren't we just predators and prey of a different sort? How long will those cattle we lost survive out here before the wolves or panthers take them down? For that matter how long will we roam this world before the vultures pick our bones?"*

"Wake up," said Etienne who suddenly rode beside him.

"I'm not asleep."

"No but you're day dreaming again."

"It's damn hot today."

"Oui, it is and likely it will be for another month or so."

"It's not this hot back home," said Maurice.

"We get more dry breezes maybe but it's still hot this time of year," answered Etienne.

"Well at home we don't have these damn gnats."

"I've seen 'em," countered Etienne, "but the swarms aren't as big. They aren't so bad here either when the wind blows."

"Well, they're bad today."

"The air is still."

"Why do you disagree with everything I say?"

"I don't, not everything, just most things," said Etienne, "cause it gets you so riled up."

Etienne paused and looked out over the prairie.

"Besides, sometimes I just want to see what you will think of next when I push you. I find it interesting. I just don't tell you. I think about stuff too. You aren't the only one."

Maurice contemplated that comment for a moment. It calmed and pleased him.

"How far do you think to Vincennes?"

"Jean says day and half to two days. Depends on how often we get confused on which fork to take or how wet things are."

"Look."

Etienne pointed. A small herd of elk moved in a line on a ridge not far off.

"Nine or ten?"

"I counted nine. They're heading for that little clump of trees. Think they will hold up in there. Could we get us one for supper? Elk steaks would be even better than passenger pigeon."

"By the time we got over there I bet we would find they moved through the trees and passed out the other side just to confuse us. Besides aren't you forgetting why we're supposed to be keeping a tight herd?"

"Well elk wouldn't be heading to those trees if Indians were there."

"You forgetting how many Indians you've seen carrying elk robes in winter?"

"There you go again disagreeing with me."

"Just trying to get you to think a few steps ahead. May keep you alive someday. Maybe today," said Etienne. "Besides if you go stalking away to hunt elk the savages might pick me off riding drag back here by myself."

Afternoon brought steady winds, which drove away the gnats. Clouds gathered in the west darkening as they rolled eastward. Soon they churned overhead and the air smelled of rain.

Lightning flashed, thunder crashed from a dark purple horizon to the north. Tall grasses lashed about in the wind. White tail deer loped away in search of cover.

Silver threads of rain were visible and Maurice could hear the big drops falling but it wasn't here yet. He thought of the canvas oiled and waxed which covered his bedroll but he didn't want his only blanket wet, besides, he'd been hot all day. The rain would cool him off.

It did cool him. It was a cold rain and the wind behind it was cold. Dark clouds shut out the sun. Maurice was shivering as the icy droplets pelted him. Eventually the rain stopped. But clouds still blocked the sunlight and the wind still blew brisk and chill.

Etienne was beside him. The boys pulled the horses up and dismounted. "Hold my horse," said Maurice, handing the reins over. Franticly he tore off his clothes.

Standing naked he fumbled to get his bedroll off from behind the saddle and pull the wool blanket out and around him. Then he took the horses and Etienne did the same. They tied the wet clothes in a bundle. In two minutes, they were remounted and repositioned behind the herd riding naked save for dry wool blankets tied over their shoulders and pulled tight the best they could.

The sun came out to brighten the surroundings but it was too low in the sky to warm the day. The boys were cold. Jean appeared riding to them.

"You two alright?"

"We're cold," said Etienne through chattering teeth.

Maurice said nothing.

"Tree up ahead. It's a little way but I sent Pierre to get a fire up. Soon as we get the herd circled, we'll get everybody warmed up."

"Can you hold on till then?"

The boys nodded.

When the herd was circled Jean rode out to send Maurice to the fire. He handed Etienne a steaming cup. It was bitter but he drank it.

"What is it?"

"The newest thing in New Orleans, coffee and chocolate. Mosiuer Buchet sent it with Pierre for medicinal purposes. There is also a touch of good French brandy. It should warm you till your turn at the fire."

There were soon two fires and half naked drovers huddled round both, drying clothes and warming themselves. Maurice hung his clothes from overhead branches near one of the fires, curled up nearby in his blanket and canvas and dozed off. It had been a long day.

Chapter 23

*T*he fires were kept burning through the night. By first light the drovers had burned up all the dry wood, which had fallen under the tree over the years. After that Jerome was hoisted up so he could climb the tree and cut off a couple dying limbs, which the woodpeckers had been visiting. This kept the fires burning for a while longer.

The sun was now up an hour. The fires and firewood were spent. The herd moved east with drovers yipping to move them along.

The morning started cool but warmed. The clouds floated thin and high. It would be a pleasant day.

They would not reach Vincennes today but everyone was hopeful about the day after.

"Your clothes dry?" asked The Parisian riding beside Maurice.

"Damp. How about your blanket?"

The Parisian had pulled his canvas covering to shield himself from the rain ahead of the storm. His success at keeping himself dry had been mixed at best. His blanket had gotten soaked. He had suffered less at first but more during the night.

"My blanket is damp too. Next time I think I'll leave it covered."

"Usually best," said Maurice, as if he were an old hand at crossing prairies.

The Parisian glanced over at the boy, started to speak, then suddenly decided to let it go unsaid. Instead, he clucked to his horse and trotted over to hustle along a straggling steer.

The hair was back up on Jean's neck. He kept his eyes on the horizon but didn't lose sight of the grass nearby. Vincennes was at least a day away. He was worried.

"If they are going to hit us it will be today, not tomorrow."

Jean had believed what he had said before; at the time he said it. Since that time, he had rolled it over in his mind so many times he wasn't sure any more. He knew Hebert thought it was the Cherokee. Jean still believed more likely the Fox, nearer and more familiar with stalking in tall grass prairie.

Whoever it was had not yet identified themselves. The Cherokee were a strong, proud people allied with the English. They would have no reason to hide their identity.

The Chickasaw had plenty of French targets along the Mississippi, why come this far north into unfamiliar territory? The Fox, however, had been hurt badly by the French campaign against them. They were much diminished and might not wish to invite retaliation. Still, their young braves hated Frenchmen.

Tobias rode up as Jean contemplated their situation.

"Seeing lots of prairie grouse flushing ahead of us. Thought I might take some loads of buckshot and get us a few for supper if that be alright with you." said Tobias.

"You not worried about our friends out there?"

"A man's got to eat. I just figure I'd rather eat grouse than jerky. I plan to be watchful. Besides if they wanted to kill me, they've had chances already. I'll be well armed and I'm not so easy to kill. If they get close enough and aren't careful, I might bag one of them instead."

"I'll ride out front with you," said Jean, "Then I can lead your horse while you stalk the birds. We can keep ahead of the herd that way and still not have you exposed. I'll go tell Hebert what we're doing. We'll stay in site of the man on point."

This was upland prairie. It was dry ground despite the rain. This far from Vincennes grouse saw few hunters. Tobias was soon blasting away. The hard part was finding the birds where they fell.

It was early again when Jean called a halt. They had enough grouse, woodcock, and quail for a good supper. Vincennes was too far to make today. He did not want to camp on wet ground between the last two rivers. The men and cattle were tired. He was looking now at a sweet valley and small stream between two woodlands filled with hickory and oak.

"This will make a good spot for our last night on the prairie."

The scouts reported. The next river was a league to the east and the Ouabache (Wabash) three leagues beyond that.

Camp was set in the trees. There was no shortage of wood. Supper was finished long before dark. Pipes were lit. Cups were filled. Blankets were dried. Jean called another four man watch, rolled up in his bed roll and went to sleep. He left Hebert instructions to wake him at midnight.

Chapter 24

The Ambush

A second nudge from Pierre woke Jean at midnight. He rose, stretching his arms above his head. The sky was clear. The stars were bright. A quarter moon cast light down on the meadow behind him. The woods were dark under a dense summer canopy.

Maurice, The Parisian, and last Alex were awakened.

"Time to go boys," said Jean, looking at Alex. "Be careful and stay alert."

Everyone knew the plan and their part in it. The drovers mounted including little Pierre and rode out to the herd. Soon Tobias, Jerome, Etienne, and Hebert rode in to camp and found Jean waiting. They dismounted and began puttering about.

"Anyone need anything?" asked Jean. "Everyone know where you are heading? Let's remember. It's most important. Don't go chasing after any savages, who might get away. The scouts are out wider. They will try to pick up any on the run. We don't want to end up shooting each other in the dark."

They all nodded. They knew the plan.

"Hebert you go first."

Hebert who was already in the shadows slipped off into the woods. Jean went next, then Tobias. Etienne and Jerome piled some more wood on the fire and then they too slipped out into the darkness.

Etienne followed Jerome on a game trail through the trees that skirted the edge of the meadow heading north to where the stream flowed out from the woods into the grass and curved to the southwest. Bullfrogs croaked and tree frogs sang as they had in this valley for ten thousand years.

The game trail turned and followed the stream into the forest. Jerome and Etienne kept on it a little way further until they reached a big smooth barked beech. Without a word exchanged Etienne stopped and Jerome moved past in the darkness. He would take up a position a few yards further facing the trail. Etienne would face the Creek. Elsewhere the others were setting up their own ambushes.

From the big beech the landscape sloped sharply downhill to the creek. Directly in front of the beech an ancient log lay across the forest floor making a natural blind. Etienne settled down behind it to wait.

Toward the left he could see the meadow clearly lit by the moonlight. He could make out the shapes of horses and riders moving round the herd and occasionally he could hear them speaking though he could not make out words.

In front, behind, and to his right, the wooded areas were dark. He could see little in those directions except for dark shapes where here and there overhead shafts of moonlight filtered in from above.

Etienne carried his two pistols, tomahawk, and knife in his belt. Tonight, he also carried a short-barreled musket Tobias had loaned him. He leaned the musket now against the log in front of him and settled in to listen.

Owls were calling. He heard a fox bark once. A little later he heard something moving away through the treetops.

The wind was still and sounds came to him clearly. Etienne listened intently to each one, no matter how small, trying to identify the nocturnal creatures that were about on their natural business and where they might be located in relation to himself.

He heard a splash from the creek below and then another. He heard a chittering sound and smiled to himself.

"Raccoons hunting crawfish."

He heard a short high-pitched scream from the meadow followed by stillness.

"One fewer rabbit."

Two hours passed. Etienne thought he heard mice and opossum moving through the leaf litter at different times.

His eyes were getting heavy. He moved his arms very slowly to the back of his neck and stretched his torso. He turned his neck slowly, like the owl does around as far as he could, peering into the darkness. He could not get all the way round as does the owl but he went both directions as far as he could, getting a good slow stretch and waking himself.

He heard a twig snap.

"Something heavy."

He listened—nothing. The sound he thought had come from in front. Minutes passed; then a quarter hour was gone. Maybe he had imagined it.

He saw movement off toward his left.

"Deer maybe coming in from the meadow? But where?"

He saw nothing.

"There."

A tree had been brushed. A shaking limb, its leaves shimmering, was backlit in the silvery light of the meadow. No other trees or branches moved.

Suddenly two silhouettes developed within the brush near the still shimmering tree. Etienne could see them now. He reached forward feeling for his musket.

"Savages. How did they get past me? Was that the twig I heard snap? I was supposed to ambush them on the creek. Is he drawing A BOW!?"

There was no time. The musket was in his hand. He raised it, cocking the hammer he took quick aim and pulled the trigger.

The musket roared. Silence followed. Frogs and insects, which had sung all night long, were instantly quiet. Sulfur smell burned his nostrils and Etienne could hear little but a ringing in his ears and the beating of his own heart.

The gun smoke cleared and he could see nothing moving where he had aimed and fired. He heard cattle lowing and moving about in the grass. He heard drovers speaking anxiously but yet could not make out words. Their shadowy shapes were no longer to be seen circling the herd.

Etienne put the musket back against the log and pulled his pistols. He waited.

An hour passed. The frogs resumed their choirs. Etienne kept watching the edge of the forest to his left. He had forgotten about the dark forest behind him. His attention was in front at the edge of the meadow.

A second hour passed since he had fired his musket. Still nothing moved. Mocking birds began to sing. It was lighter in the meadow and skyward through the tree tops, though the forest floor was still dark.

"Etienne," whispered Jerome from the darkness behind the beech tree. "I'm coming in."

"I hear you, come on," answered Etienne.

Jerome was suddenly beside him behind the log.

"Did you see something or accidentally discharge the musket."

"I saw two down by the meadow. One was drawing a bow. I had to do something. I don't know how they got past me."

"Did you get one?"

"I doubt it. I didn't have a good shot. I don't know. Maybe."

"Well, you did right. When dawn arrives Jean will call us in and we can check your kill."

Etienne sensed something in Jerome's tone. He didn't like it.

"He thinks my savages weren't real."

Minutes passed.

A breeze began to move. On it came the scent of fresh wood smoke.

"Let's check your kill."

"Wait, I have to reload. I didn't want the movement after I fired."

Jerome waited while Etienne reloaded and then they moved forward, muskets at the ready.

It all looked different in the daylight. Etienne walked a straight line to the location. He was certain this was it. But there was nobody here.

"I missed," he thought. *"Now no one will believe me."*

He looked at Jerome, who was waving his hand, waist high, back and forth through the grass.

"You hit something that bleeds," said Jerome, showing Etienne the blood on his hand.

"There is more," he said, pointing to a dark spot on the ground.

Hooves thundered behind them and Jean was seen approaching horseback at a gallop.

"Did you get one?"

"Etienne may have."

Jean dismounted and examined the signs on the ground.

"We'll track him. You go on back to camp," Jean said to Etienne.

"No," said Etienne. "It was my shot. I'll track it."

Jean thought to insist then decided not.

"I brought him to do a man's work. Now let him do it. Besides he looks determined."

Etienne was in fact quite decided.

"Wait till I get back."

Jean mounted, rode off and returned soon with Tobias. They spread out and stalked ahead, Etienne and Tobias tracking the blood. The trail was easy to follow at first but soon petered out. Jerome was able to find a few moccasin tracks after that but finally they all gave up and returned to camp empty handed.

An hour after sunup the herd moved east. Jean was satisfied with the outcome of his plan and the night. The drovers were anxious to get on to Vincennes. Etienne chose to ride alone on the left flank of the herd.

134

Chapter 25

Last Day of the Drive

"*E*tienne's quiet," said Maurice.

"Oui," answered Alex. "I guess he doesn't want to talk. Leave it go. He will tell us about it when he is ready."

"Which one of us you think that savage was getting ready to shoot?"

"Probably you," answered Alex. "You were the one closest to that side when the shot was fired. Etienne may have saved your ass."

Maurice had been thinking a lot about that very thing. He had been closest when the blast came in the darkness. It had startled him from dozing in the saddle.

The moments after the musket fired had been pandemonium, and he didn't have time to analyze what was happening. He remembered getting low over the saddle and moving to the far side of the herd to link up with Alex. He remembered the anxiety of not knowing what had happened.

The cattle had being nervous and moved about for a time after. He recalled the long two hours waiting for daylight, wondering, seeing dawn arrive, smelling the wood smoke and then learning from Pierre that Etienne had shot a savage who was drawing a bow. Jean and Tobias had gone back to help track the blood.

It was then in the saddle, circling the herd in the morning light, it dawned on Maurice, one of them might have come close to dying in the early hours before daylight. It might well have been him. If the savage had loosed the arrow, would it have struck home in his chest or back?

Would he have woken with the pain or fell from his horse dead before he hit the ground?

He didn't like to think on it but he had thought of little else this morning. He kept his horse moving mostly at a trot back and forth behind the herd. He kept glancing about and moving in the saddle. Jean had said the savages likely were gone for good. Maurice wasn't so sure and he wasn't taking chances.

"Moving targets are harder to hit," he told himself.

By mid-morning they reached the last little river before the Ouabache (Wabash). Jean and Hebert took another headcount as they crossed. No cattle had been lost. They were pleased. Maurice didn't care.

This day was heating up, returning again to real summer following the temporary respite after the storm. The wet prairie between the rivers was mushy, slow going, cattle appeared and disappeared in very tall grass.

Jean was planning to ford the Ouabache (Wabash) before dark. He was pleased with himself. He and Hebert had brought the first herd across this prairie. The boys had pulled their weight as Alex had said they would. The slaves had all been first-rate hands.

Little Pierre had been a very pleasant surprise. He had carried a full load of responsibility and saved morale at critical moments. He would be returned to Monsieur Buchet with Jean's compliments.

Even The Parisian, who Jean had accepted on Hebert's recommendation, had done his job.

Jean expected no trouble from here. He had told the drovers to prepare for friendly encounters with

Piankashaw Indians. Somewhere in this grass they likely would emerge to escort the herd to the fort.

It was a clear day with cumulus clouds forming in the west. Red-tail hawks and golden eagles circled high above, casting moving shadows on the grasslands below. Red-winged blackbirds trilled in the marshes nearby.

Alex was sleepy but he too was lost in thought. He recalled St. Philippe and the sound of the girl's laughter. The big house. The food. The first lost cattle.

He remembered the mission at Cahokia and the Jeunes dames doing laundry. What had they been dreaming of since that day? Did they remember him or did he misinterpret the smiles?

"I wonder how many girls live in Vincennes. What are the Piankashaw women like? Are they pretty?"

Old Skinny suddenly was bogged down in a narrow slough. The Parisian had tried to lead her through but she had sank instead. The herd was bunching up behind. Suddenly a loud crescendo of cries came from the grass surrounding them, and half a dozen Indians appeared. The Parisian was surprised and frightened but no one attempted to crush his skull or stab him. They were all close enough to do so. He noticed now they were smiling and laughing at his predicament.

Jean came riding up. The Michigamia scouts appeared. There was a parlay about the problem. The Parisian was shocked when he understood the Piankashaw were proposing to butcher the cow and remove her a piece at a time. Jean convinced them she was of special value and offered them another steer for a celebration meal tonight. Soon Little Pierre came up with his horses. Ropes were produced and horses employed. Old Skinny was soon back on solid ground shaking and covered in mud. The herd moved around her onward toward Vincennes. The Parisian coaxed her along behind.

Jean rode out ahead with one of the Piankashaw trotting along on foot as a guide. Half hour later he returned to tell Hebert, "Turn the herd north. They have long-lot plowlands planted ahead this side of the river. Some fenced. Some not. The ford is to the north. Commandant St. Ange will send us a guide before we cross to the holding pen. Before we get to the fields, we will circle the herd and hold them till preparations are made for us to bring them across."

The Parisian had caught up to the herd. Old Skinny was seemingly no worse for the wear. Muddy as she was, he thought it appropriate she and he should lead them over when the time came. He approached Jean with the idea. Jean smiled and nodded.

Chapter 26

Crossing the Ouabache (Wabash)

*T*he sun was low when the guide from the commandant arrived. The herd moved out immediately. In the distance Alex could see a couple houses and residential fenced lots built along this side of the river. The long-lot fields stretched out west into the prairie. The two houses were upstream of the fording place.

The village sat on the east bank of the river. But the river actually was on a wide bend and running westward. The crossing rose up out of the water on a road separating the church and fort to the right (west) from the remainder of the village built mostly to the left (east) of the river ford.

The Ouabache (Wabash) was wide compared to other rivers they had crossed, but at the ford it had a good gravel bottom. Today it was not running deep. Only a few of the smaller cattle were forced to swim a short distance near the far bank.

When Alex rode up that bank, the cattle and horses with riders cast long shadows trotting along beside them on the nearest tall fences surrounding the village residential lots. As in Kaskaskia each of these lots, enclosed roughly one arpent of land, including gardens, barns, and other habitant buildings.

Alex was disappointed. Vincennes was a trifling little village. The fort was only a blockhouse. The houses were small. The church was tiny.

Buildings were new and strait. Little had been here save the ford when Francois Marie Bisot, Sieur de Vincennes had arrived with his soldiers thirteen years before. They had come here to erect a French military and trading post on the Ouabache (Wabash). Since then, the sounds of axe, saw, adze and hammer had seldom been silent. Alex heard them working now.

The village common (for grazing animals, gathering wood and hunting) was to the southeast behind the village. It too was small. It would grow with the settlement.

The trading post and the river landing were immediately north of the crossing. Some coureur de bois lived beyond in shanties and lean-tos along the riverbank.

This village had been established as a fur trading and military outpost. It remained only a little more. The trading post was the beehive of activity and commerce in this place and it would continue so for many years.

Commandant Louis de St. Ange stood in the door of the blockhouse when the herd passed by. Jean reined his horse toward the fort. Hebert and the drovers escorted the herd toward the holding pens just inside the commons.

It was dark inside the blockhouse. There was a small table with two chairs. Candles burned from a sconce on two of the walls and one other on the table.

St. Ange was a fit and able officer. He stood now in a mostly clean uniform beside the table. Writing supplies, a report book and parchment were strewn across the tabletop.

"Bienvenue (welcome), Monsieur Verrou. My clerk is ill. I will take your report. My Piankashaw have already told me you were attacked."

"Well, I don't know I would say that exactly."

"Well, sit down, Jean and tell me about your trip. Don't leave anything important out."

Jean and the commandant sat down.

"Brandy?" the officer offered. He picked up a bottle and two cups, placing them on the table and pushing the supplies over to make room.

Jean had met Louis de St. Ange when he had been commandant at Fort de Chartres years before. But he was surprised to be remembered by him now.

Jean related the trip in some detail. When he finished, he leaned back in his chair and studied the officer. The commandant drew a breath in thought.

"Well Jean, it may very well have been the Fox as you suspect, but it could also have been any number of other tribes. Relationships are shifting again. The Anglais (English) are on the move slipping through our forests everywhere. Illegally trading. Attempting to draw our allies away. Entice them with their trinkets. It could even have been some of our own Piankashaw. A few of the young braves have pulled away and gone off to trade with these riff-raff. Wherever this scum set up a camp in the woods young men from the Miami and other tribes soon gather round and become a disgrace to their elders. After they have drunk enough rum, they begin to see their French brothers through jealous eyes, feeling they have been cheated in previous dealings. These young bucks are always looking for a perceived insult they can use as an excuse to go on the war path."

The soldier paused, contemplating whether to say more.

"Monsieur Cerree has been anxiously awaiting your arrival."

"He did the headcount with Hebert as we crossed," said Jean. "He is down at the holding pens now."

"Some of the Piankashaw will travel with his drovers taking the herd north to Fort Ouiatennon and Detroit. It should be friendly territory for us but these days you never know. When will you head back to Kaskaskia?"

"Couple days. We want to rest up and visit your tobacco fields. The horses we'll sell here. We plan to return downriver by pirogue."

"Good choice; faster—safer."

Chapter 27

Vincennes

 $\mathcal{M}$onsieur Cerree was pleased. The cattle he had been waiting for were here. Jean Verrou had brought them as promised. Here he came the man himself.

Jean rode up to the holding pens.

"What was our final count?" Jean asked Hebert.

"Same as yesterday. We didn't lose any more."

"Oui, Monsieur Verrou my count was the same. I am very happy to see you. Bienvenue a Vincennes," said Nicolas Cerree.

"You and Monsieur Hebert must be guests at my home while you remain here."

Nicolas Cerree had come to Vincennes from Kaskaskia the first year Vincennes had been established on the Ouabache (Wabash). He and Jean had not known one another then. They had met seven years past during the first war with the Chickasaw.

It was Cerree who had the contacts with powerful men in New France. It was he who had the contract to supply the beef to Ouiatenon and Detroit. And it was he who would soon drive the herd on toward Lac Erie. Jean glanced over to the drovers who were all standing near the gate to the commons.

"The cattle are inside the fence. They now belong to Monsieur Cerree. But I want you boys to camp here tonight and keep an eye on things till dawn. Then you can relax till we head home. Tobias, you're in charge. Any questions?"

There were no questions. It was too dark to go poking around much anyway. They would look things over and find the Piankashaw village tomorrow.

"Pierre, take care of our horses."

Jean and Hebert handed over the reins and strolled away with Monsieur Cerree. It was a warm evening. The breeze came off the big prairie and crossed the river bringing a unique redolence when mixed with the smells of the riverfront businesses.

The tools had stopped resounding through the village. Wood smoke, kitchen and garden smells mixed with the street odor of animal waste. It wasn't a bad smelling village except when the wind blew from the northwest across the tannery yard and slaughterhouse. Tonight, the wind blew out of the southwest and had the sweet smell of a haymow.

They walked back toward the river and turned right on Second Street. The trading post near the river had two torches burning outside on the southwest corner of the building. The door was open and a dim light shown also from within.

Loud conversations and boisterous laughter came from the riverfront. Elsewhere the hum of summer conversations could be heard in subdued tones along with the barking of dogs and the singing of whippoorwills from further up river.

There were only five streets in Vincennes and none were cobblestone yet. First Street ran along the riverfront separating businesses from the river landing. Second Street separated businesses from a row of four residential lots, all fenced with tall wooden fencing. Next was third street which fronted another row of four residential lots followed by forth street with six residential lots.

At the north end of Second Street was the Cerree home. As they walked up to the front gate, Jean could see a glow of light from the house. Monsieur Cerree lifted the wooden latch and swung the gate open to expose a brick walkway leading to the front steps of a small white house with a wrap-around porch and low overhanging roof on three sides. The porch was lit with candles in wall sconces. The side porch was set for an outdoor supper: table, chairs, candelabra, breadbasket, wine bottles, glasses.

The front garden they passed through was awash in flowers of the season including roses. In the side yard Jean could see a grape arbor and orchard though the fruit trees and vines were yet small. Madame Cerree brought cheese and summer sausage. Introductions were made. Food was served and polite conversation ensued.

Madame was a stout Canadian frontier woman whose family had raised her at Fort Ouiatenon further north on the Ouabache (Wabash). She had met and married Monsieur Cerree at age eighteen and moved with him first to Kaskaskia and a decade later here. She had born six children, which she paraded forth now, introduced, and then retired with them to the house.

Pipes were lit. Candles burned lower. A breeze continued to challenge the candle flames without quite ever winning the battle. It was a pleasant repose. Jean's thoughts wondered to Morningstar and what she might be doing now.

"The younger children would be like these children heading for bed."

"So, what did St. Ange tell you about the Anglais (English) problem?" asked Cerree.

Jean sat up in his chair and took the pipe out of his mouth.

"He said they are skulking around through our forests tempting our Indians away. It's an illegal trade and they use their cheap rum to turn the young warriors against us."

Jean paused to remember the conversation.

"He said they come down the Belle Riviere what they call the Ohio. He said there are more each year and he doesn't have the men to find and discourage them from coming."

"Well, he is right about all that," said Cerree. "And the traders and voyageurs are on his back every day to do more. They're feeling the pinch. A bigger share of their profits are lost each year to these Anglais trespassers. Something must be done. But that's not the whole problem."

His voice moderated. "I'm embarrassed to say it but their goods are often better made. They sell for less. Our traders can't compete. I've seen examples. If the Anglais are allowed into our territory we will lose our business and our income."

"Well, that's why Vincennes and his soldiers were sent here," said Hebert. "To keep the Ouabche (Wabash) safe for our traders. Maybe he shouldn't have worried so much about the Chickasaw and kept after the Anglais."

Hebert spoke rarely on such topics. He was a habitant first, a Catholic second, a Frenchman third, and a militiaman last of all. He had been with them in the recent war on the Mississippi, but he resented having been required.

"Vincennes had his orders as we all did," said Jean. "We can't fault him for following them."

"Well, he didn't have to stay behind."

"We all made our own choices that day," said Jean, "it was a bad day."

Jean gave Hebert a look across the table with a subtle turn of his head. He did not wish to offend their host. Monsieur Cerree took a few puffs on his clay pipe.

"The Governor must send us more soldiers to defend our rights," Cerree said. We have to protect these rivers from all encroachment or lose our commerce. The Anglais, the Spanish and the tribes also watch for weakness. If they see it, they will peck us to death like a feeble old hen in the henhouse. We must prepare. We must project strength. The wars will come as they always do. We must win them, punish our enemies for their arrogance, and most important of all reward our allies with plunder, scalps, and glory."

Chapter 28

2nd Day in Vincennes

Jean awakened to the singing of birds just before daylight. He had spent a comfortable night on a pallet laid down on the floor of the north porch at the Cerree home. He rose to visit the outhouse beyond the back garden. Upon his return a chorus of roosters from most of the poultry sheds in Vincennes began tuning up to great the sun. He rolled up his bed and tied it with a strip of rawhide, which had been left for the purpose. The smell of wood smoke and frying bacon floated in from elsewhere in the village. Jean left Hebert snoring, stepped off the porch and walked out through the garden and gate turning left down Second Street toward the village commons.

"Bonjour," said Jean as he approached camp a few minutes later.

"Bonjour," responded Little Pierre.

The black youth was puttering about a smoky fire. The Parisian appeared to be sleeping. Tobias and Jerome were off beside the common fence facing south and deep in a private conversation of hushed tones.

"Where are the boys?"

"The scouts left, the boys said they were going to check out the river before breakfast. They should be back in a minute."

"Well tell everyone they can charge what they need to me at the trading house. Monsieur Cerree has made arrangements. It will all come out of their wages when we settle up back home."

Little Pierre did not respond. On the frontier most business was done without hard money because there was so little coin or script to be had. Especially in the Illinois country barter and credit was the lifeblood of commerce.

"Cerree is sending a man to watch the cattle. Everyone is free to do as they please today. Tell Alex I'm going to look at the tobacco growing in what the locals call the upper prairie loglots. If he wants to come along, he'll find us there."

"I'll have bacon ready in a minute."

"No. Merci. You are a fine cook Pierre but Madame Cerree will be fixing breakfast for Hebert and I this morning."

Jean turned and sauntered back toward the village.

As he walked the main road he could see Alex, Maurice, and Etienne skirting fields of cropland to the southwest. People in Vincennes called those fields the lower prairie. For now, these were lands allotted to the church.

Jean waved to the boys. They waved back. A musket popped from somewhere across the river.

"Hunter."

Roosters continued greeted the sun, in earnest now. A soft, warm wind blew from the southwest. It was going to be another hot July day.

When the boys retuned to camp Pierre gave them Jean's message and began serving the bacon. Eggs had been found from somewhere. He hadn't mentioned the eggs to Jean. The boys ate heartily and with a smile.

"I'll bake bread today," said Pierre.

No one answered. But they all thought it was a good idea.

149

A few minutes passed. The Parisian rose. Rubbing his hands together he approached the fire.

"Bacon," he said, "wish we had eggs."

He'd missed his chance; though he never knew it. He took a share of bacon and ate it in a hurry.

"We're going to look things over," said Alex.

"I'm coming too," said The Parisian.

The smell of a smoky coal fire met them as they walked out of camp. On the way to the trading house, they heard the familiar sound of hammer striking anvil.

Like the pealing of a church bell the Blacksmith announced the start of another workday. Men shouted from the river. Pirogues grated in the gravel and then splashed into the water. Horses whinnied. Cattle lowed. Axe and saw and adze began their daily beat. Everyone knew it would be hot later in the day. This was the time to get work done.

Alex strolled past the door to the trading house where the boys entered. He walked past the other door too, the one on the river landing side of the building. He crossed the alley. He approached the blacksmith shop.

It was a small shop. Built of black locust logs hewed square and set upright —chinked between. Two large plank doors where swung outward opening most of the front wall and inviting any westerly breeze from the river to flow, through and out a large open window in the back. There was an overhanging roof in front creating an extended open-air work area. The forge, encased in brick, had a tall chimney rising out the center of the building. It was a good shop and a busy one.

"Bonjour, Monsieur Bourdon," said Alex.

The blacksmith glanced up between strikes but did not break rhythm. He kept pounding while the iron held against the anvil by his tongs was red hot. As the color faded, he placed the metal back into the fire and only then paused to look at the speaker.

"Bonjour, Alex, you have grown since last I saw you. I heard you had arrived. I knew you would not keep me waiting. Do you have something for me?"

"A package from Louis."

He handed the small package over. Joseph took it and set it carefully aside to open later.

"Merci."

Joseph took his poker and raked coals over the iron in the fire. He put the poker down and reached for the overheard handle and pulled, powering a large bellows to blow air into the fire from below.

"I'll come back to talk this afternoon," said Alex.

"Bien," answered the smith without looking up again.

With his tongs and gloved hand, Joseph pulled the red-hot metal out of the fire. He waited a moment until it stopped sparking, placed it carefully on the anvil, picked up his hammer and went back to work.

Etienne Maurice and the Parisian stumbled out of the trading post pushing one another.

"Whad-ya-get?" asked Alex.

"Peaches for now, cheese and a basket of raspberries for later and tobacco for the pipes," said Maurice. "Etienne has string and hooks. We can go upriver and fish when it gets hot."

The Parisian opened the cloth bag he carried and tossed everyone a peach.

The boys walked north on the dirt street separating the river landing from the village though there was really no clear delineation where the landing stopped and the street began. What was called Front Street was just the area closest to the buildings, hard packed earth, which by common consent everyone tried to keep open for the flow of commerce.

The river landing itself varied in size depending on how high the river flowed and how much distance there was to the water's edge. Sometimes the landing was fifty yards wide, other times one hundred.

Today there were pirogues, canoes and bateau pulled up on shore. Six men were busy unloading one of the pirogues beside the water's edge. Two other men were carting supplies from the trading post to a small bateau. A large canoe was upside down on a wooden rack away from the water. A man nearby stooped over a hot fire, stirring pine pitch, which was heating in a small iron pot.

Three canoes were visible at a distance, moving upriver almost to the bend where they would disappear as they paddled north toward Fort Ouiatenon. Maurice noticed the flashing wet paddles of the voyageurs. They had a very steady cadence, which he knew they could keep up for hours.

"Everything done right seems to have a natural rhythm," he thought. *"To be good at it you have to find the pulse."*

Skills came hard to Maurice. He was clumsy. He knew he was. It had certainly been pointed out often enough. He wanted to do things well.

"It's just a matter of timing," he thought.

"What you thinking about?" asked Etienne.

152

"Nothing," said Maurice. "Just watching those fellas building the pirogue."

"Oui, it is a big one."

"I'd bet it's nine toises (about sixty feet) long."

Two men were busy with adze hollowing out a huge cottonwood log and shaping it into a large river craft.

"You think they dragged that up here from the river with one team of oxen?" asked Maurice.

"Don't know," said Etienne. "May have taken two teams."

By mid-morning the boys had walked the village and riverfront twice. It didn't take long. There wasn't much to see.

North of the blacksmith was the village chair maker/cabinet maker/gunsmith, Monsieur Francis Bellrose. He had a small shop and worked outside for the most part in the shade of a big sycamore tree. Maple walnut and cherry blanks cured in a lean-to off the side of his building

Beyond Monsieur Bellrose's business was a rather large saw yard where Robert LeClerc had set up a pit saw operation to process logs into planks. In the river at the north end of his set-up floated several rafts of logs tied to trees on shore.

One by one the logs would be snaked up the riverbank by oxen and skidded to the pit saw. Oak, poplar, walnut were the favored woods for construction.

Today two men were hewing square logs for jobs in process about the village. There were a dozen stacks of sawn planks all about in various stages of air-drying. And there were piles and piles of posts everywhere, mostly of red cedar and black locust. These were the woods which last longest set in the ground. Vincennes like all the villages in the Illinois country needed lots of posts for the picketed fences built around the residential compounds and the fenced commons, and fenced agricultural long-lots in the upper and lower prairies.

Almost everything in the village was constructed of wood including shingles for roofs, furniture, tool handles, sleds and carts, plates to eat from and spoons to eat with. Vincennes required a steady supply of wood and the best way to get it here was to cut it upriver and float it down to Monsieur Le-Clerk's saw yard. Each year the denuded riverbanks were announcing your approach to Vincennes further and further north along the Ouabache (Wabash).

"Let's see what they caught," said Maurice, as he and Etienne approached the river.

 A boy of nine or ten stepped to shore from the bow of his pirogue and beached it alongside the bank. An old man rose slowly from the stern stepping ashore as he had done no doubt a million times before.

"Bonjour," said Maurice.

"Bonjour," responded the old man.

He had a stout grizzled look of a timeworn voyageur: short in the legs, broad in the shoulders, (previously strong) still resilient arms.

"These fish are all spoken for. You'd be the boys from Kaskaskia."

"Oui, I am Maurice, this is Etienne."

"I am Pierre Yoo of the discovery."

"What discovery?" asked Maurice.

"I was with La Salle when he discovered the portage at St. Joseph. I sell fish now. My voyageur days are through.

"You were with La Salle?" asked Etienne.

"I was sixteen years old," said the old man, "I am seventy-nine years next month."

"A long time ago," said Maurice.

"Oui," answered Pierre, "but it seems like not so long, on good days when I have a paddle in my hands coming downstream."

He paused and looked at his catch in the bottom of his pirogue. There were fifteen or twenty catfish and carp all in excess of five pounds, some closer to thirty.

"Get the cart Jacque," said Pierre.

The youth went up the bank to a site where dry fish nets were stretched between trees. He retrieved a two-wheeled wooden cart brought it back and began loading the fish.

"You deliver, I'll mend nets," said Pierre. "You boys want to sit a spell. It's getting hot."

"Oui," said Etienne, as they followed the old man to his nets.

There was a fire pit with charcoal and a few half-burned wood chips but no fire for several days by the look of it. Two short drift wood logs provided the seating. All three produced tobacco and clay pipes. Soon the smoke floated away on the warm breeze.

"So, you boys brought the cattle across the prairie, did you?"

"Oui."

"Well, that be something, I guess. Not been done before. Maybe someday when you're my age you can sit here and tell young men how you did it. Tha'd be about the turn of the next century. Who knows where we will be trading for fur by that time. Course by then everyone will likely not see the import of driving cattle cross a never before traveled prairie. People round here are pretty much tired of my old stories."

He sighed. "But they still like to eat fish and I make a pretty good living catching and selling 'em in summer. Winters are hard but I make out."

"What was it like when you were with La Salle on rivers never seen before, not knowing where they might take you, or what you might find when you got there?" asked Etienne.

"Exciting boys. Every day. Every hour. Around every bend in the river."

"And dangerous," said Maurice.

"We thought so said Pierre but, in some ways, it was safer than now."

"How could that be?" asked Etienne.

"We were breaking new territory. The Indians were curious about us. We tried not to take sides in their fights. We wanted the fur. They wanted to trade for muskets and stuff. It was like a new marriage every time we made an agreement."

"It went well for a long time. We wed their women and raised our families side by side. We had good trade. No one felt cheated. Then we got comfortable, took sides in their fights—made enemies."

156

"Now the damned Anglais have found their way into our rivers. The marriage is sour. No one is safe."

Chapter 29

"*I*s it safe out on the Ohio?" asked Miller.

"Safe as anywhere I recon," said John. "Injins are injins."

The two Englishmen were talking on the porch at Harris's Landing, on the Susquehanna River, in the English colony of Pennsylvania. Pipes were lit. Rum had been poured. It was a pleasant September day. Miller had come down to Harris's as much for news as for supplies.

"What about the French?"

"What about 'em?

"Don't they claim the territory?"

"Who cares? Virginia says it's theirs. The Quakers tell us it belongs to Pennsylvania; hell, the damn Connecticut people claim it too. I don't care who owns it. I ain't planning to build a house and raise crops like you're doing. I'm just a tradin'."

"All I know is the fur trade is there. The Indians are happy to see us. They like our goods and our liquor. A man can get rich in a few seasons. Why would I care what a few Frenchmen think? It's a big country. It's wide open. Who's gonna stop us? We ain't hurting' nobody. We take the risk. The profit should be ours."

"Is it legal?"

John set his cup down and gazed at Miller.

"I thought you said you was a farmer up on the Juniata."

"I am."

"Well, them laws you're talking about is for rich merchants and trading companies in Williamsburg and
158

Philadelphia. They try to keep all the profits fer themselves. There's enough room I figure for a few free trappers like me to make a little money too."

Miller knew that most people out away from Philadelphia felt the same way. A little money on the side, what could be the harm. People had to make a living.

"I didn't mean no offense," said Miller.

"None taken."

For a while they smoked and drank without talking.

Millar knew the authorities said they needed to control the trade with the Indians to avoid trouble. He knew about the laws. He had heard the old stories about deals gone bad, Indians feeling cheated, wars breaking out. It was a constant discussion when people got together. The folks who always got killed in those troubles were people living out in the lands between, the frontiers, places like where he lived now on the Juniata River in Pennsylvania.

Miller wasn't sure what he thought about the matter but he was certain he didn't want any trouble with Indians. He saw lots of Indians up and down the rivers he traveled. He had no quarrels with 'em. He meant to keep it that way.

Local Indians spoke some English and Dutch. He had traded a few personal items with them from time to time. Everyone did that. How could that be wrong? He was careful. He traded fair. He wanted no hard feelings. Miller planned to live here a long time.

"You ever see any Frenchmen when you are out there on the Ohio?"

"Not yet. They are mostly up north on the big lakes or way out west in what they call the Illinois country. I hear a lot about 'em but I ain't personally bumped into any."

"We usually team up in small groups when we go out. Haven't personally had need to go far down the Ohio yet. The nearest French forts are at Niagara, Detroit and some little post out on the Ouabache (Wabash). All three are six or eight hundred miles away from where we trade right now."

"How do your crops grow on the Juniata?" asked John.

"It's good ground, we do all right and we can sell any excess here or take it on to Lancaster if we want."

"I must have come right past your place when I came downriver."

"We aren't right on the river itself, we're back up a little hollow."

"That's smart. How many families in the area?"

"Maybe fifteen spread out over ten mile of river bottom."

Miller thought about that. He remembered back to his last day in Philadelphia, his meal at the town tavern with the old German immigrant fresh off the boat. That old guy was moving his family up somewhere on Perkiomen creek. He remembered thinking maybe he should reconsider the Juniata. But land was cheapest out here and he had kin here, what choice had he really had. He wondered how the old German had set himself up in the same amount of time.

"Maybe it would have been easier there," he thought.

"You ready to head home?"

It was cousin Jesse asking. They had come downriver together. He was standing before them out of money or cut off from the rum by Mr. Harris. He swayed slightly on his feet, which likely meant the latter.

"Might as well get a jump on it," said Miller, popping the bowel of his pipe on the palm of his hand and spreading the ash to the ground as he swung himself off the porch heading for their canoe pulled up on the riverbank below.

"Good luck with your tradin' Finley," he called back.

"Good luck with your corn, Zack."

Chapter 30

*H*einrich Feagley was settled on Perkiomen creek a day's ride north of Germantown on the Philadelphia Pike. His house, barn and springhouse were built, his fields fenced. He remembered his meal at the town tavern a decade before after the long voyage.

It had all been a bit of a blur at the time. Eight weeks aboard the ship Elisabeth, then the ten days waiting in Philadelphia for the rest of the family on the ships Samuel and Hope, the oaths of allegiance taken, the million and one decisions. His meal at the tavern had been a respite in the chaos of those days.

His chance meeting with the young man (Zack Miller) heading out to the Juniata had boosted Heinrich's confidence. The young man had been in this new land longer and seemed to think the Perkiomen Valley was a safe place to settle. Maybe it was. It had gone well so far. But Heinrich now had sons and grandsons eyeing cheaper land near the forks of the Delaware, in New Jersey's Valley of the Paulinskill, in the Minisink area and even down in the colony of Maryland.

Heinrich had learned in the old country that there was no place truly safe from violence. He knew also that cheap land was often cheap for a reason. In the past decade he had heard enough to know this new land like in the old country was built and maintained by violence. Cheap land often meant contested land and in the American colonies that meant sooner or later Indian problems.

Philadelphia was a city of 15,000 people, said to be the biggest metropolis in all the English colonies. As many as a dozen shiploads of new immigrants docked at its wharfs every year. The wooden docks were expanding the streets were wide and cobblestoned. There were many big houses (usually of red brick) with gardens, orchards and servants. Commerce was brisk. Furs were not the only export but they remained one of the most important.

From the Perkiomen Valley New France seemed a long way off. But Heinrich had heard about conflicts with Frenchmen up North on Lake Erie and out west in the Ohio country. If there was violence brewing, Heinrich didn't want his family in its path.

Chapter 31

March 1743

In the Wyoming Valley on the Susquehanna river

$\mathcal{T}$he snow was falling fast. It was wet snow. It clung to everything. It had started an hour before.

Otter and Red Corn had been away from the Munsee village for two days. They had yet to kill or even see a deer. It had been a hard winter. Meat was needed.

Forests and fields near the village had been hunted out for months. Now it was necessary to go farther afield to find the game. Winter travel was always difficult. The weather for the month prior had been mixed with snow, rain and even an ice storm. When they left the village, it had been cold and a hard crust had formed on top of a foot of snow. The two had traveled upstream along the river and then followed a small tributary southeast.

Otter and Red Corn had been friends since boyhood. They liked hunting together and could usually anticipate one another's moves. Gunpowder had been exhausted in the village. They hunted today with bows and arrows.

A half hour ago they crossed the track of a small herd of eight deer. They followed that trail now. Suddenly Red Corn stopped and froze in place. Otter did likewise. Neither moved. Seconds passed. Then a minute went by. Red Corn remained frozen in place. Otter knew there were animals ahead but he could not see any.

Red Corn was standing on a little rise and looking down into a bowl. If Otter could not see the deer, then likely they could not see him. But from Red Corn's imitation of a tree, the animals must be aware of his presence and he knew it.

Slowly Otter sank to a crouch and took a careful step left. The fresh snow muffled any sound. Remaining low, Otter stalked away keeping a big rock and some laurel bushes between himself and where he thought the deer stood. He knew he had to move noiselessly but swiftly. If Red Corn stirred the deer would bolt away in a second.

In a few moments Otter had circumnavigated the laurel bushes. Slowly he raised himself. His bow already had an arrow nocked in place for a shot.

He saw six deer, their heads and tails up, frozen in a stare with Red Corn. Otter was on their right flank providing a broadside view. The animals might very well have seen him had they not been mesmerized by their anticipation of danger from Red Corn.

Here was an opportunity. But it would disappear in a heartbeat. Otter pulled the bowstring tight and let fly an arrow at the deer nearest him. With the twang of the bow string the other deer turned to look at Otter before bolting away through the brush. That second of confusion gave Red Corn an opportunity to pull his own bowstring and let fly his arrow at the deer nearest him.

The muffled clatter of deer fleeing through the brush and snow lasted only a few moments and left two of the prey lying quiet on the white ground. The hunters waited, offered a silent prayer of thanks and watched for a minute more. Then almost simultaneously a war whoop came from both hunters as they trotted to their respective kills not five yards apart. The friends smiled at each other savoring the moment. Rare hunting experiences were treasured among the Munsee. Such things were thought to be very good omens. Both men knew they would likely remember this kill as long as they lived. And as friends each knew the other was recalling a similar occurrence from a decade before.

"Like you and Jorris," said Red Corn.

"Almost," said Otter, "but that time there was no snow and he had to read my imitation of a tree and take the first shot. I'm not sure I could have done as well without the silence of the snow."

"Jorris was the best stalker of us all when we were boys," said Red Corn.

The two friends drew their knives and went to work. The task was familiar and they went at it without speaking. Each man was deep in his own thoughts of past good times on the Fishkill (Delaware River).

The Fishkill was the old home of the Munsee who had lived near Minisink Island for generations until forced to move away by the Iroquois and the Pennsylvanians. Jorris Davids was a boy who lived with his family three miles north of the native village at Minisink. Jorris, Red Corn and Otter had been inseparable as boys.

The Dutch settlers had moved into the area on the east side of the Fishkill from earlier settlements on the Hudson River. The early Dutch had bought land from the Munsee and lived peacefully on the east side of the river from about 1700 until the Munsee were forced by the Pennsylvanians to move.

"I would like to see our friend Jorris," said Otter.

"We should pay him a visit."

"It is dangerous to go there now. The village elders will not approve."

"Jorris would be happy to see us. He never agreed with that walking treaty," said Red Corn.

"If we are discovered it will bring sanctions from the Iroquois. Everyone will suffer."

"They will not discover us. Jorris should know of this kill. It is a sign we share with him. We need to sit beside a fire, smoke the pipe and discuss its meaning."

The Munsee had been cheated in the land deal known as the Walking Treaty. Pennsylvania authorities and rich speculators had done the swindle. Even many of the Munsee's white neighbors knew it was wrong and spoke out against it. But Pennsylvania was allied with the Iroquois who enforced the order and insisted the Munsee move west to the Wyoming Valley on the Susquehanna.

The Munsee were a proud people but they were not as strong as either the Iroquois or the Pennsylvanians.

Profits were high for speculators selling land to new immigrants. More poor farmers came off the ships at the docks in Philadelphia every year. There was much debate about the treaty. Sermons were preached against it. But in the end the Indians living in the Minisink were forced to move to the Wyoming Valley and new immigrants bought land, which the Munsee thought they had not sold and which they did not wish to leave.

The Munsee had been wronged. Over the years they had not forgotten.

The snow fell harder by the time the hunters had finished gutting the deer, packing the inside of the carcasses with snow and building a quick sled to carry home the meat.

"We will go to the Minisink in spring, when the ground firms, but we must tell no one," said Otter.

"No one," agreed Red Corn, "and we will not be discovered."

Chapter 32

Nine years Later, 1752

Kaskaskia

No more cattle drives across the Illinois Prairie had occurred since the one in forty-three. Jean Verrou and his drovers had been famous in Kaskaskia for a couple years after that first one. But, soon enough they had been forgotten in the steady drumbeat of life's happenings.

Each drover had returned to his previous station or moved on to new adventures. Jean and Alex were back in their long-lot fields at Kaskaskia. Hebert was in his long-lots at Prairie Du Rocher. Etienne had signed onto a voyageur crew and came to visit in recent years only when his craft brought him near. Maurice had gone to work building pirogues. Little Pierre and Tobias were back serving their masters in St. Philippe, as was Jerome in Cahokia. No one had heard from The Parisian since he had left them at Vincennes.

Life in the Illinois country continued much the same and yet it was different. One day faded into another like the seasons and the years. Fields were planted and harvested. Convoys of river craft loaded with furs, bear grease, lead, wheat, and corn moved downriver to New Orleans. Manufactured products mostly made in France moved back upriver always accompanied with a few dozen new people, normally more men than women, usually but not always French in nationality. Sometimes black slaves were sent along too.

Babies were born and old people died each year. Fevers occasionally carried away even strong healthy people. With the immigrant influx the Illinois country grew its population. But it didn't grow fast. Still there were more French men and not enough French women. Most of the children born were metis (mixed Indian blood) some raised in the towns as Frenchmen, others raised as Michigamia in the Native villages. It didn't seem to matter to most people and it worked for the good of all.

Old enemies still came to call in the Illinois country, though some were not so strong as they once had been and did not come as often. The Fox, Chickasaw, Cherokee and Iroquois were still to be feared and all were encouraged and supplied by the English.

In fact, English traders seemed bolder each year in their adventures into French territory. These troublemakers drew away individuals even from French allied tribes with promises of better goods and cheaper prices. It had gone on long enough. Something had to be done. In early June 1752 it was.

In August Etienne came home for a visit. Soon after arrival in Kaskaskia he was at the Verrou house for dinner. It was late afternoon, not yet the time called early evening, too hot for mosquitoes. The meal was finished. Morning-Star remained inside the house. Jean, Etienne, and Alex were sitting outside in the shade of the east porch enjoying a light, dry, breeze coming from the west across the Mississippi.

Fieldwork was limited this time of year. Etienne sat on a short three-legged stool, Jean was sitting in his prized Windsor chair brought out from inside and Alex sat on the floor with his legs dangling over the outside edge of the elevated porch. They all smoked the standard clay pipe, but with various lengths of stem. Etienne had the longest because he had purchased his pipe only last week when passing through Vincennes on his way down the Oubache (Wabash). Jean had the shortest stem having kept his same pipe carefully for many years.

Jean spoke first. "Etienne, you said during dinner you would tell us about meeting up with The Parisian."

"I didn't think it would be polite dinner conversation," said Etienne. Then he paused to gather his thoughts. "I saw him in Detroit outside the fort. He looked healthy but he had changed. He was quiet, worn out, and more skittish than ever. You have heard about Pickawillany?"

"Oui", answered Jean, "God bless the Ottawa and the Chippewa. They destroyed bad Indians who have been killing Frenchmen on the Ouabache (Wabash) and out in the Ohio country these past few years. About time I'd say."

"Well, many of those Indians were Miami. Some were Piankashaw and Wea," said Etienne. "Many other tribes had breakaway groups living there also. Memeskia a Miami was the village leader. He had contacts with British traders. He had drawn many Indians from their home villages to Pickawillany to build his own power within the larger Miami people. There were hundreds living there with him. It was a big village. The English had helped Memeskia build two forts which they called trading houses."

'How do you know all these details?" asked Jean.

"The Parisian was there. He saw it happen."

"What was he doing there?" asked Alex.

"He was there with a friend to buy trade goods and hopefully some muskets and powder. They were planning to take them north to trade with the Huron."

"Well, he knew that was illegal," said Jean.

"He knew, but he would hardly be the first Frenchman to trade in smuggled English goods. I've known even licensed traders to have some English items mixed into their cargo by the time they arrive at Fort Niagara."

Jean nodded waving his hand in surrender of the point everyone knew but which no one wished to discuss. At least a few smuggled goods were found now in every Illinois Frenchman's home and probably at the forts too. European manufactured products in this far frontier were scarce. When goods showed up few people asked questions other than price.

"So, what happened?" asked Alex.

"The Ottawa attacked early in the morning before dawn. Hundreds of them. Led by Charles de Langlade, a metis, with an Ottawa mother from Michilamackina. They killed dozens but many Miami warriors were away hunting. In the darkness most people ran for cover or off to the woods. The Ottawa surrounded the two tiny forts where some of the English traders and dozens of Indians had taken refuge."

"Where was The Parisian?" asked Alex.

"He was asleep like everyone when it started but he made it into one of the blockhouses with a bunch of Indians, and his metis friend who has a Miami mother living at Kekionga. That made him well acquainted with at least some of their present housemates. The Parisian was the only full blood Frenchman in the place. He kept his head down and said little. The Ottawa weren't after him. They wanted the English traders and Memeskia who, lucky for The Parisian, had all taken refuge in the other blockhouse."

"For a few hours the killing and torture of captives went on outside as the Ottawa negotiated with those inside the forts. The Ottawa had taken important Miami women as hostages. They offered a trade. Fires were built in sight of the forts and threats were made."

"Just before noon there was a scuffle heard in the other blockhouse and the door there was thrown open. The four English traders and Memeskia were pushed out, unarmed. The women were brought forward and left outside the door. The exchanged prisoners were led by the Ottawa toward the fire."

"The Parisian saw all this?" asked Alex.

"Most of it. So he says. In bits and pieces through the loopholes of the blockhouse."

"They took one of the traders and Memeskia closer to the fire away from the other three prisoners. With a scream they fell upon them and cut them to death with tomahawks and knives putting some of the pieces in a big pot of water, which was already boiling on the fire. After this was done, they sat quiet around the fire as if in some kind of trance. Then bowls were produced from the village and each warrior ate from the pot."

"As each warrior finished eating his bowl, he let out a shout and ran away into the village to plunder and set fires. By midafternoon the Ottawa and their prisoners were gone, the air was filled with woodsmoke and it was quiet save for the crackling of flames and whimpering of women as Pickawillany burned."

"How did he get to Detroit?" asked Alex.

"They swung out way to the east for two days before heading back north. The Parisian kept hold of his musket and possible bag during the ruckus. He's learned a few things since we knew him. But he was shook up a good bit. Said he had never seen anything like it. Hadn't had much dealings with the Ottawa or the Chippewa and he had never heard of Charles Langlade till he got to Detroit and learned the name. But he says he will never forget the man in war paint."

Jean leaned forward in his chair and popped the bowl of his pipe onto the palm of his left hand scattering the ashes off the porch with a simultaneous swing of his arm.

"Well that will sure make a statement to the tribes and the English too. What is the Governor saying about it?" he asked.

"No one knows yet," said Etienne. "They say in Detroit that Langlade and his Ottawa were acting on their own. But everyone is cheering 'em on. They're saying it should have happened long ago before the English got their talons in so deep. Too many Frenchmen have been killed as a result of those people. The Governor must take steps to keep 'em out for good. The King needs to send us more soldiers. The English have had a taste of French profits now. They are like a wolf pack, which has tasted the blood of your herd. You may run 'em off for a while by killing some. But they likely will come back later if you didn't kill them all."

Jean spoke. "Celeron took his party down the Bella Riviere four summers ago. He ran the English out then. He planted lead plates and notices reclaiming and marking the territory at river confluences. He talked to the tribes and warned them about the English. Some listened but obviously some did not."

"Celeron did not have a large enough force to make the impression needed. He didn't kill anybody, burn any villages or eat any leaders. Maybe Langlade has sent the message and made the impression the English will remember," said Alex.

"I hope so," said Jean, "I hope so."

Chapter 33

December, 1752

Minisink Valley on the Delaware River

Mackhackemack was an isolated farm community of Dutch settlers who had come over the highlands from the Hudson River Valley around 1700. They lived technically in the colony of New York though the colony of New Jersey sometimes lay claim to the area as well. It was a problem, which had surfaced in recent years and often caused serious conflict among neighbors. Across the Delaware River (previously known as the Fishkill) the land was claimed by the Colony of Pennsylvania.

The Dutchmen of the Minisink had lived peacefully for almost forty years with the Munsee Indians as neighbors. Until 1737 when the Pennsylvanians concluded the Walking Treaty and forced the Munsee to vacate their land on the west side of the river and move further west over more mountains to the Wyoming Valley of the Susquehanna River.

Some of these Dutchmen traveled to Philadelphia at that time to speak against the injustice of the treaty. But no one in Pennsylvania government cared much what farmers from New Jersey thought about the matter. The Indians were moved by threats from the Iroquois Confederacy, who were at the time allied with the Pennsylvanians.

After the Munsee moved, not much had changed in the Minisink the past twenty-five years. Except a few Dutchmen had moved over to the west side of the river and become technically Pennsylvanians. No one here thought much about it. A few, however, knew the Munsee still claimed the land and decided it was best to remain on the east bank. Jorris Davids was one of those.

Jorris lived on a farm three miles north of Minisink Island and nine Miles south of Mackhackemack. He had grown up hunting and fishing with boys from the Munsee tribe, who had lived then in their village on the Island. Jorris' younger brother Solomon had married John Decker's daughter and built a water-powered gristmill just north of Mackhackemack. A couple years back Solomon had been found dead and murdered. Jorris and most of his family thought the cause was the dispute between New York and New Jersey. Since then no one had been found or punished.

Jorris was sick of land disputes and he was an angry man today as he rode his sorrel horse toward Mackhackemack Dutch Reformed Church. It was a small stone church about a mile up the Mackhackemack branch of the Delaware river on its west bank between the smaller branch and the larger Delaware which here took a sharp northwesterly bend heading west though more mountains.

It was the week before Christmas. Today there was to be a dinner at the church.

Beletje Davids was Jorris Davids' niece, Solomon's fourteen-year-old daughter. She was already at the church down near the small stream where her brothers had started a fire and helped get a big pot of water near boiling.

"It's time to get started," she said suddenly walking toward a pile of six live chickens bound together at their feet. Quickly she untied one of the hens being careful to retain her grip on the legs. Smoothly she swung it over and lay its head on the ground in front of her. Her younger brother, David, lay a broomstick handle across the chicken's neck and Beletje stepped on the stick, one foot on each side of the head, applied pressure with her weight, pulling upward at the same moment with a swift jerk. The follow through tossed the headless chicken out in front of her with the same movement. It was over. In a second the hen had had its head separated, but the wings still flapped and the legs still jerked for several seconds more flopping the body about the grassy area in the process. Before the first hen had stopped moving the second had its head removed in the same manner. And then the next and the next till all were done. By that time several birds were flopping about but the first bird was quite dead and still. It was all very efficient. To eat chickens they must be killed. These children had performed the task many times. They had no illusions as to where drumsticks originate.

Beletje then stepped to the first hen, picked it up by the feet and carried it to the hot water pot, which had been removed from the fire. She dipped the hen into the scalding water and moved it to a wooden stump close beside. Quickly she and her younger brother David went to work plucking the feathers from the bird.

It was smelly work. Bird feathers and hot water combined create a very unpleasant odor. To which anyone who has ever done the work of plucking a bird can attest. Beletje thought it one of the most unsavory jobs on the farm. It took a little while to complete.

When they were finished, she handed the bird to her youngest sister Elizabeth who carried it a few yards downstream to two other ladies of the church, waiting at a small wooden table with knives. They gutted the carcass saving some choice innards and passed it then to two other women who cut it into pieces sending it on to be floured and placed in a large iron skillet of grease.

Fortunately it was a sunny bright day. The ground was frozen. The fires and the sun made the work pleasant for everyone. The smell of frying chicken helped Beletje forget the earlier task and reminded her she was hungry.

Then she saw Uncle Jorris cross the stream riding his sorrel. He didn't often come to such events. She wondered about that. Beletje's brothers greeted him as he rode up in front of the church grounds. He smiled.

There was to be no sermon today. The Reverend said a few short words about the joyous season. It took only about thirty minutes. By that time the food was ready to eat. He blessed the food and the hands, which had prepared it. Dinner was served inside the church where tables and benches had been improvised by the men.

The food tasted good. The ladies had brought forth their best preserves, breads pies. There was buttermilk, eggnog, cookies. Everyone ate well but people kept glancing at Uncle Jorris. He had asked for time following the meal when he could address the congregation. That time had come.

He rose from where he had been eating and whispered in his siter-in-law Lea's ear. She whispered in the ears of a couple other women. Then she announced that the children should follow her outside for games. They did and the room got quiet as soon as they all shuffled out and the wooden door closed behind them.

Beletje stayed where she was. She wanted to hear what her Uncle Jorris had to announce.

"I was down to Dupui's trading post Monday," he began. "There was an article posted from a Philadelphia newspaper. An English trading post in the Ohio Country has been attacked and burned to the ground. English traders were tortured, hacked to death and cannibalized by Frenchmen and their savages the Ottawa and Chippewa."

He paused and some people whispered.

"The post was set up several years back by George Crogan, a Pennsylvania trader known to many of us. He was away from the post at the time and was not harmed. But several English traders were slaughtered."

"Well some of them traders don't deal square and get themselves in all kinds of trouble," said someone in the crowd. The voice sounded familiar but Beletje could not see who had spoken.

"Well Crogan is a licensed trader with a good reputation for dealing square, not some border trash trying to get rich easy. Crogan has been operating his post at a Miami town called Pickawillany near the headwaters of the Miami River, an important portage point he says for trading further north and west. He was invited to set up his post by the Miami Chief himself. Trappers called the chief Old Britton because of his love of the English traders. The Indians called him Memeskia."

"The post was so popular with the Indians that it kept growing. Small bands from several other tribes had moved in to live there. Memeskia and his people were friendly to all. Crogan says this was a golden opportunity for us to improve our relationships with the Indians of the Ohio country."

"Maybe Old Britton will invite the traders back," offered John Decker.

"He was killed and eaten with the traders, John. The whole town was burned to the ground. The savages went on a killing spree like a weasel in a hen house. All the Miami and the others were killed. The Frenchmen and their Ottawa dogs are roaming through the Ohio country right now hunting any English trader they can find."

"Well it's good to know but I don't see this has got anything to do with us. It sounds like Pennsylvania business to me or maybe Virginia. They're the people who lay claim to that Ohio country," said the voice speaking from the crowd.

"No," said John Decker. "What Jorris is telling us is important. We have to remember what them Frenchmen have done to us before, up in Schenectady, and plenty other places not that far away or long ago. We better start focusing on our Militia preparations. Albany may call on us. I just thank God the Iroquois hate the Ottawa and Chippewa as much as they hate the Huron and the French. If that ever changes, we're in big trouble living here."

"What about the Munsee?" asked the voice.

"They're loyal to Pennsylvania," said Jorris.

But when he said it, he wondered to himself if that loyalty might change. He knew in his heart they had been wronged. He knew also they were a capable and proud people.

Chapter 34

New French Forts

$\mathcal{T}$he smell of wood smoke greeted them as they rounded the turn and paddled into the bay at Pesque Isle on the south shore of Lake Erie. Maurice looked back at Pierre and smiled. The older man looked tired but smiled back. They were the only two in the canoe from Kaskaskia. The other six were soldiers from Fort De Chartres. The eight men in the canoe following them were all Frenchmen from Vincennes.

A mile away they could see smoke rising and hundreds of men scurrying about like ants on the hillsides. They could hear axes and adze chopping and trees crashing. As they got closer, they could hear voices shouting directions. Some of the voices sounded angry others cautious and even a few who sounded mirthful.

It was a big operation. Bigger than anything Maurice had ever seen until earlier this year when workers had started to rebuild Fort De Chartres. All five communities in the Illinois country were busy on that project now. He resented having been pulled away and sent here.

He could hear saws cutting now and chisels being tapped. There were even a couple teams of small oxen, chains clanging, pulling logs up the hills driven by shouting teamsters. Gangs of men were pulling other logs. All these timbers were moving toward a single point on the bluff ahead. The spot was about three hundred yards from the shoreline and maybe three hundred feet above the water's edge. This would, by the look of things, soon be the new French Fort at Presque Isle.

New France's temporary governor Baron de Longueuil had been shocked into action following the burning of

Pickawillany last June. He had only assumed the role of Governor after the death of Governor Maquis de la Jonquiuere. He hoped he might later be appointed permanently. Rumors however suggested he had taken his eyes off the prize out west in favor of business activities closer to Montreal.

He couldn't have talk like that. It might get back to King Louis. Quickly, he recommended Charles Langlade for a commission in the French Colonial Militia.

The Baron de Langueuil might not have bothered. King Louis had already sent his replacement even before news of this summer could be sent back across the Atlantic. The Marquis Duquesne assumed Governorship in August and took charge immediately. He approved the recommendation for Charles Langlade and added a lifetime pension for his important services.

By October the new Governor had decided on a more grand strategy. Before winter ice could close river travel and communications, he sent orders from Montreal, up the Lakes and down the Ouabache to all the French Military posts, as far away as Fort de Chartres. Fort De Chartres and Post Vincennes were in Northern Louisianna and therefore technically not under his command but this was no time to quibble over such details. This was a time for action. Four important new forts would be built from Lac Erie to the Belle Riviere.

Even St. Ange the commandant at tiny post Vincennes redirected some of his meager manpower to help build these new forts and a few more of his men to help in the work being done to build a grand stone fort at De Chartres.

St. Ange knew that many from his local Piankashaw tribe had been tempted away to live at Pickawillany. The elders told him they were slinking home now to live peacefully with their French 'fathers'. The Commandant was happy to hear the wayward braves had come home to their village outside Vincennes. But he wondered what they might be doing now had Langlade and his Ottawa not eaten Memeskia and burned his town to the ground.

A grand show of strength was needed now to cement Indian loyalty. What could do better than a string of new French forts with cannon, and soldiers to enforce the law. How better to keep English traders on their own side of the mountains and out of French territory.

Presque Isle was only the first of four new forts planned to be built this summer to protect a portage called The Venango Way. This path was from Lake Erie overland to the headwaters of French Creek, down that water to its confluence with the Allegheny and then down the Allegheny to its confluence with the Monongahela River, which then formed The Bella Riviere. With this portage opened and protected it would provide safe passage down the Belle Riviere, a branch of the Ouabache (Wabash), which flowed to the Mississippi, Fort De Chartres and eventually all the way to New Orleans and the Gulf of Mexico.

It was a good strategy but it required resources, leadership, cooperation and speed. The first three hundred men had arrived from Montreal May third and started work the same day. Now other men were arriving almost weekly. The plan was coming together. Maurice and Pierre were part of that plan. When they beached their craft, they were met by a grizzled soldier in part of a uniform, who had at least some semblance of military manor.

"Bonjour messieurs, passing through or have orders?" he asked.

"We have orders from the commandant at Fort De Chartres," said Pierre.

"Take your gear and report to the command post up that trail a little beyond the top of the ridge," said the soldier pointing. Then he turned suddenly and walked on down the shore toward a work crew.

Maurice looked beyond the soldier, along the shoreline. He noticed tiny waves slapping gravel on a narrow beach like they had for thousands of years. It was a pretty late spring day. Dogwoods were in bloom the air smelled sweet. A big adventure lay ahead.

Chapter 35

May 1753

Presque Isle

$\mathcal{T}$he view from atop the bluff was impressive. The bay below opened at the east end presenting a northeastward view of Lac Erie. The peninsula forming the bay stretched out into the lake from the west end. It had a tree-covered ridge of its own. This feature blocked the prevailing winds, and most storms. Presque Isle's Bay was a fine natural harbor for shipping.

Thirty-eight leagues (115 miles) to the northeast, at the far end of Lake Erie, western waters flowed into the Niagara River. After seven leagues (21 miles) more those waters rushed over the great falls. Every Frenchman had heard of those falls. Five leagues (fifteen miles) beyond the falls the river opened into Lake Ontario and at that juncture stood Old Fort Niagara topping a bluff on the rivers east bank facing the Lake. This old French post had been fist built in 1679 of wood. It had been rebuilt twenty-six years ago in 1727 of stone.

This post commanded another strategic choke point for water travel, communication and commerce. It required a stronghold and Fort Niagara was just that. From here, downstream, northeast, one hundred thirty- eight leagues (four hundred fifteen miles), through sometimes-dangerous waters, on its own bluff above the St. Lawrence River lay Quebec City capital of New France.

Maurice and Pierre hauled their gear up the bluff to the command post at Presque Isle. It was a large wall tent with a French flag flapping occasionally on a pole outside. The tent was roped off on posts and separated from the other tents by about ten paces on each side. A single soldier stood in front of the only opening in the pretend fence. What looked to be an officer sat at a table outside the tent on a three-legged rough-cut stool.

"We were sent up to report. We have orders from Fort De Chartres," said Maurice to the soldier.

The soldier spun around to address the officer.

"I heard," said the officer curtly, "send 'em down to Chambo's crew for today. The captain will see them in the morning. He'll be busy all day. Chambo can fix 'em' up till tomorrow." He turned back into his tent.

The soldier turned back to face Maurice and Pierre with a sheepish grin.

"That's Captain Michel Pean, second in command," he said. Then, under his breath, he added, "His usual nasty mood".

"Chambo's crew is over on the left side of the build site, stripping bark from logs."

The soldier was talking now in a normal tone. "Just ask if you don't find them. The commanding officer is Captain Henri Marin. He is out working with the men. He won't be in till late. He will have a look at your orders then and make your assignment. I hope you came prepared to work."

"Merci," said Maurice, picking up his gear and trudging off the way, the soldier directed.

"That Captain Pean wasn't too friendly considering how far we came to help, now was he?" asked Pierre.

"No," answered Maurice. "But, I guess he came a far distance too. Everyone here looks tired when you see 'em up close. They've already been here working a few weeks from the look of things."

"Well, we all better get used to it and smile," said Pierre, "cause from what I'm seeing this job is far from over."

They found Chambo's crew with only a couple redirections. The crew wasn't exactly where they had started the day. They had moved to a better spot, some shade and closer to the cutting. It was better to have the logs dragged here, stripped of bark and then moved on to the build site.

"Better for us and better for the project," Chambo had told everyone who asked.

"The captain will agree I'm sure."

He hoped it was true. He did not wish to displease the captain.

It was a small work crew, only four men plus their leader. Chambo was a big man, a head taller than the others.

"We were told to help out till we see the Captain Marin," said Pierre.

"What's your craft?" asked Chambo.

"Came to build dugout canoes or pirogues of any kind," answered Pierre.

"Any good at it?"

"Some say we are," answered Maurice.

"Well, you must be able to debark logs," said Chamo. "Grab an axe or a spud and pitch in. These logs here will be smaller than your use to, but the process is the same". He pointed to some extra tools.

"You got enough tools," said Maurice looking at the pile.

"Oui," said Chambo. "Axes are one of the few things they didn't short us on. At least for now we have plenty before they get spread out to the other sites. This isn't the only fort were going to build you know".

Pierre and Maurice didn't answer they just pick up an axe and a spud and went to work. It felt good to be out of a canoe with something other than a paddle in their hands. It had been almost a month since they had left Kaskaskia and headed upriver to get here.

The work that first afternoon at Presque Isle limbered up Maurice's stiff back. He and Pierre enjoyed being on solid ground again, out of the cramped positions of the canoes. The temperature wavered between warm and hot. They shed coats and worked only in linen shirts, with the sleeves rolled up. Sweat felt good even after they finally stopped. The sun was low in the west, shadows were long but there were no color changes yet in the sky. It would be a while before the cool of the evening. By then the sweat would dry.

It was the time of day to get camp arranged, sharpen tools and prepare food. Late flocks of geese honked at high altitude. Ducks quacked passing overhead barely above the trees swerving left and right in case someone was tempted to take a shot. A few pops from muskets were heard but none nearby.

Chambo showed them where his work crew camped. There were four tents set up and one was an extra, which he assigned to Maurice and Pierre.

"Captain often sends us extra men till he gets 'em assigned to their regular duties," he said. "Sometimes they stay a day, sometimes two, longest was a week. That's the tent they use so it's yours for now. That's our fire". He pointed. "Down yonder, is where we get our supper". He pointed again down a row of tents to a big cook-fire, with various pots hanging above and positioned in it. A couple Indian women were carefully tending to the process.

Maurice and Pierre inspected their tent. They tightened the sagging ropes and Pierre retied a couple knots to his liking. Then they began to store their gear as best they could for the night. It was a clear day but they weren't just off a ship from the old country.

Chambo watched. The rest of the crew went about sharpening tools and puttering around camp.

"Where you from?" he asked.

"Kaskaskia," answered Maurice. "you?"

"Montreal."

"That's a long haul for an expedition this size," said Pierre.

"Oui, it is," said Chambo. "You do not know the half of it." He let out a big sigh.

"We paddled and hauled all this gear over rivers, lakes and portages nearly breaking our backs to get here in record time. When we arrive, proud of our effort, and start to unpack, what do we find? The officials in charge of supply shorted us on critical items and packed us tight with frivolities. We have items totally useless to us out here. We have instruments for a five-piece band at each fort and enough parasols for every whore in Parris. We are short on shovels, and files. We have tents but little rope. Most important we are short on food if we have a poor crop this summer. Where will we find time to clear and plant fields while we build forts? Someone back home is getting fat."

"What does Captain Marin say?" asked Maurice.

"Not much to us. But he's mad about it that's for sure. He works just as hard as the men do. He may be an old man but he is a tough bird. He's French-Canadian like many here, born in the province. He knows the rivers lakes and woods. Knows how to treat the Indians. He's a good commander. He says resupply is on the way. We trust him. We're just not sure we can trust the merchants to send what he requests. One thing is for sure though, since Governor Duquesne took control the royal coffers have opened. He aims to arm our frontier and bring the renegade savages back to our side. He seems to want it done yesterday."

"The Frenchmen of the Illinois country agree with that," said Maurice. "A new larger stone fort is being built at Fort de Chartres. A new wooden fort is being built on the Oabache (Wabash) right after its confluence with the Bella Riviere.[2] On our way here we saw the new fort Miami being built on the St. Joseph River to replace the one burned by renegades a few years back on the St Mary's."

Pierre nodded and said: "It's good the King has recognized our need to keep out the English. They've robbed us long enough and some of the bad Indians were listening to 'em and causing all sorts of mischief. This is important work. I hope the Captain and his engineers know what they're doing,"

"Don't worry about the captain," said Chambo. "He has experienced engineers and builders. If the Governor can keep us supplied from Montreal and Quebec, Merin can

---

[2] At this time the lower Ohio River was thought by the French to be a tributary of the Wabash River rather than the other way round.

build these forts. He also knows how to impress Indians and that may be more important than anything until we have finished walls, strong gates, and mounted cannon."

Chapter 36

July 12, 1753

On French Creek Above the Allegheny River

Maurice was in the woods this afternoon digging in the duff with a sharpened stick. He was searching for vine roots, which could be used for lashings in building of canoes. Much lashing was needed for even a single canoe and they were building many. It was women's work or so said the Indian men. Mostly the Indian women had been doing it. But the need for lashings had once more out stripped supply. So here he was harvesting the stuff himself.

When he located the vines growing up a tree it was simple to find roots just below the surface of the forest floor, in that dark colored layer where leaves turned back into soil. The roots were easy enough dislodged in ten-foot-long pliable lengths, a little-finger's width in diameter. He rolled them into rope like coils and bound them together. He had several such coils in a pile already. He would split and process the roots when he returned to camp.

For July, Maurice found this pleasant work in the cool shade of the deep forest. Where he worked today, giant chestnut trees towered over the smaller oaks and hickories. Vines were plentiful. The ground was moist but not wet. The familiar musky odor suddenly reminded him of giant mushrooms he always found back home in Kaskaskia.

Maurice was homesick. He missed familiar places and people. And he was tired. The work had been hard. Captain Marin drove men like he drove himself.

Chambo had proved right. Captain Marin was a tough old bird but he was fair. Most of the men liked him. So did Maurice and Pierre. They all followed his orders whether they liked them or not.

The Fort at Presque Isle was nearing some form of completion. The walls were mostly up. The walls were twelve to fifteen feet high in a one hundred -twenty-foot square configuration. The front gate faced the Lake and the rear gate opened onto the road to French Creek. There was a stone powder magazine almost built but it still didn't have a roof. Wood chips and saw dust covered the ground and the place smelled like a lumber mill from all the fresh cut green timbers. The ten-foot-wide opening for the front gate was being fitted with heavy swinging wooden doors two days ago when Maurice and Pierre left to come here.

Maurice and Pierre had been sent south to the build site for the next fort. The road was really only a widened pathway for half a league (mile and half) south of the back gate at Presque Isle, then it went back to being a narrow track winding its way south through deep woods and rocky terrain.

Most of the men dispatched down to French creek were coming to start the build for the next fort: Fort Le Boeuf. Maurice and Pierre however weren't coming to strip bark. They had been tasked to begin building a river fleet.

After the second fort would get under work but long before its completion, the third fort would need to break ground. French creek was navigable by small watercraft to the Allegheny River four league (twelve mile) downstream, the chosen site for what would be called Fort Machault: the third fort.

Bark canoes, pirogues and even bateau of various sizes would be needed to transport goods on the creek below Fort Le Boeuf. They were needed yesterday according to their direction from Captain Marin and even more would be required as time progressed.

The final fort planed for construction by this expedition would be built at the junction of the Allegheny and the Monongahela Rivers twenty-two league (67 mile) down river from Fort Machault. A fleet would be required and the only way to get watercraft in those numbers and sizes was to build them.

It was a huge undertaking and Maurice thought about that now as he picked up his coils of root and began his tramp back to the clearing near the creek. The captain had promised more craftsmen to help. The forests were vast. Indians had built bark canoes and dugouts in this vicinity for thousands of years, but never on this scale. The felling crews had strict instruction to select and save the biggest and best logs and lumber for the river fleet.

Maurice was exhausted beyond anything he had ever known and so was Pierre. So were all the men and so was the captain. How much longer could they go on at this pace?

When he broke out of the forest into the clearing Maurice could see Pierre hacking away with his adze on a long poplar log. Other axes in the surrounding forest had begun to grow silent as the sun sank low. Still Pierre worked on. There was a man standing near Pierre watching. He looked familiar. He glanced over when he saw the movement coming out of the woods. Then he smiled. It was Etienne.

"Where have you come from?" asked Maurice.

He, Etienne and Pierre sat around a small fire kindled for light. Their pipes were lit. The rum was poured. The sun had set.

"Fort Frontenac with supplies and ammunition," answered Etienne.

"Where is that?" asked Maurice.

"North end of Lake Ontario."

"When were you last in Kaskaskia?"

"Two months ago," said Etienne. "Jean and Alex are busy with the rebuilding of Fort De Chartres. Most everyone back home is working to build the new fort of stone. It will be massive when it gets finished."

"How are Jean and Alex helping?"

"Jean has three teams of oxen hauling stone from the rock quarry in the bluff to the lake where it is loaded on pirogues and floated closer to the fort. They work two teams and rest one. It pays well."

He paused to pick up a small log and place it on the fire. Then he continued. "Seems like we're building or rebuilding forts all over New France. Fort Frontenac is getting new supply warehouses and a contingent of seventy marines."

"Why are they doing that?" asked Pierre. "Why not reinforce fort Niagara?[3]"

"Likely to counter the fort which the Iroquois have allowed the English to build on the Mohawk Portage. They call it Fort Oswego. We have to keep Lake Ontario

---

[3] Fort Niagara was the French fort built in the 1720's at the southwest end of Lake Ontario where the Niagara River empties into the lake. The fort guarded the important portage around the great falls in the Niagara River, which connected Lake Ontario and Lake Erie.

open for French travel. Fort Niagara is being reinforced too. Then there is the big effort here to protect the Venango Way. The traders are making lots of money selling goods, services and transportation to The Crown. This year trading for furs is not the only way to get rich."

"Well we have needed these forts for a long time," said Pierre. "We need to keep the English out, if it's not too late. Thank God the King and the Governor have finally opened the royal purse."

Chapter 37

August 1753

Fort Machault

$\mathcal{F}$ollowing Etienne's visit last month, Maurice had been even more homesick. Today he was at the new build site. Named Mauchault it would be the third fort to be built. Construction had just begun.

The fort would sit on a hill seventy yards up from the Allegheny River at its confluence with, and on the west bank of, French Creek. The front gate would face the river. Maurice could tell all that only from whitewashed stakes, which had been driven into the ground.

He had expected to find a scene very like this, but there was a surprise. Inside the marked off, to-be-built walls of the fort sat a well-used log house, today flying a very new French flag. Beside the house stood a smaller log built shed hosting a stone chimney and blacksmith's forge.

"Whose house?" Maurice inquired of a fellow debarking a log nearby.

"Some English named John Fraser," answered the man. "Said he came here ten years ago to trade with the Delaware at Venango and fix their iron. Probably a spy. I saw the soldiers run him off. He packed up quick but he didn't look happy about it. Told me he'd be back, but he didn't say that to the soldiers."

'The place looks like it has been here ten years," said Maurice.

'Maybe," said the man, "but it's soon going to be a French blacksmith pounding iron on that anvil. And pretty quick after that, he will be shaping iron from inside a new French fort."

"The Munsee at Venango can trade with Frenchmen instead of Englishman. This is our country. The English better start believing it," he said with a smile.

Maurice on his trip here had paddled past the village of Venango just north about two miles above, on French Creek. It was a Lenni Lenape village (mostly Munsee) but the English called them Delaware Indians because the English had renamed the river where the Munsee had once lived (The Delaware River).

Frenchmen identified the Indians by the name the Indians called themselves — Munsee.

These particular Munsee people had cousins still living in the Wyoming Valley to the east and others in the Ohio country farther west. Unlike the Mohawk who were strongly attached by treaty to the English and the Ottawa closely bound to the French by many marriages, the Munsee people, like many tribes, were uncommitted. They had reasons enough to trust neither European group nor their Indian allies. But the Munsee like everyone relied upon trade with the white people for manufactured goods, which made their lives easier than the old ways.

These were difficult times on the frontier. Rumors of war were on the wing like little birds between the villages of both white men and Indian. The English had been pressing in on the Munsee at Venango from the south and east for several years now bringing their trade. The English blacksmith named Fraser had been a good neighbor. Now the French had come with many solders and workmen to build forts. They had even brought with them something never before seen in these valleys— cannon. Obviously they had come to stay. The Frenchmen were running the English away. The balance of power once again was shifting.

197

Chapter 38

December 6, 1753

Fort Le Boeuf

𝓐 sullen sky made it seem colder, and it was already cold. The past week's weather had alternated between rain, snow or sleet depending on nature's whim. Maurice was tired and his bare hands were frigid, as he turned the brace and bit drilling the last hole deeper into the timber. He laid the drill aside and checked the hole's depth. The depth was right. The hole was the fourth he had drilled in a neat row all connected to one another. Pausing he blew on his hands to warm them. Picking up his chisel and mallet, he began to square the interior edges of the mortise joint.

Maurice and Pierre were back at Le Boeuf. Most Frenchmen had left Fort Machault

in early September. The project was barely begun when they were ordered to stop building.

The Munsee at Venango objected to Fort Machault. The tribes were unsure about these intrusions into their territory. Surrounding tribes sent emissaries to complain as well. That would have been bad enough but then a strange fever came to camp.

Many men came down with the sickness including Pierre and Captain Marin. Pierre recovered. Captain Marin died. He had been the driving force of the expedition to this point. Now he was gone. For the expedition, it was the worst of misfortunes.

Captain Michel Pean took command. He had neither the charisma nor the wisdom of Captain Marin but he did his best. Work continued on Forts Presque Isle and Le Boeuf.

Reports were sent to Quebec City. Further instruction was requested.

As they awaited direction from the governor some of the men were sent to Fort Niagara and others to Fort Detroit. The remainder of the expedition including Pierre and Maurice settled in at Le Boeuf for winter.

December 11, 1753

"Bonsoir monsieur, parles tu anglaise?" came a call from across French Creek.

It was a strange request from somewhere out in the brush. Maurice peered into the woods. A man suddenly stepped into the open. He was young, clean-shaven, dressed in frontier attire. He carried a musket, possibles bag, shot pouch and powder horn. As he stood his ground an older man, similarly equipped, came forward to the creek bank opposite of where Maurice had just broken the thin ice along the edge and dipped his wooden pail full of water.

Maurice, unsure how to respond, stood still and stared at the men. In the quiet he thought he could hear his own heart beating over the rippling of the stream. Neither of the strangers across the way had taken any aggressive stance and they had alerted him to their presence of which he had not been at all aware. But they were Englishmen of that he felt certain.

In broken French the older man identified himself as Christopher Gist, he introduced the younger man as Major George Washington who had come with an important message from Governor Dinwiddie of the English colony of Virginia. He asked for a canoe to bring them over and permission to meet with the officer in command.

Maurice was surprised and frightened. The enemy across the way could easily have shot him dead if that had been their intention. How many more were over in the brush? Was the fort already surrounded? Were these two here to demand its surrender?

The defenses were not yet ready for a full assault. Maurice knew no one expected an army to move against any fort in winter.

"Wait where you are," said Maurice.

He turned to get soldiers from the fort. As he spun about he saw the two strangers fade slowly, quietly back into the shadows of the brush. It was dusk. Light was fading quickly. Hurriedly he marched up the hill spilling more than a little of his water along the way. *It will be dark in few minutes,* thought Maurice.

It was fully dark when Maurice led the soldiers back to where he had seen the Englishmen. The soldiers and officers inside the fort quickly alerted one another as well as the soldiers in the other barracks—the ones outside the walls of the fort. A canoe was brought down to the creek.

In the darkness the strangers were hailed and answered. They repeated their request and the canoe was launched and sent over to pick them up. The sky was clear and a three-quarter moon rising when the canoe came back. The men debarked and climbed up the bank.

The young major was a big man, tall and broad of shoulders. He towered at least a head above any man present. As he strode up the hill toward the fort, Maurice noticed a long stride and erect posture in the young officer, denoting, he concluded, a confidence in himself and his mission.

The older man named Gist was smaller but moved with the smooth surefooted gate of a man comfortable in his present surroundings. This was obviously not his first visit to the camp of an enemy.

The door to the officers' quarters was open. The fireplace and candles on the table backlit the entrance. The two strangers entered and the heavy wooden door closed leaving Maurice alone, standing in the dark.

December 13, 1753, Fort Le Boeuf

There had been no attack on the fort. No more Englishmen were found in the woods. Young Major Washington and Mr. Gist were the talk around camp.

They had traveled over five hundred miles from Virginia through mountains, crossing rivers and streams, enduring winter rain, ice and snow. It was a trek. Every Frenchman who observed them about camp the past two days looked upon them with at least a bit of respect.

Rumor had it they were leaving tomorrow to return over the same rivers and mountains to Williamsburg, if they didn't freeze to death along the way. Maurice did not envy their journey.

"Do you think they will make it home to Williamsburg?" he asked.

Pierre and Maurice were inside their barracks near the stone fireplace riving roots to use as lacing for building canoes.

"It's a long way," said Pierre. "They did it coming. I guess they can make it going back. But who can tell about winter weather. It's a dangerous undertaking. I heard they have a couple Indian guides out in the brush, who chose not to come in to the fort with them. Maybe they cached some supplies on their way here. They look like they're used to living in the woods, especially Gist. Did you hear what the Sargent said of their purpose?

"No," answered Maurice.

"He said the Major claims this is Virginia land and therefore belongs to King George. The letter he carried here from his Governor demands we stop building our forts and leave. Can you believe that?"

"What did the officers tell him?"

"That this was French territory claimed by La Salle and marked off by Celeron. We will continue to build, thank you very much. But they also told him that they would deliver his letter to Quebec City and Governor Duquesne. It was a pleasant meeting according to the Sargent. The officers allowed the two could enjoy French hospitality for three days of rest, before their return home. However, they strongly suggested to the Major that he not return unless he wished a trip to Quebec City as a suspected spy.

"Do you think he is a spy?"

"I think he is what he claims to be. But his eyes are taking in all he can while he paces about on his daily walks. I suspect our fort will be well described in his reports. Yes, on that I believe we can be assured. He appears no one's fool but also arrogant, like most Englishmen. It might be best for us if he and his companion vanish in the woods and never reach home."

"I wish we were home," said Maurice.

Kaskaskia, in the French Illinois Country, December 31, 1753

Nearing midnight a large group of men quietly stalked toward the home of Jean Verrou. They wore painted faces and strange attire. Stealthily they strode up the steps onto the porch bunching at the front door of the house. It was a dark night without a moonrise. Owls hooted in the distance.

Jean and Morning-Star were asleep in their bed. Alex Verrou sat beside the fireplace whittling a stick and smoking his pipe. Christmas had passed quietly and he was thinking of his boyhood friends Maurice and Etienne. Where were they tonight?

Suddenly shouts and demands of "open the door" rang out in the stillness of the winters' night. Rough hands pounded on the wooden door. Not a single hand but many.

Alex rose and walked to the door. When the lock clunked back, before he swung the door open, a fiddle began to play outside the door. Various catcalls and demands for rum rang out.

Jean and Morning-Star were out of bed in their nightshirts. Before retiring for the evening they had decided, because of the late hour, they were to be spared the expense this year. But it was not to be.

Frenchmen of the Illinois country had little entertainment in their rough lives except parties they threw for themselves. So they knew how to get up a party. And they had many throughout the year.

This one was special coming in winter. It was called La Guiannee. Occurring annually on New Year's Eve, roving bands of revelers marched through the streets often singing as they went, stopping at random houses, demanding refreshments for their parched throats. It was all in fun. People were expected to be ready with the drinks or suffer the tricks of a rowdy crowd.

When Alex opened the door at least forty people young and old, men and women rushed in. The house was filled and others hung about on the surrounding porches. The costumes and painted faces were colorful and crazy. There was laughter and singing, fiddle music and dancing. Jean quickly fetched two jugs from the cellar and began filling mugs. Everyone carried a mug.

Jean had nearly emptied the second jug when someone yelled for quiet. Everyone hushed. The fiddles stopped playing. King Louis' bell at the Church of the Immaculate Conception was ringing. It was midnight. The New Year had arrived. When the bell rang its final stroke of midnight everyone cheered and congratulated one another for surviving to greet another new year— January 1, 1754.

Slowly the revelers began to move off the porch and out of the Verrou house. The crowd was breaking up, each person heading for their particular abode. The laughter and conversation faded slowly away until the hoot of the owls returned.

Jean smiled at Morning-Star and Alex, pouring them all a small drink of the little remaining rum. From the porch they looked up at bright stars in a dark sky. Each member of the family wondered to themselves what this new year might bring.

Over a thousand miles east at the same moment Maurice stared up at an identical sky, wishing he were at home in Kaskaskia.

Chapter 39

Spring 1754

Presque Isle on Lake Erie

Joincare came from Quebec with reinforcements and supplies. He took command of the expedition. Governor Duquesne intended the mission to proceed as planned.

Presents were sent for the local Munsee at Venango. Talks were held. Promises were made. The work on Fort Machault resumed.

The fleet at Le Boeuf consisted now of dozens of newly built canoes and pirogues ready for use. New men and additional supplies arrived almost daily from posts all over New France. The French governments in Quebec City and New Orleans promised more men and material were on the way. The English must be kept out of French territory.

Today Maurice was back at Fort Machault with a work crew. He had been tasked with making wooden shakes for the roofs of the buildings. Other men brought the blanks (round logs cut to length) and dropped them in a pile for his use. He had set up a chopping block and begun splitting with a froe and mallet.

It was a simple job. Place the blank on the chopping block, apply the froe, drive it in with the mallet, twist the froe handle, slide the froe down the crack created and twist again, till the wood snapped and a new shingle broke away. Replicate the process thousands of times until there are enough shingles to roof the buildings.

"You Maurice?" a young man asked.

"Oui."

"I was sent to help. I'll stack." He picked up some shingles and began.

The young man looked to be in his teens, strong, hair long and dark like most metis (mixed blood) men from the Illinois country but this one was taller than average. He went to the work with the agility of the young. He looked to be a good worker and Maurice was happy to see it. Many he had encountered here were slackers when not pushed and prodded by the officers. Maurice wanted to get the job finished so he could hopefully go home this fall.

"Where you from?" asked Maurice.

"Vincennes, my name is Jacque."

"I think I remember you. I was in Vincennes a few years back. We brought the cattle from Kaskaskia. You were helping a fishmonger peddle his fish. You were just a boy then. You've grown."

"Oui, I remember the cattle drovers from Kaskaskia. You were one of them?"

"I was," answered Maurice.

"Are the others here as well?" asked Jacque.

"No, but there are other men from Kaskaskia here. Most of the drovers who were with me at Vincennes are still back in the Illinois country. Two have gone off to be voyageurs and coureur des bois. One has passed through but the other has not been heard from of late."

"Other canoes were rumored to be coming behind us on the rivers from Fort De Chartres," said Jacque. "I heard the voyageurs talk of it. Some of your friends may arrive in a day or two?"

"It's possible," said Maurice. "But I would rather this job were done and I was heading home." He twisted his froe and snapped off another shingle.

Two Days Later

The day was warm but not hot. Trees were newly in leaf. Catkins and pollen were sifting through the understory to fall on the forest floor. Jacque and Maurice had been harvesting roots again. The pirogue building had shifted south to Fort Machault and Pierre had come with it. The bigger trees required for dugouts and canoes were all used up nearer Le Boeuf.

"Did you hear the news?" asked Pierre, as the boys walked into his worksite to drop the coils of root.

"What?" asked Maurice.

"The English have beaten us to the forks. They've built a fort there already."

"How do you know?"

"Scouting party. Two Ottawa and Captain Marin's brother came back with the news."

"The captain had a brother?"

"He did, but we've never seen him because he is always out scouting. Looked more Indian than French when he came out of the brush. I heard him telling one of the officers. I guess it's a small affair, maybe fifty or sixty men with a little stockade, but it's there all right. Right where we should already have been."

"What will it mean?"

"I don't know but Joincare isn't going to be happy about it. I'm sure. It will be harder to run off fifty or sixty from a stockade than it was to get rid of that English blacksmith here."

Maurice thought about that for a moment. From inside Fort Machault's new stockade walls he could hear the ring of a hammer pounding iron on Fraser's anvil. It was a French blacksmith now as had been foretold last fall when Maurice had first observed the site.

"Will there be a fight? Are there English soldiers there?" asked Maurice. He was thinking about the young Major Washington. Had he returned with these soldiers?

"I don't know about that. Nothing was said of Redcoats (English Soldiers). But, Joincare cannot allow them to remain on French land. Not at The Forks. We are to build 'our' fort there and we are about ready to start the move. We didn't build all these pirogue to trade with Englishmen. Besides the cannon are almost all delivered to Le Boeuf. I don't think anyone wants to haul them back to the lake. If the English won't go peaceably Joincare will have them moved by force. They must learn. The land along these rivers belongs to New France and King Louis."

In April Joincare made his move against the English at Trent's Fort. Eight hundred French soldiers boarded canoes and pirogues for the attack. It was the greatest flotilla ever seen on these waters or any rivers west of Niagara.

The boats full of men and equipment launched first from Le Boeuf and came down French Creek to Fort Machault. Troops debarked for the night and shoved off again next morning at dawn. It took half an hour to get them all in the water. Then the pirogues and canoes from Machault followed loaded with their men and cargo: tools, supplies, weapons tents and half a dozen cannon in six special made dugouts.

This was a big logistical nightmare. Officers, soldiers, engineers and workmen toiled long hours in planning and execution. No one born here in the Province had seen anything like it. Maurice and Pierre were proud to be a part of such a grand foray.

When the entire flotilla was in the river it took an hour to pass by one or two crafts abreast. The event had been planned to make an impression on the local tribes and it certainly accomplished that. It also had an impact upon the Englishmen at Trent's Fort when they observed it coming down the Allegheny River two days later.

The first canoes landed men on shore upriver from the little fort and began unloading with their weapons. A few minutes later there were men enough in battle lines to take the fort by storming. More Frenchmen were landing every minute.

After an hour four hundred of the soldiers were deployed in front of the fort with another four hundred Indian allies behind them and more canoes still visible coming downriver.

Trent's Fort was a small stockade with only about fifty defenders. Captain Trent and some of the men were away. Ensign Edward Ward was left in command and had been busy hanging one of the front gates when the first enemy soldiers were spotted coming downriver. Soon every English militiaman was at the walls weapons in hand. Lieutenant John Fraser (the blacksmith) was one of them.

After a few minutes Ensign Ward glanced over at the Lieutenant.

"I sure never saw that many," said Fraser "There weren't more than a few dozen who ran me off. I didn't know there were that many Frenchmen this side of Quebec City."

"Well we can't hold them off for ten minutes. Even if we sell dear every life in this fort," said Ward. "Hell they can blow us to bits with those cannon they just unloaded, and let the Indians pick up the pieces."

"Here come the junior officers under a flag of truce," said Fraser.

"Let's hope they give us an offer to save our hair," said Ward. "If they do I'm going to grab it."

Chapter 40

May, 1754

$\mathcal{T}$he new fort would be called Duqeusne after the Governor. Trent's Fort had been dismantled in three days after Ensign Ward and Lieutenant Fraser led their men out on the long homeward trek, back over the Appalachian Mountains. If the Virginia militia remained where they belonged there need not be any more trouble.

The construction of Fort Duquesne was underway. It was to be an even more impressive fortification than the other French forts along the Venango Way. It would command the confluence of two large rivers: the Allegheny and Monongahela. At this fork the two rivers flowing together formed what the French called the Belle Riviere. The English had named it the Ohio River.

The point of land between rivers where the fort was to sit had long since been cleared of timber. But, not far upstream on either tributary were more than ample stands of trees. Work crews were busy now marking and cutting. Logs were floating down both rivers every hour or two. A pit sawmill had been erected to turn out planking.

The walls of the fort had been staked off and the trenches for the palisades were being dug. It would take time to finish. But all efforts of the entire expedition were directed here now. This was the strategic point. Details and strengthening at the other forts would have to wait.

Already there were reports coming in from scouts and friendly Indians. More Englishmen were in the woods this side (the French side) of the mountains. Who they were and exactly where they were heading no one seemed to know. Native allegiances were shifting toward the French, who seemed more in command (for the moment), but there were holdouts among the 'savages'. Frenchmen were sometimes suspicious of the Indians' accounts.

Tanacharison was one leader for a tribe who lived up Mingo creek, a tributary to the Monongahela about 15 miles south east of the forks. The Mingo were a band of Iroquois who had moved near to the forks and intermarried heavily with other local native people. Like the Iroquois in the east they felt bound to the English by the covenant chain (tradition and treaties of long standing, remembered through wampum belts retained by their people).

Moreover Tanacharison had additional reasons to prefer the British over the French. His father had been killed at Pickawillany in the raid by Charles Langlade and the Ottawa. Tanacharison wished to build his personal reputation as a warrior, and to keep face among his people he must have revenge.

He had met the Englishman George Washington who came on previous surveying forays into the local country. He was impressed with the young man's presentation and felt he might advance his own standing by association and trade opportunities with the young Virginian.

On his part Washington recognized Tanacharison, whom the local Indians called The Half King, as an important leader. Washington needed allies. He had courted Tanacharison with gifts and flattery on previous trips. Christopher Gist was wary of the relationship.

Now Washington was back west of the mountains, promoted to the new rank of Lieutenant Colonel. This time he had Virginia militiamen with him and promises of more troops to follow from New York and South Carolina. He had orders to expel the French from what Governor Dinwiddie said was clearly Virginia land.

Washington had encountered Captain Trent, Ensign Ward and Lieutenant Fraser in their retreat. He had listened to their frightening story and had folded their men into his own force. The Virginians were camped at a place called Great Meadows. Washington awaited reinforcements from the east and contact with the Half King. He needed more troops before he made his next move.

"Who is that?" asked Maurice.

He was referring to a young French officer gathering a group of thirty or so soldiers at the riverbank on the Monongahela.

"Ensign Jumonville," answered Pierre who was stitching the seams on another canoe build. "He is from Fort De Chartres I think. De Villers family as I recall. His father and an older brother were killed fighting the Fox a few years back. Canadian military family. Respected in Quebec City. Bright future I would bet. Looks fashionable don't you think?"

Maurice took note of the young man and his smart uniform.

"The captain insists his officers look the part to impress the Indians," answered Maurice. "Where they heading?"

"Upriver it appears like. Probably looking for those Englishmen we keep hearing about but no one ever sees. I think it's just Indians exaggerating the truth to wedge open the captain's gift box for good Indians. Probably some free trappers or maybe long-hunters looking for deer hides. If we can get this last fort finished we may get to go home this fall," he said.

Pierre tugged hard on the riven root strapping. He was sewing two of the bark pieces, binding them together as a part of the canoe's outer skin. For today's work the strapping was steamed in a big pot of boiling water to make it pliable for the sewing. That was Maurice's job. In a few days after the seams had fully dried they would be sealed water tight with pine pitch. When that pitch cured over, hard but not brittle, another canoe would be river ready.

"Do you think the Captain will ever have enough water craft?" asked Maurice.

"I don't know," said Pierre, "but we aren't the only ones building them."

"No but ours may be the best," answered Maurice with a smile and wink at the old man.

Pierre didn't answer but he did smile and nod his head.

Ensign Jumonville's men were boarding their river craft. Soon they shoved off heading up stream paddling against the current. The clear water they rode upon looked green from reflection of verdant hillsides rising both sides of the river. The men and canoes grew smaller as they paddled south. Finally they disappeared one after the other around a far bend.

Maurice wondered what they might find.

Chapter 41

June 1754

Near the Forks of the Ohio

$\mathcal{D}$rums were beating soldiers to assembly. Englishmen and Indians had attacked Ensign Jumonville and his men at dawn four weeks ago. All but one were killed or captured. Jumonville was among the dead. One Frenchman had been a short distance from camp when the attack occurred. He evaded discovery and arrived at the forks a few days later with the news. Scouts had been sent out. The English had been discovered.

Reports said at least four hundred Englishmen were camped at a place called Great Meadows. An attack force of six hundred Frenchmen and one hundred Indian allies were ordered to drive them back over the mountains or kill them. Ensign Jumonville's older brother Captain Louis Coulon de Villers was in command.

Maurice had been pressed into a militia unit and was going along. He had been issued a new musket, possible bag, powder horn and bullet pouch. He was scared. He had never been to war. He was here as a laborer not a soldier. He was supposed to build canoes and pirogues.

Soon the point of the column moved out single file into the woods on a trail, which would follow along the river bank a few miles before heading inland through the forest. Flankers were out either side of the column to guard against surprise.

Maurice moved with his unit in the middle of the long line of soldiers. Jacque and Pierre would stay behind with others to guard the new fort. Today they were waiting at the edge of the cleared land, where the deforested field of fire for the new fort gave way to old growth trees. As

Maurice walked by in the column of soldiers, Jacque nodded his head. Pierre raised his chin to attention and made a fist in front of his chest, then smiled. Maurice took his point, raised his head, and marched into the deep woods with the soldiers.

A few days later, on the morning of July 3, 1754, the drums were beating again as French soldiers and their Indian allies positioned themselves in the forests surrounding Great Meadows.

During the past month the English had built a small circular stockade fort around a small log storage building in the middle of the meadow. It was a minor creation not capable of withstanding a strong assault. Around the stockade they had dug a trench throwing the dirt up on the outside edge making an earthworks from which they hoped to defend themselves.

Twenty-one-year-old George Washington had been promoted again in June, this time to the rank of full Colonel. In dispatches he had described Great Meadows as a charming place, well suited for battle.

Two hundred ninety-three Virginians were under Washington's command. Recently one hundred additional militiamen from South Carolina under command of Captain James Macay had reinforced him. Best of all the Englishmen had nine swivel guns (small cannon built to rotate on a post). These weapons were excellent to defend against a charge by massed attackers.

Washington had reported to Dinwiddie of the Jumonville affair. Tanacharison had killed the young Canadian officer in the fight. The Indian with a group of warriors had guided the English to the French encampment. Colonel Washington neglected to mention the

Frenchman had been tomahawked after he had surrendered and the fight was over.

The Half King was not with Washington today. He and his braves refused to fight from a tiny fort in open ground. They quickly faded away into the forest at the first discovery of approaching danger. They would not be back today.

Washington deployed his men in formation in front of the fort. Quickly he discovered that the French did not plan to fight in the accustomed manner. (They were no doubt aware of his swivel guns.) They remained concealed in the trees, which, unfortunately, the English soon realized, were within musket range of the fort. The Virginian pulled his men back to the trenches and both sides settled in for a longer fight.

Maurice was positioned on the west side of the meadow on slightly elevated ground. The old growth forest here had a mixture of large and small trees: chestnut, hickory and oak. Walnut, cherry and dogwood predominated at the meadow's edge. It was as Washington had said in his dispatches, a charming place of tall ferns and laurel bushes. The undulating ground was covered with a thick spongy forest duff (decaying organic matter). Fallen logs and even some hog-sized boulders were strewn about, making excellent protection from the English musket balls buzzing now through the air, cutting leaves, pounding into wood, ricocheting off stone.

Maurice had found himself a secure place. He had dropped down behind a huge ancient log, fallen long ago. The log rested against a big beech tree. It was easy for him to reload behind the beech and then slip his musket over the log to either the right or left of the tree and fire. His view was obscured somewhat by tall bracken ferns and laurel bushes to his front, between he and his targets. But, he felt no need to move closer for a better shot.

Maurice had soon shot three times at men he could see in the trenches surrounding the little fort. He did not think he had hit any. It was hard to tell. They popped up only for a moment, fired their piece and then dropped out of sight. Then another would pop up and fire from somewhere else along the embankment or from inside the stockade through a crack between the logs of the palisade or through a loophole which was cut in the wall for shooting purposes.

Only occasionally did a ball tear into flesh as the morning progressed.

"I can do this," thought Maurice.

Then the roar of a swivel gun sounded and a barrage of shots came flying through the forest a few yards to his left. It had a sobering sound unlike the whizzing song of the musket balls.

"I hope the captain doesn't send us in a charge against that," he thought.

De Villers was a good commander. He saw no need to waist men in a frontal assault. He had the English right where he wanted them. He was in no hurry.

It was a hot sultry day by noon. There were dark clouds in the west. The stink of gunpowder in the air masked the smell of approaching rain. Men had been shot on both sides but more on the English side. English and French were dead or dying. Others were wounded and suffering in pain. Curses and insults were shouted continuously between combatants. Maurice noticed some of his fellow soldiers climbing trees for a better shot. But then he saw a soldier in a tree shot dead and watched his limp body fall to the ground.

Maurice remained where he was behind the log. About one of the clock he raised up over his log on the right side of the beech to take another shot. An English musket-ball slapped loudly into the tree inches from his head. He ducked down without firing his musket. He remained down for a long while, thinking.

For the rest of the fight Maurice crawled for a little distance along the fallen log right or left after reloading behind the tree. It was a long log there was no need to fire from the same position very often. He promised himself he would fight smarter. He had learned a lesson. He was a better soldier now. He was frightened again.

About two of the clock in the afternoon the rain came. It was a heavy rain. The meadow was low ground and it filled with water, especially in the trenches where the English were fighting. The firing from both sides slowed during the rainstorm and the loudest noise for a while was thunderclaps overhead.

The air cleared of smoke for a time. There were only occasional shots after the storm. The rain didn't stop, it only slowed to a steady drizzle. The blackpowder smoke, which came again, hung like a damp cloud over the battlefield. Slowly Maurice watched men risk harm to themselves for the chance to kill their enemy. Some were successful. Others ran out of luck themselves. The killing went on at a slow but steady pace.

Maurice was exhausted and hungry. He was tired of shooting and almost out of musket-balls. He had managed to keep his powder dry, of which he was rightly proud. Many at Great Meadows on this day had not been so fortunate.

At dusk, De Villers ordered a ceasefire from the French side. When the English noticed they stopped shooting too. Two young French officers went forward under a flag of truce to the little fort with demands for surrender of the English.

When they came back orders passed along the line that the French troops were to rest in place tonight where they now were until the English considered terms. The fighting was likely over for today unless the English decided to fight their way out during the night. Maurice hunkered down. He did not go to sleep.

About midnight he heard three hurrahs from the direction of De Villers command tent. Soon word passed down the line again. The English had surrendered. The battle was over. No one else need die or be wounded. Maurice was relieved but he remained behind his log, and he didn't relax until the first pink light had shown in the east and he could smell frying bacon.

On the morning of July 4,1754 Washington's Virginians and South Carolinians quickly buried their dead and loaded their wounded onto carts. According to the terms they were allowed to leave with all their baggage and weapons excepting the nine swivel guns, which Captain de Villers intended to keep for use at the French Forts along the Venango Way. De Villers' terms were gracious considering the treatment of his brother. His superiors wanted no war with the English. They just intended to keep them out of French territory.

The French soldiers lined the trail this morning as the English moved off on their way back across the mountains to Wills Creek (Cumberland Maryland). Young Colonel George Washington walked at the head of the column. The big man looked tired but he stared straight ahead and held his head high as he marched behind the color bearers to the step of the drumbeat.

Was he proud or arrogant? Maurice couldn't tell, but he was happy to see him go. Hopefully they would see no more of him, and Maurice and Pierre could go home this fall.

Chapter 42

June, 1755

Forks of the Ohio

The work continued. Fort Duquesne was beginning to be the major fortification intended. Maurice and Pierre did not go home as they had hoped. They remained here. Today they were splitting shake shingles with Jacque Ravellette.

"Do you think the English will come against us this summer?" asked Jacque.

"Word is they're on the way now, cutting a road through the forest for their supply train as they come," said Maurice.

"Can they haul wagons over the mountains?" asked Jacque.

"Of course they can," said Pierre. " And cannon too. They do it in the old country, they can do it here. It might be a bit further distances but the English can do it if they set their mind to it."

"Well, we may have a surprise for them when they get here," said Maurice. "More Frenchmen arrive daily at Presque Isle."

"Rumor says it's a big army the English are bringing."

"Lots can happen between here and where they are now," answered Maurice "They could get delayed".

"Maybe they're coming to build a fort on their side of the mountain," said Jacque.

"No one believes that," said Pierre. "They have announced their intention. War is declared between

England and France. The English have sent General Braddock and his army to America for one reason. To help the Virginians drive us off our land here at the forks. We had best get ready. From what I heard yesterday they are about to crest the mountains any day now."

"Maybe they will build a fort at Great Meadows," offered Maurice.

"You boys can keep thinking that if you want," said Pierre. "But I'm telling you they're coming to take this fort from us."

It had been almost a year since the battle at Great Meadows had expelled the English. King George had responded quickly to support his colonial forces in defense of his lands. General Braddock had been dispatched with two thousand regular army troops to be reinforced by another thousand colonial troops. Pierre was right. The main English objective this year was the destruction of Fort Duquesne.

July 8, 1755

Etienne had returned to camp in June with a group of reinforcements from Fort De Chartres. He told Pierre and Maurice that the new stone fort on the Mississippi was nearing completion. He told them Alex and Jean Verrou were using their oxen to assist the stonecutter's haul from the quarry on the bluff to the little lake. The slabs of stone were next transferred to rafts and floated nearer the fort. It had been a huge undertaking.

"What do they hear about us? Do they know about the English coming?"

"They get the flying news like everyone in New France and Louisiana. Voyageurs pass through. Not as often as before all this building but regular. The soldiers get their dispatches. They are reluctant to share but the information soon leaks out. Indians pass along their tall tales some of which are accurate."

He paused to think what else to say.

"Alex told me all of Kaskaskia knew about the fight last year at Great Meadows within three weeks of it happening. The bells at the church rang for an hour in celebration."

"Do they know about this English army?" asked Maurice.

"That's why we're here with men from all over the province. Won't General Braddock be surprised? There are more soldiers coming behind us from Louisiana. I wish they had got here for this fight," he said with a sigh. "But, I guess we have enough without them."

"Looks like a lot of us alright. I've never seen so many Frenchmen in one place," said Maurice looking about him at the masses of men gathering all around Fort Duquesne. "Or Indians either."

Maurice and Etienne were on the roof of one of the interior buildings bringing shingles to the roofer, Pierre, who was finishing his job for the day. It was late afternoon. The sun was low. The sky overhead was blue. Everywhere there were groups of Frenchmen and bands of Indian allies. Some men were frantic in last minute preparation. Others loitered about awaiting orders.

The English were close. Scouts said they were crossing the Monongahela upstream to avoid difficult terrain. They would have to cross back a few miles south east of the fort. They would arrive tomorrow. The French commanders had decided to meet them in battle before they were within sight of the fort. The battle would begin in the forest.

Unbeknown to Maurice or Etienne, the English had the French outnumbered and if they ever got artillery into place, their cannon were bigger than the French cannon and they had more of them. General Braddock was a seasoned successful military campaigner. He had planned and provisioned well. He was a brave soldier respected by his men and his superiors. But, in his arrogance he had made mistakes.

Braddock had disrespected potential native allies considering them ineffective and unnecessary. The Indians had left the army in disgust, much to the chagrin of young Colonel George Washington who served Braddock as a colonial aide-de-camp.

More recently The General had made a second mistake, which no one seemed yet to have noticed. In his haste to confront the enemy he had come forward of his main body with a 'flying column' of fourteen hundred men. Today, they were well ahead of the main body of English soldiers, their supply train, and most of the cannon.

War cries rang out suddenly near the edge of the cleared ground where large groups of Ottawas were camped.

"What's going on over there?" asked Maurice.

"I hear they're preparing a big war dance for tonight and Captain Beaujeu has agreed to attend. Everyone is invited. Maybe we should go watch," said Etienne. "Beaujeu was commandant at Fort Niagara before the governor sent him here. He understands Indians. They like him."

Captain Beaujeu would lead the French forces in tomorrow morning's attack. After dark had settled he appeared at the ceremonial fire the Ottawas had prepared. He came bare chested, in war paint.

"I will fight," he said, "as my brothers, the Ottawa, the Ojibwa, and the Pottawatomi."

These three tribes of northern Indians were the main allies who had come to support the French in tomorrows' fight. There were small bands from other more local tribes here too. These others, however, were small in number and thought to be less reliable. Beaujeu knew their continued allegiance would be greatly impacted by the outcome of tomorrow's fight.

The Indian drums began. The flames of the fire leapt high. Beaujeu slapped the war post many times as he danced. The smoky night air cast strange, foreboding shadows on nearby trees. War cries rang out loud and clear. After more than an hour, Beaujeu collapsed, sweaty, gasping for air, and satisfied. The allies were ready. They would meet the English in battle. Tomorrow they would have a great victory.

July 9, 1755

French drums called men to their stations. The enemy was crossing the Monongahela a second time, back to this side. They were moving fast. They would follow the road to the fort. They would advance into the French ambush. It was time.

"You two come with me," shouted a French Marine officer.

He was pointing to Maurice and Etienne. They picked up their gear and followed. They were to be part of the attack but they thought they would be fighting with their militia group. They had gotten to know those men in the past two weeks. Where was this guy taking them?

"This is Lieutenant Marin," said the officer.

A savage looking man in Indian dress with war paint stepped forward and smiled. It was Captain Marin's brother.

"Gentilhomme, I need you to fight with me and my Ojibwa brothers today," he said pointing to a group of about thirty warriors standing nearby, painted for war. "They are good fighters but they sometimes get very excited in battle and forget our larger strategy. You two, I assume, can identify a British officer?"

Etienne and Maurice nodded.

"Good. Your militia captain says you can shoot well. That is your whole job today. You shoot only at officers. Do you understand?"

"I think so," said Maurice. But, he wasn't sure he really did.

"What if we don't see any officers?" said Etienne.

"Look for them. They'll be there. It's your job to find them. Don't waste your powder on anything else. My warriors and I will do the rest."

"You will fire from behind us. I have found you a good position. We will take care of most of the fighting in front, draw the fire and cover your ass. You shoot the officers. That will make our job much easier. Understand?"

"I think so," said Etienne.

"Good, let's go. Be sure to keep up."

That said, Lieutenant Marin raised his musket into the air and shouted something to his Ojibwa brothers. They came trotting, and the lieutenant led the group at a quick pace into the forest with Maurice and Etienne bringing up the rear.

As they moved into the trees Maurice heard a number of war cries from the Ottawa camp. He glanced over that way and saw Captain Beaujeu, at a distance, delivering a much-animated speech whipping the Ottawa into a frenzy. Behind that scene French soldiers marched in formation to the beat of drums, down the main road heading straight for the oncoming English.

Lieutenant Marin's men moved quietly through the forest for some minutes along a brush-covered ridge. Maurice could see little except the Indian ahead of him and sometimes one or two others ahead of that man. Suddenly the warrior froze in place and remained still.

Nothing moved about them except the wind in the trees. Maurice noticed it was a warm morning. He could hear a woodpecker drumming a tree off in the distance behind him.

Lieutenant Marin pushed through the laurel bushes to retrieve Maurice and Etienne.

"Follow me," he said. He led them forward to the midpoint of his line of warriors who were positioned down the backside of the ridge they had been traveling.

"See that ridge?' He pointed to another ridge fifty yards away running roughly parallel to the ridge they were standing on.

"Oui," said Etienne. Maurice nodded.

"Well beyond that about forty yards is the road. The British flankers will follow that ridge as their army approaches on the road. It's higher than this ridge. We will hide here until the flankers pass. When Beaujeu attacks, the British head on, we will move forward to that high ground and fire down on the English from their flank."

"There is a wide spot in the road just over there," he said, pointing again. "The English will try to make a stand at that spot where they can deploy their troops and maybe bring up one or two cannon. When they do, we will have them for a moment in a barrel." He smiled and winked at Etienne.

"You see those two oaks on the ridge?"

"Oui," they said in unison.

"Those are your positions. When we move forward, you get behind those trees and do your job. I scouted it well. You will have a good shot and the slope on the far side is steep. They will be unlikely to charge up at that point. Kill their officers. Leave the rest to me and my warriors."

"Oui," said Etienne, but he didn't feel good about it.

The British red-coated flankers came down the other ridge just as the lieutenant had predicted. There were a dozen or so strung out single file a few yards apart. They were big men with fixed bayonets on the end of their muskets.

"There might be others behind them," thought Maurice. *"Or they might come back along that ridge. I wonder if the Lieutenant has planned for that".*

The rattle of musketry a few moments later announced Captain Beaujeu's attack on the head of the British military column. It was a distance away but war cries were audible through the forest. Lieutenant Marin natives moved forward down the ridge in front of them. At the bottom was a small stream they had to cross.

Maurice suddenly wondered *"what if we get to the top of this next ridge only to meet Englishmen climbing up the opposite slope? Better to get up there first,"* he thought, as he scurried up the slope ahead.

Approaching the top near one of the designated oak trees, he slowed and lowered himself till he could peek over cautiously. He could hear Englishmen barking orders to their troops below on the road. There was the rustle of heavy movement in the forest. The scent of gunpowder arrived now with the familiar smells of deep woods mixed on the morning breeze. Musket fire seemed closer. War cries were louder but still muffled. The shouted orders ahead of him were clear and distinct.

He peeked over through some tall bracken ferns. The scene below shocked him.

There were red-coated soldiers everywhere along the road ahead. It was an anthill of flurried activity. Soldiers struggled to deploy themselves to advantage at the wide spot in the road and bring cannon up along the narrow road from behind them. Ahead some retreating troops were running headlong into officers who stopped their retreat and quickly reposition them into their fast-establishing current line of defense. There was order within the chaos.

Lieutenant Marin then came along the back of the ridge below its crest out of the enemy's sight. He moved quietly but quickly gesturing to his native warriors to wait. Maurice and Etienne, a few yards apart behind their respective oak trees, exchanged worried looks. Then Etienne smiled and they both turned back to face the enemy.

The rattle of musketry was loader and the war cries distinct. The fighting was closer. The smell of gunpowder had replaced all others. The July air was thick and hot.

Maurice took another peek over the hill through the ferns. The English defensive line was formed but holding its fire. Out in front, the forest was alive with a horrifying ballet of retreating red-coated soldiers in a rout toward any safe place they could find. Men leaped over fallen trees and fallen comrades, they crashed through laurel thickets, bumping into trees and one another as they came. Behind could be seen Ottawa warriors and French soldiers firing their muskets, hardly stopping to reload but attempting to do so as they came on in a hot pursuit.

The forest was alive with the screams of the wounded and the war cries of the advancing defenders of New France. These Frenchmen and their Indian allies suddenly sensed the smell and sound of victory in the agony of the English, many of whom were now running away.

Maurice took careful aim at a red-coated officer near a cannon.

"Fire!" came the loud clear voice of Lieutenant Marin standing not far to Maurice's left.

Maurice squeezed the trigger of his musket. The musket roared as the shot was fired. The British officer fell. Maurice ducked behind his tree to reload.

The forest was now totally engulfed in powder smoke and the screams of men and blasts from musket fire. It was so loud that it made it hard to think. Then suddenly came the roar of three cannon from below and then delayed slightly a fourth cannon was fired. Maurice's killing of the officer had only delayed its deadly response.

Reloaded, he came around the tree for a second shot. Quickly he identified another officer near the cannon and fired. The man spun around and fell. Maurice dodged behind the oak to reload.

And so it continued for what seemed a long time to Maurice but was in reality likely only a few minutes. One by one the cannon stopped firing.

Maurice looked down on the English for his seventh shot. A big officer, mounted horseback, attempted to rally the English troops and hold the line while cannoneers frantically attempted to hitch horses to two of the cannon so as to move them down the road in a quick retreat.

The big man sat tall in the saddle and then Maurice recognized the young Colonel. Slowly he took aim at the Virginian.

"You arrogant son of a bitch," he thought to himself. *"This will be your last time to kill Frenchmen."* He fired.

His shot went wide and high, singing past the big man's nose close enough to make him jerk back his head violently. His horse, feeling the motion, reared up at the very second Etienne also fired at the big officer. That ball tore through the officer's saddle pommel, missing the flesh of either man or beast.

Maurice struggled to ram another ball down the barrel of his musket. It was tight from exploded powder residue. When he was reloaded, he turned to seek another target. The big officer was gone. Vanished down the road with most of the English soldiers and one of the English cannon. Below some of the Ottawa and Ojebwa warriors were scalping the slain red coats and seeking plunder from among the dead and wounded.

Etienne glanced a woeful look at Maurice, who stood beside his tree staring back. They were unclear what to do next. Neither wanted scalps or plunder. The threat was gone for the moment.

But, the battle was not over. It had just moved on back toward the river crossing. Musketry could be heard raging still off in that direction. Lieutenant Marin was suddenly beside them.

"We will let them gather a few more scalps," he said, referring to the warriors, "then we'll get back in the fight. We must destroy this part of their army before they can cross back over the river. I know a short cut to the crossing. Then we will see." He paused to think. "Clean your muskets. The English are on the run, we can't let them stop till they get back to Virginia. We may be able to destroy their whole army. This is a great day. I wonder where Captain Beaujeu is?"

The lieutenant trotted off to converse with some Ottawa seen coming down the road. A few minutes later he came back looking forlorn. Captain Beaujeu is killed he said. Then he yelled something to his Ojibwa warriors who came trotting toward him.

"Allons-y (let's go)," he said to Maurice and Etienne gesturing the Indians to follow. Then off he trotted into the forest on the other side of the road. Soon they were back in the fight, sniping at the English always from cover and usually from higher ground. The lieutenant knew these forests well.

All day the outcome was the same. English soldiers in the rear guard would turn and fight until they heard conflict behind them. Then, rather than be cut off, they would turn and retreat as quickly as they could to catch up to their main column. There was order to it but not much determination. At every stand, they left dead and wounded behind them. This British army was defeated. The French and their native allies intended to bleed it as long as they could unless the English asked for terms of surrender. And so the killing went on even during the night and into the next morning.

Many of the English officers were dead on the field of battle strewn along the narrow road. Most of the officers

233

still alive were unhorsed and running afoot like their soldiers. Still they were leaders trying hard to rally their frightened men. Maurice and Etienne had orders at every engagement to seek them out as targets. They did their duty.

Maurice saw no more of the Virginia colonel.

Washington had kept his mount and his hair. Several musket balls had come perilously close but miraculously he had escaped so far untouched. He was ahead, escorting General Braddock, who traveled now in a cart, having been grievously wounded.

The young colonial had done a great deal to rally English troops to some order, but they were defeated and everyone knew it. The goal now was to escape with as many English lives as possible. If they kept moving, complete surrender of the army might yet be avoided. All was not lost. There was still hope.

Finally the battle ran out of steam. The French had chased the English for almost forty miles. The fighting had lessened. The opportunities for looting baggage wagons and scalping the dead had enticed the native warriors away from the fighting. Their blood lust had been satiated.

French officers encouraged the Indians to continue but everyone was tired. Etienne and Maurice finally stopped to rest beside a wagon turned on its side in the middle of the road. Lieutenant Marin went on ahead with a half dozen warriors still willing to fight. Maurice sat on the tongue of the wagon, gazing about in an exhausted stupor.

The body of the teamster lay scalped in the road a short distance away. The horses were long gone. The wagon's load of buckwheat flour in twenty-five pound cloth bags was strewn around the wagon. Some had been carried off, trailing flour dust as they left. The wagon was branded by the army with letters and numbers painted onto the tongue. Maurice twisted his neck to read it: wagon 310 Property of Hienrich Feagley, Perkiomen Valley, driver Benjamin Grabber.

Maurice guessed at the translation. He guessed also that was Benjamin Grabber lying dead in the road. *"I think Mr. Feagley may be short one of his wagons from now on,"* he thought. *"I bet this one is soon sat right and pulled to Duquesne with what's left of this load of buckwheat flour."*

The Battle of the Monongahela was over. It had been a massacre of the English. The defeat of this British army was complete. General Braddock himself had been mortally wounded during the fight.

The French forts would remain. Nonaligned Indian tribes were already on the way to congratulate the Frenchmen and pledge allegiance. The English frontier would face a new and greater danger. The Venango Pathway was secured for Frenchmen to travel.

"It's a great day." thought Maurice.

Chapter 43

July, 1755

After the Battle

$\mathcal{T}$he earliest news to reach Fort Cumberland at Wills Creek came from mounted teamsters who had abandoned their wagons and the army. They had fled immediately at the understanding of what was happening to the troops ahead of them on the road. They weren't the most reliable witnesses, having personally seen little of the actual battle, but they were the first to get back.

Soon freshly mounted riders were on the roads from Wills Creek carrying the news east. Braddock's army was destroyed. Indian hordes were expected to attack English settlements in the backcountry of Virginia, Maryland, and Pennsylvania at any moment.

A few days later units of the bedraggled, exhausted army began to stumble in at Fort Cumberland. All had not been lost, but Braddock's army had been soundly defeated, of that there was no doubt. The Virginia Colonel was noted in reports as one of the surviving officers who had maintained some order to the retreat, keeping the army from total collapse.

Still the dead and many of the wounded had been abandoned to the savages. It was hard to put a sunny face on that. Many cannon, as well as all the baggage and supplies, had been left behind to the enemy. Even the general's body had been forsaken, buried hastily in the road in the hope it would not be discovered by the savages. For the English, The Battle at the Monongahela River had been a monumental disaster.

The Morrison Family heard about it from a neighbor who had been at Fort Cumberland when the original reports were received. They heard the harshest version of the story made worse by honest fear in the voice of the man telling it.

The Morrisons lived in a log cabin on Little Owen Creek in the backcountry of Maryland. They talked of heading east that night at supper and all the next day as they went about their chores. But they had nowhere to go back to and crops here in the fields. The drought did not promise much of a harvest this fall, but what would they have if they left everything behind and fled east?

The Morrison farm was out of the way. The enemy had no reason to come this direction. They decided to stay and take their chances.

Heinrich Feagley in the Perkiomen Valley of Pennsylvania heard about Braddock's defeat from his neighbor Ezekiel Graber. Ezekiel was worried about his son Benjamin. The boy had driven his father's team of horses hitched to Heinrick Fegley's wagon to haul supplies for the army. It was a business venture they had all hoped would pay well. Nothing had been heard from Benjamin.

"It's not a good sign," said Ezekiel. "He would send word if he was able."

"There's still time," said Heinrich. "You said yourself the news about the battle just came from Philadelphia through Germantown yesterday. Benjamin hasn't had time to get word to us yet."

But Heinrick was worried too and not for his wagon. He had two extra wagons. Ezekiel had other horses. But, his friend had no more sons.

The news spread from farm-to-farm, town-to-town, village-to-village. The Pennsylvania Gazette in Philadelphia printed the story. Soon the account was reprinted in one form or another by every newspaper in the colonies. General Braddock was dead. Dozens of his officers were dead. Over a thousand of his men were killed. The army was defeated. The wounded, many of the camp followers, and others had been slaughtered or drug off by savages to an almost certainly horrible fate. The French had loosed their savage allies on the frontier.

Jake Kuckendahal heard the story in Easton, Pennsylvania, and carried the news north along the Delaware River. He stopped at Dupui's Trading Post at Shawnee on the Delaware long enough to share the story with Samuel Dupui. Then he headed north to warn the Dutch settlers at the Minisink.

Young Beletje Davids was sitting with her grandfather John Decker when Kuckendhal shared the news with the people at Mechackemac Dutch Reformed Church. Her family and neighbors knew old Jake. His words carried weight. If Jake said it was so, then it was true. But that wasn't all. The measured way Jake spoke told another story he wasn't saying out loud. He was worried.

Beletje glanced up at Grandfather Decker. She had seen that expression before. He was worried and now suddenly she was too.

The Shawnee, Mingo, and Delaware Indians living near the forks of the Ohio had for the most part been reluctant to choose sides in this struggle between the French and English. They had learned through generations of previous treaties to be wary of alliances with white men. They had grievances with both sides and they knew whose villages sat closest to the presently contested area.

Their warriors had not been involved in the battle but they had been close by to observe.

Now the decisions suddenly become clearer. Quickly councils were called in village after village. They would ally with the victorious Frenchmen and drive the English away. They would reclaim old homelands and settle old scores. The time to strike was now. It was time they paint themselves for war.

Kaskaskia

It took almost three weeks for canoes to travel downriver and up the Mississippi to Kaskaskia. Suddenly, one hot, dry morning, the bell at the Church of the Immaculate Conception began ringing and kept on ringing. Alex was at home training a new young team of oxen, hoping to take them in a few days north to the stone quarry near Prairie Du Rocher. He heard the bell, rushed the team to the barn, and hurried off to see what had happened.

Have the armies clashed? he wondered. *"Have we won or lost? How is Pierre and Maurice and Etienne?"*

As he approached and made a turn up the street, a boy came running toward him from the direction of the church.

"We won the battle!" he shouted at Alex as he ran passed and down the street.

Alex had missed the big announcement from the priest. He was late. Now he would hear the news second hand.

But then he saw an old man limping toward him. It was Pierre, though older, looking tired and used up. But Pierre's old weathered face was wearing a big smile and his twinkling eyes told a story of their own. He literally fell into Alex's arms as they met. "We won. We won. We won," he blubbered.

Alex wondered about Pierre as he helped him back to the house. The man had been old when he had left to go east. Now he seemed ancient, almost fragile though anxious, proud, and happy at the same time. He looked like he needed to rest, but he couldn't stop talking. He had to share the news of the wondrous victory at the Monongahela River.

The forts were some finished, others still in progress, he told Alex. The English had come to attack them.

"They had cannon bigger and more numerous than we. Our boys were outnumbered three to one, even counting the Indians. But we won. We won," he kept saying like he couldn't believe it himself.

Soon he sat at the table in a straight-backed chair eating stew from a crock bowl with a wooden spoon. Morning-Star had handed the food to him with a smile and a pat on the shoulder. Now she sat across from Pierre watching him eat.

"Are Etienne and Maurice well?" asked Alex dreading the answer, which might come.

"Oui, Oui," answered the old man. "Both well. Though they were in the thick of the action, neither got so much as a scratch. I was kept at the fort. I didn't see the fight. But Etienne and Maurice told me about it. We won," he said with his voice trailing off. "We won," he said again softly as he slumped in his chair fading off to sleep.

Alex helped Pierre to a bed. The bell had still not stopped ringing.

"I'm going back to the church," Alex told his mother rushing out the door.

Later that afternoon people heard six cannon blasts reverberating up and down the river valley from Fort De Chartres. The news had reached the fort and celebrations had begun.

Two hundred miles northeast on the Ouabache (Wabash) River the news had reached Post Vincennes yesterday coming downstream from the north. Celebrations there had gone throughout the night and continued on a more subdued level all of today.

Frenchmen were proud and happy. The battle at the Monongahela River was a great victory. The news was flying across New France as quickly as canoes could be paddled. This was reason to have a party. The fiddles played. The people laughed, danced, drank, and sang songs.

Chapter 44

Fall, 1755

French Fort Duquesne

$\mathcal{T}$he Venango Way was open for business. French shipping could portage from Lake Erie at Fort Presque Isle to French Creek at Fort Le Boeuf, follow that stream to the Allegheny River at Fort Machault (sometimes called Venango because of the Indian village at that place), and from there float down to the confluence with the Monongahela river, protected now by French Fort Duqesne. From that place, river traffic could follow what the French called the Bella Rivierre (the English called it the Ohio) nine hundred miles southwest to the Ouabache (Wabash) River, the Mississippi River, and the French Illinois country: Post Vincennes, Kaskaskia, St Genevieve, Cahokia, Prairie Du Rocher, St. Pillippe, and Fort De Chartres.

Etienne and Maurice remained splitting shingles and building pirogues at Fort Duquesne. Efforts on the other new French forts slowed almost to a stop. Fort Duquesne was thought to be most important and French exertions centered there.

But the real priority that fall was prosecuting the war against the English frontier. Since the defeat of Braddock in July, war-parties were sent east almost daily from Fort Duquesne. They were usually small groups of a dozen or so warriors sometimes led or accompanied by French soldiers or coureur de bois.

Their mission was simple: go east, find Englishmen, kill or capture them. Destroy their farms and homes, steal or kill their animals. Move fast, stealthily. Ambush the enemy. Finish the fight quickly and move on immediately, putting great distance between yourself and any pursuers. Spread terror. Force the English to flee eastward.

It was usual frontier warfare. The type of conflict many of them had seen before. The French and their native allies were good at it. But, so were the English. No one expected an easy fight.

"Did you see that bunch who came in this afternoon?" asked Jacque Ravelette.

He had just walked up to the fire where Maurice and Etienne were boiling root as Pierre had taught them for use in lashing the bark skins to the canoe they had under construction.

"Didn't notice," said Etienne. "Coming or going?"

Now days more parties were coming back in to Fort Duquesne from having been to war than going out to fight. Winter would soon be upon them.

"Coming in," said Jacque. "Mostly Ottawa I think. With a long string of prisoners and all kind of plunder. There will be some dancing and whooping tonight I bet. A soldier told me the leader was Charles Langlade himself. I saw him. He looked tough enough but not so big as I thought he would be."

"Well Langlade is one of our best officers," said Maurice. "I hear the Governor has rewarded him with a nice block of land and a house. Not to mention an officer's pension for life."

They all thought about that for a moment. Etienne stirred the pot and Maurice added more root which had been split into half strips, as Pierre taught, making one side flat, a nice fit against the ribs or gunnels of the canoe when tied into place.

"Well I hope there's no more burned at the stake," said Etienne.

"No," said Jacque. "I think the captain has forbidden any more of that near the fort. Some of those prisoners may be taken back home to villages where they may suffer the fate, but most will likely be sold, ransomed, or adopted into tribes. They're most all young and strong. The ones who could keep up."

Etienne and Maurice knew that the old and weak had been killed if they couldn't keep pace with the warriors. It was war. Their warriors could not afford to be slowed down in their movements. Speed and distance was a form of security.

The soldier said they had gone all the way to the Minisink and brought back scalps just to show the Munsee it could be done. "They stopped In the Wyoming Valley at a big Munsee village. That village is still trying to stay neutral like the Iroquois up north of them but our warriors put some shame on them and their young men are beginning to listen. They've been wronged by the Pennsylvanians but they still don't trust us either. If all keeps going well I bet they will see the light and come over to our side."

"Let's hope they do," said Maurice. "I hear there are lots more Englishmen this side of the Atlantic than there are Frenchmen."

Chapter 45

Spring, 1756

Fort Duquesne

*I*t was early May. The war was going well for the French, at least so far as anyone here could tell. Warriors had begun arriving from the western tribes in March. They were supplied with powder and lead from the fort's ammunitions and encouraged to set out against the English settlements immediately.

The English frontier, being contested at this time, spread out in a great fan shape emanating from Philadelphia. From the Shenandoah Valley of Virginia up through the backcountry of Maryland and central Pennsylvania all the way north to the Minisink valley where the colonies of New York, New Jersey, and Pennsylvania intersect was ablaze with hundreds of burning homes and barns. The English frontiers farther north had not yet erupted into conflict, as it would later. For now, the fight in America was centered here, near the forks of the Ohio. Fort Duquesne was command and supply center for the French and native forces.

Nothing succeeds like success. Fort Duquesne was alive with activity. The French had won the first big fight. Their forts seemed secure. All the western and local tribes had become fast allies to fight the English.

Now young warriors wished to win glory for themselves in battle. Experienced warriors wanted to burnish their reputations and expand their influence. Even the old men and women of the villages demanded their warriors avenge previous wrongs and settle the score from perceived and actual injustices of the past. The time for debate and half measures was behind them. It was now a time for war. The enemy must pay with their lives and treasure.

This morning was cool for May. The Parisian was in a tree where he could see over the laurel bushes. In the clearing ahead he noticed a dim light coming through a narrow crack where interior shudders didn't quite come together to cover a window in the small cabin made of logs. What served as a barn was actually a three-sided shed not far removed from the cabin. It was still dark in the trees but light was beginning to come to the morning. The buildings were distinguishable, obscured in a light fog. There was a springhouse and a rick of cut wood still held over from the long winter. It was a modest homestead.

The Parisian was part of a war party of a dozen Shawnee led by a warrior named Snaggle Tooth and a French-Canadian Lieutenant named Lafollette. They had passed through Fort Duquesne ten days ago. They were now somewhere in the Colony of Virginia. Three of the warriors were standing with Lafollette beside the tree The Parisian had just climbed. The other warriors had surrounded a larger homestead a mile or so to the east in a different clearing.

"What do you see, Squirrel?" whispered Lafollette from below.

"Just a dim light from the window," answered The Parisian. He didn't much like being called Squirrel but the Indians had christened him so because they didn't like calling him The Parisian. They decided on Squirrel because he was so quick to climb trees. Now he answered to either. He had concluded through the years it didn't much matter what you were called so long as no disrespect was intended.

The Parisian had, over the years, earned some measure of respect on the rivers of New France. Following his first job as a cattle drover he had worked as a voyageur. He had done a little trapping and trading. He had tried smuggling English goods. He had learned to hunt and become a good shot with a musket.

He was not a true coureur de bois like the lieutenant and others born in Canada or Louisiana but he was learning. For a man born on the streets of Paris, he had come a long way toward making the transition to frontier life. Finally, he was being accepted as a good hand by Canadians like Lafollette.

The Parisian very much wanted to fit in and do his part. But warfare was a new experience for him.

He was worried he might not measure up. He had been in a few fist-fights and even one or two where knives were involved. He had been cut and had the scar to prove it. He had once stabbed another man in the arm. But he had never killed anyone.

He wasn't sure he really wanted to. And yet he knew that was why they had come to this place. That is why he was up in the tree watching the cabin now: to see how many would come out to do the morning chores, where they could be killed more easily. That was why the warriors with Snaggle Tooth had surrounded the other cabin.

This was warfare on the frontier. He had heard the stories and the boasts around the campfires. Now he was here with these others to find out, first hand, how the stories were earned.

"When today is over, will I have a story to tell?" he wondered. *"Or will I be lying on the cold ground, shot dead by a Pennsylvania rifle?"*

He had heard about the rifles being made in Pennsylvania. He had seen a few demonstrated. They were deadly at long distances. Not every English farmer had one, but some on the frontier did. And, they knew how to use them.

Suddenly he heard the clunk of a wooden door latch and the squeak of a heavy door swinging open. For a moment he could see inside the cabin backlit by a fire being rekindled in a fireplace. At that instant he smelled wood smoke rising from the chimney though he could not yet see it against the sky. A silhouette of a man blocked the interior view before he could count how many others might be inside. The man paused and looked about with what appeared to be a long rifle in his hands. Then he stepped to the ground and strode off quickly toward the barn closing the door behind him. As he walked the window shudders in the cabin opened. Another rifle peeked out from inside to cover the man's short trip to the barn. These farmers weren't taking any chances. They seemed alert to possible danger.

"This might not be the right time or place for an ambush," thought Squirrel.

Pop! Pop!----Pop! came the muffled report of muskets being fired across a distance. The man in the barn appeared in a flash with his rifle in hand. Suddenly he sprinted back to the cabin. The door opened just before he got to the step and he dodged inside.

There was more musket fire in the distance. Obviously Snaggle Tooth and his warriors were in a fight bigger than they had expected.

"What do you see?" whispered Lafollette.

"One man went to the barn then ran back to the cabin when the shooting began," answered The Parisian. "There are at least two others in the cabin".

Suddenly the door at the cabin opened and six men armed with what looked to be long rifles surged out and loped off to the nearby tree-line disappearing into the brush. The door at the cabin closed behind them. A rifle still peeked out at the window.

The Parisian almost fell out of the tree as he scurried down, whispering the story loudly as he came.

"It's a trap," said Lafollette.

Before Squirrel could retrieve his musket and gear, Lafollette was disappearing stealthily into the laurel thicket, the three warriors at his heals. Squirrel grabbed his stuff and followed. This was no time to tarry.

They hurried back the way they had come in the dark. It was daylight now. Back toward a big ridge to the west they moved quickly, quietly. Back toward their camp of the night before. Snaggle Tooth and his warriors would meet them there. If they were able.

The Parisian was breathing hard in the steady climb upslope through brush and over boulders and fallen logs. It was obvious to The Parisian the ambush they had planned had fallen apart. They had been surprised themselves. Maybe that had happened to Snaggle Tooth and his warriors after they had committed themselves to their attack. If so they were all in trouble.

From the sounds of the muffled musket reports Snaggle Tooth and his warriors were still engaged in a fight. That meant only one thing: they were being hotly pursued. And, that indicated far more Englishmen than any of them had expected. They had stirred a hornet's nest. There were but two things to do now: put distance between you and the hornet's and try your best not to get stung.

Chapter 46

June, 1757

At Fort Duquesne

The war had gone well for the French in 1756 and early 1757. War-parties directed against the English from Fort Duquesne increased with great success, sending thousands of English settlers fleeing eastward. Fresh warriors still continued to arrive from western tribes. The English colonies failed to mount an adequate line of defense. Frenchmen and their allies raided effectively and often with only limited casualties of their own.

Last summer King Louis XV had sent Louis Joseph de Montcalm to assume leadership as the French Commander in Chief for French forces in New France. Last August his army attacked and overcame the defenders of the British Fort Oswego on lake Ontario. It was another great victory. Again bells rang in Vincennes, Kaskaskia, and around the Illinois country, people sang, danced, and played their fiddles.

The lakes were now secured for Frenchmen to travel. Supplies were shipped past Fort Niagara, up lake Erie, and down the Venango Way to Fort Duquesne supporting the war effort against the English in Virginia, Maryland, and Pennsylvania. Other commerce began to use the new route as well. Fur trading convoys stopped often at Fort Duquesne and floated on down La Belle Riviere, avoiding head winds on Lake Erie and fighting against upstream currents on the Maumee River. Coming back northeast they would travel up the Ouabache (Wabash) and carry over at Fort Miami to take advantage of the same currents they wished to avoid when traveling west. The new route saved time and effort. How much time and effort was saved depended on the rains and the wind.

The need for new and repaired pirogues never slowed. Maurice and Etienne were kept busy working. Neither had been sent out to fight since the great Battle of the Monongahela.

Maurice didn't speak of that day. He'd had his fill of war. He wasn't sure how many Englishmen he had killed but he knew he had shot at more than a few and some of those had fallen. He had done his duty. The buzz of lead balls flying through the air and men screaming in pain held no charm for him. He hoped he was never asked to do it again. Still he was happy and proud with the news of more French victories.

"I heard some news," said Etienne, as he walked up to camp where Maurice sat, his back against a small tree.

"What?"

"Well first they are building a new fort on the Ouabache (Wabash) just after the confluence with La Belle Riviere. It's to be called Fort de La Ascension. [4] They say Fort de Chartres is nearly finished being rebuilt of stone."

"Are you sure?"

"Some fur traders just came up river tonight. That's what they say. I wonder if Alex will be working on the new fort."

"Maybe? Is it to be a stone fort too?"

"No, just a picket fort on a high bluff. But it will be equipped with cannon. They are being shipped upriver from New Orleans. Pretty soon no one will challenge

---

[4] It would be renamed fort Massac two years later.

251

Frenchmen on these rivers. The fur trade will be ours for good. As it should be."

Etienne paused to think. "Word is our supplies might be slowing down. There is some kind of need out East. I heard some soldiers at the fort say the Indians are being limited on powder and ball. They don't like it."

"Why do you think the Governor would limit our gunpowder," asked Maurice.

"I don't know. Maybe Montcalm needs to resupply his regulars. There has been rumor of fighting near Lake George again. Them regulars like to travel with cannon and cannon take lots of gunpowder. Something is up. I'm just happy it's not me telling the Shawnee they have a limit. Or, the Delaware either. Did you see that chief they call Shingas come in the other day? He looks tougher than nails and I hear his Munsee warriors have been ripping into the Pennsylvanians."

"I saw him. He was slow to join us but he is all in now. I hear the English call him Shingas The Terrible," said Maurice. "I'm glad he is on our side."

Weeks passed. On a hot afternoon in late August a call of "bonjour messieurs (good day gentlemen)" greeted their camp. The voice was familiar but neither Maurice nor Etienne could quite connect it with someone they knew. The man stood a short distance away looking like a hundred other coureur des bois who passed through Fort Duquesne every week. This one looked particularly worn and dirty. Maurice noted he had three scalps hanging from his belt and a Pennsylvania longrifle in his left hand.

The stranger did not smile or move forward. Maurice looked around to see if the call was intended for someone nearby. But there was no one close enough to have been addressed. It was strange. Maybe the man had need of a canoe?

Then the man smiled and Etienne chuckled.

"The Parisian," said Etienne.

"Oui, mes vieux amis (yes, my old friends)."

"It was," thought Maurice. *"The Parisian from the cattle drive to Vincennes. He's changed. But it's him."*

Maurice and Etienne finished the day's work sealing seams with a pine tar and charcoal mixture. The Parisian sat nearby watching.

"You build all these canoes?" he asked pointing.

"Oui," said Etienne. "Maurice learned the trade from an old man back in Kaskaskia. Now he's teaching me."

"Looks like you have learned a bit since I knew you," The Parisian observed.

"Looks like you have too," said Maurice glancing at the scalps hanging from the belt The Parisian wore.

"Oui," answered the Parisian. "It is war time. Things must be done. I am learning how to survive in these forests. But some things like killing are not so much different than in Europe."

"Where you been?" asked Maurice.

"Virginia, Maryland, Pennsylvania."

"Is that where you got the longrifle?" asked Etienne.

"Oui."

"How many war parties?" asked Maurice.

"Six times," answered The Parisian.

"All through Fort Duquesne?" asked Maurice. "How did we never bump into one-another?"

"Only five from here, the first was out of Fort Niagara. I never thought to inquire about men from the Illinois country till this time."

"We might have passed each other and not known it," said Maurice.

"Were you here for the battle?" asked Etienne.

"No, were either of you?"

"Both of us," Etienne answered, glancing at Maurice.

The conversation lagged for a moment as each man searched for words.

"What of Alex and Jean?" asked the Parisian. "And the others."

"All back in the Illinois country so far as we know," answered Etienne. "We have not had word in a while. They could show up on a supply convoy any day, but Alex and Jean have been busy the last couple years hauling stone for the new Fort de Chartres. We figure they may be working on the new Fort de La Ascension on the Ouabache (Wabash)[5]. Did you hear about it?"

---

[5] So far as these Frenchmen were concerned La Belle Riviere (the Ohio of today) was a tributary of the Ouabache (Wabash River) not the other way around. So the river after the confluence of the two was considered by them to be the Ouabache (Wabash) they had traveled for generations, not the Ohio as it is thought of in modern times. Therefore, Fort Massac was built on the 'Ouabache'

"Oui," answered The Parisian. Suddenly a cannon roared from the fort followed by three more.

"I wonder what that is about," said Maurice.

Cheers were heard and a runner was seen coming from the direction of the fort up along the Monongahela River where they were working. As he got closer he shouted to them. "Montcalm has taken Fort William Henry on Lake George. It was a great victory."

The runner ran on along the river to spread the big news. The celebration commenced. The fiddles came out even before the rum. Men could be heard tuning their instruments. Everyone was smiling.

"Well I guess we know now where our gunpowder and lead have been redirected," said Maurice.

Riviere' even though today it sits on what is called the Ohio River. It is simply a matter of perspective and language.

Chapter 47

Summer, 1758

It was true. A new English army was headed for Fort Duquesne. They were building a different road coming through Pennsylvania this time, but they were coming. Their new general was named Forbs. He had more than twice the size of Braddock's army, and he was cautious.

Virginia's young Colonel Washington was with this army once again. It was his fourth attempt in four years to force Frenchmen to leave the area. He hoped this time would be successful.

The war was different this year. The English had finally gotten up a defense. A long string of frontier forts had been erected through Virginia across Maryland and Pennsylvania and up the Delaware River along the New Jersey boarder to New York. Local rangers worked between these posts to detect and deter attack. Sometimes these fighters were a threat to Frenchmen and their native allies. French casualties were beginning to increase.

The Iroquois had remained mostly loyal to the English.

Four years of nonstop warfare had begun to seem like a long time. Native people were used to warring with one another but not on such a scale or for this duration. Young braves continued to arrive from tribes out west hoping to prove themselves against the English. But, the numbers were fewer each month. Others who had come earlier stopped raiding and simply went home to bask in their newly found glory. It was not their custom to fight for years at a time.

The French and English were fighting, not just in America but worldwide, wherever French and or English colonies existed and could be seized: Europe, Africa, India, the West Indies.

Here in America the English frontier settlers stopped fleeing eastward. They fortified stockades. They organized counter attacks and offensives.

The fighting in the north nearer Lake Ontario increased, redirecting many French resources. The English attacked Frenchmen living in Acadia and captured Louisburg, a major French fortification and supply depot, opening a threat to the St. Lawrence River and Quebec City.

The English King sent more soldiers. The colonial governments raised, trained, and equipped troops of their own. The fight became more desperate and brutal on both sides.

Forts on the Venango Way felt the pinch. Indians reporting at Forts Presque Isle, Le Boeuf, Venango and even Duquesne found gunpowder and lead musket balls in short supply. Shipments from the French Illinois country were critical to supply the war effort. Prisoners to be ransomed, trade goods, and war bootie were transported downriver to Fort de Chartres.

The Parisian today was deep into Pennsylvania country with the Frenchman Lafollette and a band of eight Shawnee led by a warrior called Cut Nose Peter. It was late in the evening just before dark. They had surrounded a small homestead: log cabin, barn, springhouse, a few acres cleared with growing corn in the field. It was like hundreds of other English farms The Parisian had seen since the war began.

The surprise was complete. The killing was brutal and swift. In twenty minutes the English settler and most of his family lay dead near where they had toiled a few minutes before. It wasn't much of a fight.

Two teenage girls and a small boy were left alive. They were already bound, ropes tied to their necks and packs on their backs. Tear stains and shock covered their faces. Quickly they were trotted away from their home into the forest like a string of pack animals.

It was dark now. The buildings were set ablaze. Smoke began to rise. Flames inside the cabin popped and cracked as they crawled out the window and licked their way up the sidewall toward the clapboard roof. Soon the conflagration had lit the clearing and strange shadows danced in the cornfield and among the trees where the forest began.

The Parisian had seen all this before in other places— many times. He had grown weary of it.

At the beginning of the war he understood the strategy of spreading such terror to force the English to leave the land they had stolen and flee eastward back from where they had come. It had worked—for a while. But after four years of such warfare it didn't seem to be working any more.

"This is no longer war," he thought. *"It's more like revenge killing."*

The little English boy stumbled ahead of him. The Parisian leaped forward to steady and redirect him along the track. The boy had to keep up or Cut Nose would kill him. No one could slow them down now that they had exposed their presence by the attack.

The challenge was to escape. That was not as easy as it had been a couple years before. Rescue parties would soon be organized and on their trail. The Frenchmen and Indians had a long way to travel. Their pursuers (likely relatives and neighbors of these young people) would be determined to catch them. If the English succeeded, no quarter would be given to the French or their allies. The Parisian was tired of killing, but he was not ready to die. All effort must be made to move fast. Nothing could be allowed which might slow them down.

Chapter 48

General Forbs' British army had continued its progress toward the forks of the Ohio all summer, building their new road as they came. The mountain terrain had proved tougher than expected. It had taken more time than they had hoped. Still advanced elements were now only about fifty miles southeast of Fort Duquesne. French scouts kept close watch.

Forbs had learned from the previous debacle, which General Braddock had experienced. The Scotsman planned not to suffer a similar fate. This time as the army-built road they also constructed fortified positions every fifty miles or so as a fall back in case of attack. That took more time, but Forbs was a cautious man. He had a larger army than Braddock but he was determined not to waste it fighting in this wilderness.

Today the advanced units were constructing what was expected to be the last fortification needed at Loyalhanna Creek.[6] The rest of the army was spread out over roughly seventy miles behind them with Forbs himself near the rear. He had sent orders for a reconnaissance in force to assess the situation ahead of his army.

September 14

---

[6] Later christened Fort Ligonier.

It was a hot day. Maurice and Etienne were in the war again. Englishmen had come against Fort Duquesne. They had attacked the fort with a portion of their army. The fight had lasted all day. It was late afternoon. Now the Englishmen were surrounded.

Maurice and Etienne were fighting with their militia unit this time and not shooting only at officers. Actually they had been sent first here and then there and had done no shooting at all. The heavy fighting seemed to be always somewhere nearby but constantly moving in the forests ahead of them. The woods were full of the noise and smell of battle but always somewhere a little further off.

By the end of the day the battle was over. Maurice and Etienne had seen a handful of dead and scalped British soldiers but no live ones. After dark they came marching back into the gate of Fort Duquesne, happy but confused.

Soon the fiddles were playing and the rum had been brought out. It had been another great victory. Hundreds of Englishmen had been killed with only light French casualties. Hundreds of other Englishmen were fleeing now in the darkness with Shawnee and Ottawa warriors in pursuit. Why the English had not brought more of their army no one seemed to know and tonight no one seemed to care.

Later, back in their tent and about to go to sleep, Maurice asked Etienne, "Do you think more English will come tomorrow?"

"I doubt it after the beating they took today."

"Maybe that was just a test of our defenses," said Maurice. "Maybe there are more lurking out there tonight just getting ready."

"Scouts say they are on the run and no more about."

"Well the scouts didn't seem to notice these guys coming till they were almost here," said Maurice.

"You worry too much. Besides you don't know what the commandant was told. He doesn't share information with us until he needs to. He may have known they were coming for days. If this was a test of our resolve they found out we intend to stay here. These are French forts and we will defend them."

"Well what are we going to defend it with? I have only ten musket balls in my pouch. More supplies better get here soon." He yawned. "And food rations are getting slim too."

Throughout the night Major James Grant's troops were in fact making a hasty retreat from the terrible defeat they had suffered. There were no more Englishmen lurking in the forests around Fort Duquesne. Fortunately safety waited if they could quickly get back within the walls of the fort being built at Loyalhanna Creek.

Major Grant himself spent his night as a prisoner inside Fort Duquesne. At least he was not dead on the field of battle like many of his men. As a prisoner he was also relieved of the obligation to explain to General Forbes why he had chosen to exceed his orders and attack Fort Duquesne. One can only wonder how he slept that night.

Chapter 49

September 16, 1758

"What's that?" asked Maurice.

"Looks like a head," answered Etienne with a shrug and grimace.

"Do you think the commandant knows about it?"

"I expect he does," answered Etienne. "Look, more."

Etienne pointed his finger following along the fort palisade. Other heads were clearly visible at intervals stuck upon the sharpened points of the picket posts. Birds flocked around more than one.

"Englishmen I guess," said Etienne. "I bet the Ottawa did it."

"Well I don't like it," said Maurice. "They will smell up the place and I bet the good father doesn't like it either."

"I wouldn't be so sure about that," said Etienne. "I've heard the priest talk about English Red Coats. If they didn't want their head on a spike they should not come all this way to kill Frenchmen."

"You boys got a fast canoe for us?" came a shout from behind them.

It was a Sargent of marines, neither knew, approaching from direction of the commandant's quarters. They were just outside the front gate looking back.

Three other men rushed along behind the Sargent trying to keep pace and carry their gear.

"We have to catch up to that convoy that left yesterday heading downriver," said the Sargent as he caught up to the two Kaskaskia men.

"Down along the river," answered Maurice, with a motion of his head.

They turned and paced quickly up the Monongahela River toward their building location. The other men followed struggling with the gear.

The convoy had left following the defeat of Grant's Englishmen. It was a jubilant party bound west for Fort De Chartres with the victorious news and a variety of war booty and prisoners.

"What's so important Sargent?" asked Etienne.

"Some new dispatches from up north that have to get to the Illinois country," answered the Sargent.

Nothing more was said as the Sargent and his men piled their gear into the canoe, jumped nimbly in themselves, and quickly paddled down river. The rapid paddle strokes told their own story.

"They were in a hurry," said Etienne, as he watched the flashing paddles move the canoe quickly downstream.

"Oui," answered Maurice. "I'd like to know what's in those dispatches."

What the Sargent had not told them was that he had just brought bad news to the Commandant. No supplies would come from New France any time soon. The English had taken Fort Frontenac, on the north end of Lake Ontario. Frontenac was a big supply depot and important strategic point. Fort Niagara between here and Frontenac had nothing they could spare from their own supplies. With the north end of Lake Ontario controlled now by the English, any hope of resupply must come from the west and its connections downriver to New Orleans and the rest of Louisiana. Survival of the Venango way, Fort Niagara and possibly New France now depended on help from Fort De Chartres and the Illinois country.

In the next few weeks the news that had traveled downriver with the Sargent and his men leaked out of the commandant's quarters and became commonly known around Fort Duquesne and the other forts of the Venango Way. Anxious eyes watched river traffic coming upstream on the Belle Rivierre or downstream on the Allegheny. It would take weeks for the message to travel downstream nearly a thousand miles. Days would be required to put together supplies at Fort De Chartres and weeks more for those supplies to come back upstream via either the Belle Rivierre or the Ouabache (Wabash).

It was fall. Not only were the English approaching, but so too was winter. Survival for both armies now became a race against time. Armies must have resupply especially during winter, and both of these armies were far from their base of supply. The French depended on a very long river route and the English were risking all upon a shorter, newly built road over very treacherous terrain. Neither army was well equipped for cold weather.

In early October, unusual for the season, rain began to fall in the area. It had little effect on river currents, but it played havoc with mountain roads; turning clay soils into a slick, sloshy mess, and making movement of the British army impossible for days at a time.

The possibility of an attack on Fort Duquesne this season began to be questioned. Forbes and his officers started to discuss the probability of a required winter quarters at

Fort Ligonier and the other forts along the road. Frenchmen at Fort Duquesne began to pray for more rain.

Etienne and Maurice were upriver on the Monongahela in their dugout. They were running limb lines for catfish like they had done so often as boys.

"Too bad Alex isn't here. It would be like old times," said Maurice.

"Oui, it would, mon ami. But Alex is better off in Kaskaskia than here with us."

"Oui, But he would be impressed with the catch today," answered Maurice.

Maurice and Etienne were fishing often these days to help feed the soldiers. Deer and most forest animals had been hunted out near the forts long ago. Fish had become an important source of protein.

The fall bird migration was in progress. Wildfowl was plentiful along the rivers. Gunpowder however was in short supply. Only a few of the best hunters were allotted powder to shoot game. Others were discouraged from shooting at birds unless a flock of passengers pigeons suddenly darkened the sky. That had happened a couple times in September but not since. Rations were low. Their catch of fish would be needed.

About noon-time they approached the landing at Fort Duquesne. A tall savage stood nearby, waiting. As they brought the dugout to shore Maurice saw that it was in fact Lieutenant Marin whom they had fought alongside during the great battle three years ago.

The lieutenant smiled as they dragged the dugout on shore.

266

"Bonjour," he said. "I will require your help again today. Get your weapons and gear for a day out in the woods and meet me at the front gate."

"When?" asked Maurice.

"Now." answered the lieutenant as he turned and strolled quickly away toward the fort.

"What about the fish?" yelled Etienne.

"Leave them." responded the lieutenant.

Etienne glanced at Maurice and Maurice gazed back. Both shrugged. They took their muskets and gear from the dugout and hurried away to retrieve the packs and blankets they had been issued.

Half an hour later they found Lieutenant Marin and his band of savage allies. Other regular units of French marines and Canadian soldiers were forming up all over the parade ground and outside the fort too. Hundreds of men were preparing to go into battle.

"Where is the attack coming Lieutenant?" asked Maurice.

"We're leading it," answered Marin. "We're taking the fight to the English this time."

Drums began to beat. Maurice noticed Captain Charles Aubry lead the first column of men through the front gate with flags whipping in a cool fall breeze, with colorful leaves blowing about them. The Frenchmen stepped off smartly moving eastward to the beat of the drums.

Chapter 50

October 12, 1758

Near the Advanced British Post on Loyalhanna Creek[7]

Maurice was tired. They had traveled nearly fifty miles.

As the army marched, Lieutenant Marin's men were out as flankers on the left side of the main column, moving through the thickets rarely on anything which could be called a trail. It had been a brutal march but it had been successful. The English had not detected their approach.

It was late morning. In the air hung still a bit of fog. A slight misty rain fell. The French army was in position.

Lieutenant Marin's Ojibwa warriors were set in a woods to the west of a small meadow where the English were grazing about two hundred horses and near fifty oxen. The English had posted a "grass guard" mostly on the west side of the meadow to keep the animals from straying. Beyond the meadow, visible over a slight hill, and across Loyalhanna Creek lay the fort itself. Still under construction and commanded by Colonel James Burd.

The remainder of the French army was positioned to the left and right of the meadow with others to the rear of Lieutenant Marin's men. Maurice and Etienne were set behind different trees about thirty yards apart with the same instructions: shoot only officers. Maurice felt exposed being forward of the main force.

"Why are we out here in front?" he wondered.

---

[7] Later to be named Fort Ligonier.

The signal was to be the sound of Lieutenant Marin's musket.

Maurice had an officer, mounted horseback, identified as his target about sixty yards out into the meadow. Maurice's position was about ten yards into the trees making it a seventy-yard shot. It was a long shot for a musket but no one had offered him a long rifle. So he would have to do his best. There were other Redcoats closer but those men were not officers. He had his orders. The orders were clear.

The lieutenant fired and so did his men. Maurice's target went down with his horse. After the rattle of musketry a shout from the savages went up and some Otttawa braves who had been hiding inside the meadow since before dawn emerged to stampede the horse herd right toward Maurice's position.

"Hold tight," yelled Lieutenant Marin. "Let them come." Soon the frightened horses with thundering hooves had come crashing through the trees and ran on behind Maurice with the Ottawa close at their rear pushing them along. A handful of horses not wanting to run into the woods bolted around the warriors and headed back toward the English fort. Maurice noticed the warriors shoot two of those and then begin to shoot the oxen deeper into the grass who were lumbering back toward the English side of the meadow.

"Where is the rest of our army?" wondered Maurice. "We should have killed every Redcoat in this meadow." Obviously there were still Redcoats visible on the far side of the meadow now attempting to herd the surviving oxen and horses back toward the fort. Other English soldiers were running from all directions, in all manner of full and partial uniform to come to the aid of the grass guards. Drums were beating and men were yelling inside the fort. Still there was only intermittent shooting out in the meadow.

"Only we and the Ottawa warriors are engaged," realized Maurice. *"Where is everyone else?"*

There were no more British officers within range to target so after he had reloaded Maurice watched and waited.

Soon a line of Englishmen came out on the far side of the meadow and began marching across toward the Indians. The warriors, who were just out of range, taunted the English as they came. Then a second and third line of Englishmen marched out and started over.

"That's a lot of soldiers," thought Maurice, *"where are our soldiers?"*

There were now plenty of officers for Maurice to target. And they were closing the distance quickly.

"Which one should I shoot first? Where is the French army we came with?"

The Ojibwa warriors suddenly ran back into the trees and were soon out of sight.

Maurice turned to follow them. It was then he saw the French army coming forward only a few paces behind him. Lieutenant Marin appeared smiling before him.

"Remain here, let them pass," he said. "Do your job from here. We're about to teach these arrogant bastards another lesson."

The Frenchmen marched past out into the open meadow and formed up quickly two lines deep. The English halted briefly out in the grass. The officers shouted commands and the soldiers came on at a steady pace to the beat of a single drummer who had suddenly appeared.

When the battle lines fired into one another it was a horrendous thunder and a sudden shock to both sides. Men were screaming in pain. Orders were shouted. Reloading began and the second lines stepped forward, raising their muskets on command.

"Fire!" came the command from the very officer in Maurice's musket sight. Maurice pulled his trigger. The sound of his own weapon was lost in the roar of the English muskets. The British officer pitched backward and fell dead before he could assess the damage done by his own soldiers upon the Frenchmen.

Maurice felt a little sick. But he didn't have time for that now. He had a job to finish. Quickly he reloaded.

The English soon realized they were outnumbered and retreated back across the meadow. But still more English troops were filing out of the fort and heading toward the meadow. The fight went on like this for almost three hours.

Twice more the English came across the meadow only to find more Frenchmen appear suddenly to face them. Finally they organized the biggest formation of the day and this time brought cannon with them.

The Frenchmen retreated back into the trees moving away from the fort. The rest of the day had been a series of light skirmishes in the forests.

It was nearing dark and the French army had found British troops trying to get around behind and encircle them. Captain Aubrey ordered a full retreat back to Fort Duquesne.

Maurice in his haste somehow became separated from his countrymen and lost. Suddenly he had Englishmen ahead and behind him in the woods. He hid quickly near a big bolder within a laurel thicket and stopped moving.

He watched a game trail ahead as English stalked along it. Suddenly a big man appeared and stopped on the trail for a moment to watch and listen.

"Did I make a sound?" thought Maurice. "Does he sense somehow that I am here?"

Then Maurice gasped. He recognized the man ahead. It was the big Virginian.

"Was that audible?" Maurice wondered. "Did he hear me?"

The Virginia colonel stood in the fading light a moment more listening. Then he stalked off.

Soon the last Englishmen had moved along the trail and Maurice thought it safe to cross. When he did, Lieutenant Marin appeared in front of him only a few paces away.

"This way," he said pointing in slow motion to the west. "We have to catch up."

"I saw the Virginia Colonel Washington in that group just now," he whispered to Marin.

"He must think he's gotten behind us," said Marin. "But he's too late. The only thing he will find in that direction are more English. Now let's go. Keep quiet, keep up."

When they had traveled only a short distance a barrage of musket fire came from behind them.

"Had more Frenchmen been left behind?"

Marin who had stopped to listen turned with a smile.

"I think they are fighting each other," he whispered with a little chuckle.[8]

---

[8] George Washington would write long after the Revolutionary war that this friendly fire incident in the war with the French was likely the closest he ever came to being killed in battle. Two officers and thirty-two men were killed that evening in that incident. None were Frenchmen.

Chapter 51

October, 1758

Near the Forks of the Ohio

*T*he battle at Loyalhanna Creek was yesterday. Maurice and Lieutenant Marin had caught up to the retreating French army. The army had marched till after midnight. The men slept in their gear wherever they could find a soft spot in the wet leaves on the forest floor.

Birds now were beginning to sing around them. It was a cool, damp morning. Daylight crept into the forest through the thinning canopy above them. Pemmican and beef jerky had been procured and distributed. Men were busy eating and preparing for a hard day's march.

Maurice found Etienne, who was looking also for Maurice. They shook hands and smiled at one another. Neither spoke.

Maurice watched the officers as they assessed the condition of their men and took count of the losses. After action reports would wait till they were back at Fort Duquesne but stories were being told already among the men.

It had been a hot action. Some were disappointed they had not taken the fort at Loyalhanna. Others were happy the retreat was called. They were the soldiers who had taken note of the cannon coming out against them.

Maurice was disappointed they had not taken the fort but he had seen the fight close up. He had seen the size of the last British battle formation and he had noted the cannon. He was pleased to be heading back to Duquesne.

But Maurice was confused about something. He had taken note that the officers seemed in unusually good spirits for a defeat. Lieutenant Marin was standing beside a small fire attempting to dry a wet spot in a wool blanket. Maurice stepped closer.

"Why are the officers not more upset?" he asked.

"We accomplished much," said the Lieutenant. "Our losses seem small."

"But we didn't take the fort."

"No but we stole many horses, ran off and killed many others not to speak of the oxen killed. The English army is far bigger than ours right now, but it's strung out for miles. They have to travel and bring their gear to concentrate sufficient amounts to attack us. Horses and oxen make that easier. Winter is almost here. We needed to slow them down till the weather can stop them. We need time to get resupplied and reinforced. Yesterday bought us time and taught them a lesson. We lost some good men but the English were surprised repeatedly and lost far more. The Captain decided we had accomplished enough. He could see we were outmatched by numbers and cannon. He was smart enough to call retreat just in time and march us home. It's called good leadership. A good commander knows when to cut his losses and save his army to fight another day. That's why the officers are not upset."

By the time the Lieutenant had finished his impromptu speech, a small knot of men had formed up to listen. Now, quietly, they all wondered away, nodding their heads, and dispersing out among the army.

A light rain began to fall.

In Early November good news came to General Forbs. The Delaware Indians had signed a treaty with the English at a peace conference held in October at Easton

Pennsylvania on the Delaware River. This treaty would remove many of the local Indians near the Forks of the Ohio from their alliance with the French. It was indeed good news if the treaty held.

Forbs needed good news. The weather had not been helpful in October. More rain, snow and sleet had bedeviled their advance. The general was grievously ill and bed bound much of the time.

On November 11 General Forbs called his officers together at the fort on Loyalhanna creek. He had recently renamed the fortification Fort Ligonier after his superior officer back home in England. Forbs had also moved his command center to this forward position. Included in his personal equipment was his sick bed.

At the meeting it was decided to prepare for wintering the army in place and to postpone attack on Duquesne until spring. It was a somber meeting. Afterward there was grumbling in the army.

November 24, 1758

At Fort Duquesne

Maurice and Etienne were exhausted. For two days they had been loading supplies into a convoy being formed at the Monongahela River Landing. At the Allegheny Landing on the opposite side of the fort men were loading an even larger convoy.

Fort Duquesne was being abandoned.

The order had come from the Commandant. Since then, there had been little time for rest. Everything usable was to be taken with them or destroyed. Nothing was to be left behind for the English.

In mid-November the weather had improved. New information had become available to the British concerning the reduced strength of the French garrison. General Forbes quickly recalculated his situation. He saw opportunity and seized it. His army was immediately set in motion toward Fort Duquesne.

Most of the French Indians had left yesterday with the horses, after the oxen were slaughtered. Mainly it was Frenchmen remaining to destroy what, for four years, they had worked to build. It was a sobering task and Maurice was sick of it.

"Smoke is getting thick," said Maurice, as Etienne came up pushing a two-wheeled handcart.

"They set fire to the palisades on the east side," said Etienne. "The wind shifted after they got it going good."

"Well I wish they had waited till we got away and downriver. What's in the cart?"

"Two of the last kegs of gunpowder. They'll need the remainder to blow up the armory."

He picked up a small keg, hoisted it to his shoulder and carried it down the bank to a big dugout canoe they were loading. There were a total of 32 pirogues, dugouts and bark canoes in this convoy. Lieutenant Marin was in command. A few of the Ojibwa warriors would come along.

It was a breezy late fall afternoon. Most of the leaf canopy was off the hardwood forests allowing more visibility to a stark, cold, landscape. Upon Lieutenant Marin's command ,Maurice and Etienne took their position in their canoe and shoved out into the cold waters of the Monongahela River. They coasted downstream. Etienne, in the stern, steered the craft.

Suddenly it was quiet. The hustle and bustle of the moments before was replaced by the sounds of the river's flowing water. Everyone was watching the fort burn. The wind had shifted again and was blowing the smoke eastward. The lead craft of their convoy was nearing the point where the two rivers converged to form a single waterway.

Suddenly there was a large explosion. Debris and smoke shot high into the air from inside the fort.

"There goes the powder magazine," said Etienne. "It won't be useful for the English."

"Took a lot longer to build than to blow up," said Maurice.

A few moments later Maurice and Etienne's canoe was nearing "The Point". They were the last canoe. Their convoy was ahead of them now heading downstream on the Belle Riviere. For a few moments, Maurice could see up the Allegheny River where the other convoy was strung out, heading upstream toward Fort Machault some seventy miles north. Those Frenchmen would spend the winter there and plan how to fight the English come spring. Then, the other convoy slid out of his sight as the trees of the north shore blocked the view.

Maurice turned back for a final look at the fort. A handful of men were setting fire to the west wall now. The brush piled against the wall was lit. The wind blowing the fire drove it quickly upward. The whole of the fort seamed instantly engulfed in flames. Above it all raised a dark cloud of grey smoke in an otherwise bright blue sky.

"Well, I guess we're finally going home," said Maurice, turning back to resume paddling.

Etienne didn't answer.

Soon they rounded the next bend in the river. Eagles soared high above them. Geese honked off in the distance. The air was crisp. The river currents worked with them, pushing their craft along as they paddled. Kaskaskia was only a little over nine hundred miles southwest. It would be good to be home.

The End

Afterword

The French and Indian War did not end with the burning of Fort Duquesne in 1758. Frenchmen from the Illinois country would return to the Venango Way the following spring. Much fighting was yet to come. The war between the French and English would continue for five more long years. During these times the Illinois country continued to be a part of Upper Louisiana, a French colony.

In 1763, the peace treaty between England and France would transfer to England all New France and other French lands east of the Mississippi River. However, it took three more years, until 1766, before British troops finally were able to accept control of Fort de Chartres from the French officer still in command. British engineers in their reports of the time declared the stone fort to be the most impressive fortification in all North America.

After 1763 many Frenchmen moved to the west bank of the Mississippi to Ste. Genevieve and the newly settled St. Louis, thinking they would remain under French rule. Others remained where they had lived and farmed, accepting English control. Descendants are there still.

In 1779, George Rodgers Clark of Virginia seized the Illinois country from the English by capturing Kaskaskia, Cahokia, and Vincennes for the new United States.

In 1803, President Thomas Jefferson concluded the Louisiana Purchase. Later the same year, Captains Meriwether Louis and William Clark began their exploratory expedition up the Missouri River. A Frenchman named Charbano and his Indian wife Sacajawea were recruited to go along. A metis (mixed blood) named George Drulliard was hired to be a sign talker and hunter.

Frenchmen had been paddling up this river for almost a century. Most of those have been forgotten by history. It is good to remember.

About the Author

Michael Phegley's love of history began in John Hodge's sixth grade class, Busseron Township School, Oaktown, Indiana. Later he lived for sixteen years in Vincennes, the oldest continuously inhabited community in the state.

The author is an amateur historian and genealogist. He is or has been during his life a hunter, fly fisherman, backpacker, canoer of rivers, farmer, antique collector, poet, husband, father, and grandfather.

Phegley holds an Associate of Science degree from Vincennes University, a Bachelor of Science degree from Indiana State University and a Master's Degree from Southern Illinois University.

The author has traced his family roots back to the eighteenth century Delaware River Valley. As a genealogist he has never been satisfied finding documents and cemetery markers. He must locate parcels of land and stand on those farmsteads to personally experience the natural surroundings his ancestors had known.

It was these deeply personal pilgrimages and the subsequent questions awakened in the authors imagination that has inspired him to write his stories: First **_Storms at Kendiamong,_** second **_Bloody Scalps and Cuckoo Clocks_** and now this book, **_The Venango Way._**

Phegley lives now with his wife and two dogs in Evansville, Indiana.

stormsatkendiamong@gmail.com

Acknowledgments

The closest we get to truth in our history is when we read original source material written or told of by actual participants or contemporary witnesses. Even then facts are skewed by prejudices and opinion.

I am grateful for letters, journals, diaries, baptismal records, land registrations, newspapers, and other original documents. I appreciate the people throughout the years who have secured, protected, and preserved these treasures for us.

I want to especially thank:

Knox County Public Library, McGrady Brochman House, 614n 7th St., Vincennes, IN.

Les Amis du Fort de Chartres "Friends of Fort de Chartres" PO box 366, Prairie du Rocher, IL.

Fort de Chartres State Historic Site, 1350 State Route 155, Prairie du Rocher, IL.

Randolph County Historical Society, Chester, IL.

Randolph County IL. Genealogical Society, 13 Westwood drive, Steeleville, IL.

Fort Necessity National Battlefield, Farmington, PA.

Fort Ligonier Historic Site, Ligonier, PA.

Sussex County Historical Society; 82 Main St., Newton, NJ.

Minisink Valley Historical Society; 125-133 West Main St., Port Jervis, NY.

Montague Association of the Restoration of Community History; Foster Armstong House, Montague, NJ.

Sandyston Township Historical Society; Sandyston Township, NJ.

Bibliography

French Roots in the Illinois Country (The Mississippi Frontier in Colonial Times), By Carl J. Ekberg, University of Illinois Press, Champaign IL 2000

For King and country (the maturing of George Washington 1748-1760); by Thomas A. Lewis; Harper Collins, publishing; New York 1993

The First Peoples of Ohio and Indiana; by Jessica Diemer Eaton; Diemer Eaton Publishing, Bloomington 2001

King of the Delawares, Teedyuscung 1700-1763, by Anthony F.C. Wallace; Syracuse University press, 1949

Peaceable Kingdom Lost (The Paxton Boys and the Destruction of William Penn's holy Experiment); by Kevin Kenny, Oxford University Press, 2009

The Indian Chiefs of Pennsylvania; by C. Hale Sipe; Wennawoods Publishing, Louisburg Pennsylvania,1999

Minisink Valley Reformed Dutch Church Records, 1716-1830; the New York Genealogical and Biographical Society; Edited by Royden Woodward Vosburgh; a reprint published by Heritage Books Inc.; Westminster Maryland, 2004

History of Sussex and Warren Counties, NJ; by: James Snell; published by Everts and Peck; Philadelphia; 1881

History of Wayne, Pike and Monroe Counties Pennsylvania; by Alfred Mathews; R.T. Peck, Publisher; Philadelphia 1886

History of Orange County, New York ; by Russel Headley; Van Dusen & Elms, Publisher; Middletown New York 1908

Orange County History; by Edward Manning Ruttenber and Lois H. Clark; Everts & Peck publisher; Philadelphia 188

The Indians of New Jersey (Dicken Among The Lenape); by M. R. Harrington Rutgers University Press; New Brunswick NJ 1966

Documents relating to the Colonial History of the State of New Jersey, Volume XX, Extracts From American Newpapers , relating to New Jersey Vol. IV. 1756-1761; The Call Printing and Publishing Company; Patterson New Jersey 1898